Spire
of
Tyranny

S.G. Campbell

Edition: 1
ISBN-13: 978-1979331272
ISBN-10: 1979331278
Printed by: CreateSpace

Cover designer: Nathaniel Lewis
Manuscript editor: Kelly McGough
Proofreaders: Tom C, Brenda T, Dave C, Elaine R
Typeface: Constantia

For the one who gave it all,
so that I could be set free
and forgiven

CONTENTS

Chapter 1: **ONSET**

E li stood up straight, examining himself in the mirror. His reflection showed a young man of average height, twenty years of age, with a toned build and blond hair, outfitted in armor. He tightened his belt, adjusted his scabbard, and tugged at the ends of his hauberk. The sounds of a cheering crowd were faint coming from the arena in the distance. He closed his eyes, listening to the villagers' muffled chanting. Eli would need all the confidence he could muster for the challenge he was about to face.

He walked a few steps to a basin of water and gave himself a cold splash in the face. He wiped his brow, dried his hands, and then resumed the pacing that had consumed his morning. Eli hadn't slept last night, but his nerves were too potent to feel fatigued.

His pacing stopped abruptly as he heard the gathered villagers in the arena burst into cheers. Eli's opponent was being introduced. He scooped up his helmet and thrust it over his head, then fought back the tremor in his limbs as he stood at the opening of the arena.

His name was shouted by the championship's conductor, and he marched into the bright, sunbaked arena. Raising an armored hand over his head, he gave the spectators a wave as he searched the stands for his family. He caught sight of his father Abner, who was holding tightly to his frightened mother and younger sister. Abner beamed at him and gave a small nod. Eli returned the gesture and then snapped the helmet's visor over his eyes.

Eli's gaze met his opponent's, Wade, a fellow finalist in the championship's swordsmen duels. The winner today would go on to face Kadmiel for the title.

He began to size up his rival as they approached the center of the arena, noting his sheer mass. Wade strutted forward, silent but smug. Eli took the opportunity to observe which leg he preferred and if he had sustained any injuries from previous rounds in the tournament. His pace looked uninterrupted but perhaps a bit slower than in preceding duels. He had watched most of Wade's victories as he advanced through the competition. He was a merciless foe, nearly disqualified on a number of occasions for pushing his opponents past the point of submission.

Eli slowed to a halt on the hard-packed ground, his eyes locked with Wade's, who stood three feet opposite him. His hands felt sweaty inside of his gloves, but Eli didn't let his trepidation show by averting his gaze. Both swordsmen extended their fists and clanked their armored gloves together, then retreated a few paces with their hands on their hilts, lowering into a ready stance.

The roar of the crowd was deafening, the villagers' favorite pick for winner indistinguishable amidst the cheers. Eli had taken the champion title twice before, but Wade had tremendous support as the underdog. His performance had never been so powerful as this year, and he looked determined to be declared the victor.

"Engage!" the conductor bellowed.

By the time Eli's sword was drawn, Wade was already barreling toward him. His fist struck Eli square in the breastplate, pushing him back and nearly toppling him. Eli regained his balance and jumped to the side, dodging another blow, and then retaliated by shoving with his shield. His opponent didn't budge far, and that was when Eli fully appreciated that Wade was a head taller. The man seemed to be smirking behind his helmet's visor as he drew his sword to block Eli's vertical strike. Using his speed to his advantage, Eli struck three more times in rapid succession, landing blows on Wade's greave, shoulder

Chapter 1: ONSET

plate, and thigh. All competitors were heavily outfitted and thus were not easily injured in these duels. Endurance decided the victor as often as injuries did, and for that reason, Eli allowed his aggression to dissipate and prepared himself for defense. Wade approached him with an onslaught of slices, stabs, and shoves that drove him closer and closer to the arena's barrier. A young woman screamed Wade's name in a clear show of admiration, and Eli used the distraction to strike his helmet. Eli's opponent growled in frustration as he batted Eli's sword aside, glaring at him with contempt.

Wade held his gaze for a few tense moments while Eli regained his footing, slowly rotating so that his back was not to the arena wall. Wade lowered his sword, pulled back his other arm, and then threw his shield with an enormous grunt. Eli ducked the brunt of the attack, but the shield clipped the top of his helmet, knocking it askew and distorting his vision. Eli dropped his own shield and frantically removed his helmet as he heard pounding footsteps approaching; next he felt his legs being swept out from under him. Eli crashed to the ground with a bone-jarring crunch, wincing as Wade towered over him, his sword pointed at Eli's chest. Behind Wade, Eli could see the championship conductor standing at the ready to intervene if needed. Both contestants breathed heavily as they tried to anticipate each other's next move. If Eli did not react quickly, he would be declared incapacitated and Wade would be victorious.

Eli began to raise his sword in retaliation, but Wade lifted his giant boot and smashed it to the ground, wrenching his wrist and bending his blade. Eli made a split-second decision and pulled up on the hilt of his sword with all his might, breaking the blade underneath Wade's full weight. With the jagged few inches of steel attached to his hilt, Eli drove the broken blade through the edge of Wade's boot. Eli had been careful not to stab the foot, knowing that kind of attack would get him disqualified. The man was unharmed, but pinned to the ground.

Before his opponent could wrestle free, Eli sprang to his feet and circled behind him, twisted his sword arm, and took the weapon. He raised the sword horizontally to Wade's neck, grappled with him as he tried to break free, and nodded to the conductor.

The conductor shouted, "Victory to Eli Abnerson! Wade has been defeated!" and the crowd erupted into cheers.

Eli dropped the sword, removed his glove, and extended a hand to Wade, who acknowledged him not. With both hands, he tore the destroyed blade out of his boot and up from the ground, then he tossed it aside and departed the arena with his head downcast.

Eli looked up to see his family approaching from the stands. Little Gabbi looked shocked. His mother Lana was a mess of tears, and his father looked as proud as ever. Lana reached him first, scooping him into a motherly embrace, while Abner clapped him on the shoulder and smiled out at the crowd.

"Another uneventful year at the Championship of Warriors, I suppose," muttered one old man to another, sharing a table across the pub from Eli. It was a loud and dark place filled with smoke and half-aware people, the perfect place for Eli to come when he wished to escape notice and the general hustle and bustle of the village. He had stopped in for a visit to relax and recuperate after his fierce battle, but it turned out that he was in store for quite an earful. It seemed that the pub's regulars made a point to find *something* to complain about over a pint at the day's end.

"Kadmiel against Eli, always the same. Always the same outcome. Why doesn't the boy just give up?"

Eli smirked to himself and sipped his tea. One doesn't stay a hero for long, it seemed. It was true that he had performed

Chapter 1: ONSET

remarkably well in the past two championships held in their village, and had defeated his rival Kadmiel in the final duel each time. Kadmiel was the best swordsman he had ever met; he was cunning, quick, and merciless—all the characteristics of a deadly opponent. Eli actually thought it was outstanding that he was able to prevail in the past, but apparently the older folks were tired of seeing the same outcome. That, and they were probably too drunk to notice that Eli himself was only a few tables away, able to hear their every word.

"Archers aren't looking too bad this year. Jousters were a pathetic show. Now if only they had allowed the sorcery competition that was proposed—*that* would make for one interesting championship!" The old man leaned back in his chair and raised his eyebrows at his companion, who nodded in agreement. Eli stopped mid-sip and spun in his seat to face the man who would suggest such a thing.

The bartender, Rufus, joined in. "Not a chance. We'll see you old souls take the swordsman championship title before sorcery is ever sanctioned, let alone involved in the Championship of Warriors!"

"Says who?" spat a man around the pipe in his mouth.

"Says the High King!" said Rufus.

The old men scoffed, then one spoke up. "The High King? You mean the *Missing* King. You realize last week marks a quarter *century* since His Highness has even been seen? Well?!"

Rufus shook his head, pulled out a rag, and began drying a glass. "That may be true but his law still stands, and you'd best watch what you say when discussing things of this nature. No more talk of sorcery in my pub tonight!" He turned away to wait on other customers, leaving the old men muttering under their breath.

Eli leaned back in his chair, contemplating what he had overheard. His parents had told him little about sorcery, only that it was an outlawed art in the kingdom by order of the

High King. With that in mind, who would try to get sorcery accepted as a competition in the championships?

Eli stood up, stretched his back, and made his way to the exit. He had enough on his mind with the upcoming battle against Kadmiel for the title. Eli opened the pub door leading to the town's main dirt road but bumped into someone on their way in.

"Excuse me—oh, Eli!" It was Tabitha, a neighbor and friend of his family. Her curly black hair bounced as she stopped abruptly in the doorway. She beamed at him. "You were amazing today! Stabbing Wade's boot with half a sword—my goodness." She punched Eli in the chest.

"Hello, Tabitha," Eli replied, bemused.

"Sorry your sword broke, though. I loved that hilt with the gems..."

For both of the previous championships he had won, Eli had been awarded gems that were added to the pommel of his sword by the town's smith. "I didn't fight with that sword today—I figured Wade would break it, actually."

"There's that smart mind! How are you feeling?" she asked eagerly.

"Sore. I almost wish Wade had finished me off so I wouldn't have to fight Kadmiel for a third time."

Tabitha laughed as though she thought Eli were joking. "You'll do great, Eli. Don't underestimate yourself. After all the practice you've put in and all the experience you have, Kadmiel won't stand a chance. Just one more day and then you'll be a three-time champion!" She smiled then darted past Eli before he could say anything else.

Eli grinned, thankful for the support. Sticking his hands in his pockets, he set a course for home.

Chapter 1: ONSET

The night hours dragged by slowly before the sun crept through the curtains into Eli's small bedroom. He lived on the upper floor of his parents' house, which was situated near their fishing hut on the outskirts of the village. Eli yawned, not feeling rested after hours of wakefulness and anticipation. He rolled over—then jumped with a start. Staring down at him were two large, unblinking eyes. It was Gabbi. Eli's heart resumed beating and he let out his pent-up breath, pulling his sister into a hug.

"What's up, Gab?"

"Just wowried about you... You fight Kadmiel today—he's stwong."

Eli grinned at her attempts to pronounce words without her top two teeth. "Yeah, he is strong. But I've beaten him before!" he said reassuringly.

"So how come he keeps twying to win?" asked Gabbi.

He sat up and considered her question. "You know... I don't think Kadmiel is the kind of man that will ever stop until he wins."

Eli didn't know Kadmiel personally, but from what he had heard, Kadmiel was a hard man. He was only a year and a half older than Eli, but he had experienced a thoroughly difficult upbringing. Kadmiel's father had passed away, leaving him to take care of and provide for his mother. He never had time for recreation, sport, or any such luxuries. Rumor was that Kadmiel wanted to win the Championship of Warriors to land himself a well-paying job.

Eli stood up and stretched, then tousled Gabbi's hair. "Don't worry about me, sis. With you cheering for me, I know that I won't lose." She smiled, showing gaps where her baby teeth had been. "Come on. I smell breakfast!"

Despite Eli's reassurances given to his sister, he felt more unsure this year than he had before. He wasn't able to eat much, and had soon excused himself to walk outside.

The morning was cool and still. Waves crashing against the beach and seagulls circling above provided a familiar backdrop of noise that allowed Eli to quiet his mind and sort his thoughts. Thinking of Kadmiel had troubled him. The village viewed them as rivals, due to the fact that each previous swordsman title match had come down to the two of them. But something about the situation didn't sit well with Eli.

I don't really want to win as badly as Kadmiel does. And I know it.

Eli had already been the victor. It certainly came with its perks—a fair amount of prize money, recognition, opportunities to join various warrior guilds, and more. Thus far Eli had opted to remain home, where he enjoyed working at his family's fishing hut, spending time with his parents, sister, and friends in the village.

Why is it so unheard of to just be... content? wondered Eli. Everyone else seemed to have grand aspirations. *Perhaps I'm still too young to know exactly what I want. Just because I'm a good swordsman doesn't mean it's what I want to do the rest of my life.*

Eli sighed and picked up his scabbard; his champion's sword now sheathed inside it, replacing the broken blade from yesterday. He would need to purchase another backup in town. Eli unsheathed the sword and squared his stance.

"You can't let him win, son."

Eli spun around to see that his father Abner had joined him outside their home. He looked down and pawed the dirt with his boot. "How did you know?"

"How did I know that you are having second thoughts about the competition?" asked Abner. "I've known you long enough to see when your heart is in something or not. Listen..." He put a hand on Eli's shoulder. "Eli, you are a natural at what you do. You were born with these gifts for a reason. You must use them to the best of your abilities, and your confrontation with Kadmiel

Chapter 1: ONSET

today will be the largest test you have ever faced." Abner let go of Eli's shoulder and began pacing with his hands behind his back, next to the garden behind their house.

"If Kadmiel defeats you without your best effort put forth, you are only shaming him. Besides, these battles are extremely beneficial for the both of you..." Abner trailed off and took Eli's sword out of his hands.

Abner held the blade up before his eyes and studied its edge, which gleamed red in the rising sunlight. "Iron sharpens iron, Eli. This competition is doing more than improving your skills with a sword, but it is a test of your character. Now"—Abner tossed the sword to Eli, who caught it around the hilt—"go sharpen your sword. Familiarize yourself with its weight and balance. You have a trial ahead of yourself, but I believe you will succeed."

Eli smiled at the sparkle in his father's eye, then nodded and did as he was charged. He knew his father was right. He needed to fight for the championship with all his strength; not doing so would be a disservice to him, his opponent, his family, the tournament conductors, his supporters in the crowd—everyone.

Eli spent the morning refining his resolve and his stances, and he destroyed a number of dummy targets. He had caught sight of Kadmiel briefly that day, watching from behind as the warrior walked brusquely through town, stopping to speak with no one. Eli's nerves were starting to rise, so he focused on his breathing, slowing his heart. If there was one thing that had allowed him to prevail in the past, it was a razor-sharp focus.

Eli arrived at the competitors' tents before noon that day, where a large crowd had already gathered outside in the stands, whipping up a frenzy of chants and cheers. The entire town would be watching his confrontation with Kadmiel, and the conclusion of the match would mark the closure of the entire

9

Championship of Warriors for the year, which always ended in a massive feast celebrating the victors. Kadmiel had not attended the feast before, which Eli thought was unfortunate.

There's nothing to be ashamed of with second place anyway, he thought.

Eli could faintly hear the tournament conductor outside, building up the upcoming match and getting the crowd even more excited; the gathered villagers sounded as if they were preparing for war. Eli began to strap on his armor piece by piece, thankful for the protection it provided. While he had taken home the previous championship titles, he had also left the arena with an assortment of vicious injuries—severed tendons, a broken arm, and a broken nose, in recent memory. Eli took a long drink from his waterskin, sat down on a stool, and closed his eyes, focusing again on reining in the wild beating of his heart.

The entrance flap of the competitors' tent was brushed aside, and someone entered. Eli turned to see the visitor.

Kadmiel stood in the entrance, outfitted in full armor, his sword sheathed with his hand on the pommel. Eli rose to his feet instinctively, reaching for his sword. Kadmiel gazed at him flatly as he picked up his weapon. After a few uncomfortable beats when Eli determined that Kadmiel was not going to attempt to harm him, he strapped the scabbard to his waist and tried to appear casual.

"Hey, Kadmiel... how are you?"

The tall, calculated swordsman was ominous standing in the entrance to Eli's tent. He responded without much inflection in his voice. "I just wanted you to be aware that something suspicious is going on outside. I've seen those sorcerers of old from the village, who say they've reformed, lurking around the arena today. I don't trust them. I'm hoping they don't intend to interfere with our match one way or another, but who knows—maybe they've collected bets on one of us and have a horse in the race."

Eli was intrigued. "But sorcery is outlawed, and there are hundreds of people watching all around. You don't suppose they'll actually try anything, do you?" he asked. "The King's royal officers would stop them."

Kadmiel shrugged. "Sure, they've avoided trouble with the law for years by staying quiet and keeping to themselves, but they are old and tricky men. Any enchantments of theirs may be subtle and unnoticeable to the crowd."

Eli did not like the sound of sorcerers using illegal magic to aid either one of them in their duel. "I have an idea—if either of us senses that we are being given an unfair advantage from an external source, or someone is inhibiting our competition, we will call a respite and discuss it with the arena security."

Kadmiel nodded once. "Fair enough—you have my word." He extended a hand and Eli shook it, surprised.

Kadmiel turned to leave, and Eli was about to thank him when an enormous boom sounded, followed by a quake that shook the tent. Eli's knees buckled, and he and Kadmiel fell to the floor. The screams coming from the arena suddenly turned from cheers to cries of terror. Eli's mind raced as he tried to regain his footing, thinking of Gabbi, Lana, Abner, and Tabitha. Another great boom reverberated from outside the tent as he stood up tentatively. Kadmiel was on his hands and knees, and Eli grasped him by the forearm and pulled him up. Both swordsmen crossed the distance to the tent's entrance flap and thrust it open, searching for the source of the calamity.

Eli's stomach churned at what he saw. Sorcerers were terrorizing the gathered spectators, casting vicious spells, hurling missiles of fire into the crowd, immobilizing those attempting to flee, and causing warriors' own weapons to turn against them.

"Where's my family?" Eli gasped. Kadmiel looked speechless.

Eli's gaze roamed over the stands, where his parents and sister had watched his battle with Wade the day before. It was next to impossible to recognize specific people in the crowd— everyone was in a panic, clutching their loved ones and trying to back away from the tyrants closing in.

Chapter 2: **INCURSION**

A lready bodies were lying strewn around the arena. Eli had to get to his family before the sorcerers did. He set off in a run but was halted immediately, as Kadmiel caught his arm and dragged him back into the tent.

"What are you doing?" demanded Eli. "I can't stand here while my family is in danger!"

"Look," said Kadmiel, pointing to the limp bodies through the entrance flap. "See who they're attacking?"

While the group of sorcerers—three, it looked like—were trying to confine and capture the spectators, it seemed the fatal strikes were aimed at royal officers and the championship participants: armed individuals, the archery title-holder, the jousting finalists...

"All the same," said Eli slowly. He pulled free from Kadmiel's grip. "I have to do something... Help me."

Kadmiel turned to look out from the tent, and around him Eli caught glimpses of the chaos; now unnaturally tall flames were rising to block all exits from the arena as an old sorcerer seemed to command them with his wrinkled hands, laughing as the villagers were trapped. The other two magic-wielders responsible for the destruction had split up and spread out throughout the stands, stamping out any attempted uprisings. A cold touch of fear shot down Eli's spine as he realized just how helpless he felt against these sorcerers, but he tried to ignore the thought.

Just as Eli decided a course of action, one of the sorcerers, a short man in a dark blue vest, spun to face them. Kadmiel blocked the entrance protectively and obscured Eli's view of what was happening. There was a bright light and a blur, then

Eli suddenly felt his ribs crunch and his feet leave the ground as Kadmiel tackled him backward into the tent. A moment later flames exploded all around, sending a heat wave that washed over them. Eli's head hit the ground hard on impact, and his consciousness seeped into a deep black; the sounds of terror from the arena faded into the distance.

Eli's head throbbed as he slowly regained awareness. He tried to open his eyes, but they stung from smoke in the air—the smell was pungent. Eli rolled off his back, got to his hands and knees, and attempted to get his bearings. Kadmiel was stirring as well, groaning. Eli stood up and offered Kadmiel a hand. They took a brief look around the collapsed and charred tent, then hurried outside.

Eli gasped. The arena was in pieces, littered with dead men and women. The destruction was unbelievable; his village had enjoyed a few decades of peace during Eli's short lifetime, even with the High King absent from the throne. All of that, undone in mere moments.

Kadmiel turned his eyes downward and put his hands on his hips.

Feeling numb, Eli stumbled forward to the nearest victim. The face was downturned, but long blonde hair revealed that it was a woman. *Please, not my mother,* he thought desperately as he approached the prone figure wrapped in burnt clothing. *Please don't be her,* he silently pleaded, bending to examine the body. Eli released his pent-up breath when he saw it was not Lana, but dread came over him as he recognized one of their neighbors lying nearby.

"Hello?" Eli asked futilely. Nothing moved in the arena.

Eli rushed from person to person, hoping not to find his loved ones among the dead but unable to keep from looking. His nerves were on edge and his heart fluttered each time he recognized someone from the Southern Shores.

Chapter 2: INCURSION

Just when he thought he had inspected the entire arena, his eyes fell upon a girl.

Young, beautiful, unmoving. Eli fell to his knees, and tears began to stream down his cheeks. He held his face in his hands and cried until he heard footsteps coming from behind.

"Yours?" Kadmiel asked quietly.

"No." Eli sobbed. "Not Gabbi. But it could have been."

Kadmiel offered a hand and pulled Eli up. "They still need us."

Eli wiped his face on his sleeve. "Did your family make it, Kadmiel?"

"Yes. It appears they were targeting warriors," he stated.

Eli shook his head. "Not only warriors, there are a few townspeople here," he said shakily.

"Perhaps those that opposed the sorcerers," added Kadmiel. He looked down at the girl and frowned. "Must have just gotten caught in the battle," he muttered.

Eli had to look away. "So where are they?" He began to pace, surveying the surrounding areas of town. There was no sign of the sorcerers or villagers.

"Gone," said Kadmiel.

Eli didn't want to believe it. "The sorcerers *took* them?"

Kadmiel walked over to a fallen swordsman and nudged the body with his boot. It looked as if had been run through by a bolt of lightning. "They chose the perfect time to strike, the Championship of Warriors, when all the strongest combatants in the land were gathered and distracted."

"Thank you," said Eli, "for saving me—for coming and warning me about those men."

Kadmiel nodded. "What do you know about them?"

Eli searched his mind for any knowledge from his childhood. "I haven't had much interaction with them—now that I think about it, my father always seemed to give our family a wide berth from suspicious men like those. I think the short one with the blue vest is Barid, the one throwing fire. And then there was a tall one—Edmond?"

"Edric," Kadmiel corrected him. "And the old, mad one's name is Fathi. These are a very dangerous group of sorcerers."

"And they have our families, our neighbors," said Eli.

"But they don't have us," said Kadmiel. They locked eyes.

In that moment, Eli knew that they needed to do something—to attempt a rescue. But a deep knot formed in his stomach just as the idea entered his mind.

Eli shook his head sadly. "We have no idea what we're up against—what the extent of their powers is. It all happened so fast; I saw the sorcerers tossing flames around, controlling lightning, moving people's own weapons and turning them against them... What hope do we have?"

Kadmiel's expression was blank at Eli's protests, as if the warrior had already made up his mind. "You're right, Eli—we need to know what we are up against so that we can prepare to confront them. Come on." Kadmiel set off toward the arena's southern exit, toward town.

Eli took one last glance at the fallen swordsmen, archers, and jousters—some of whom had been friends—then followed behind Kadmiel.

"What do you have in mind?" asked Eli.

"Raiding their hideout," said Kadmiel.

"You know where they meet?"

"I have a pretty good idea." He led them toward a single shack that was in flames; its neighbors were all untouched.

"Suspicious, no? They're hiding something—covering up their tracks," said Kadmiel. "Let's find out what it is before it's gone."

Eli paused, his hand gripping the door to the sorcerers' hideout. It was hot from the flames eating away at the house from the inside. In many ways, this felt like the door that led to a new and frightening chapter of his life. By opening it and entering their property, he and Kadmiel were essentially declaring themselves enemies of Fathi, Barid, and Edric, and setting themselves on a collision course with forces much stronger than themselves.

But what choice was there? The sorcerers had their families and neighbors, and they had already started the war. With a pounding heart, Eli pushed the door open and stepped over the threshold. He and Kadmiel peered inside through the thick black smoke. Flames were spreading out from each corner of the shack, though no firewood blazed beneath them. Raising sleeves to cover their mouths, they ventured further in. Kadmiel began unlocking and opening each window in an attempt to clear the air.

The place was an absolute mess. Every wall was lined with bookshelves, but the books had either fallen to the ground along with collapsed shelves, or were being incinerated. Handwritten notes and pieces of parchment covered the kitchen table, which was as of yet untouched. What struck Eli most was in the center of the living room floor.

"Kadmiel, come look at this."

Kadmiel set down the parchment he had been examining and stood at Eli's side. "What is that?" he asked, bewildered.

Burned into the carpet were arcane shapes and symbols that Eli had never seen before. The most prominent feature was a shape made of intersecting diamonds, like a four-pointed star. Eli didn't know how to interpret the star or any of the surrounding circles and symbols, but he knew one thing...

"This is unnatural, Kadmiel."

"Supernatural," Kadmiel stated.

Their eyes snapped up from the floor at the great groaning sound of the wall, opposite the entrance, beginning to collapse.

"We have to go!" said Eli.

"Wait." Kadmiel crossed the room to a crate of documents that was aflame. He bent down to retrieve something from the burning box and withdrew his hand quickly, clutching a completely undamaged scroll. It was small, but beautiful and ornate.

"Protected by magic. If anything in this demon's nest is important, it's this," said Kadmiel, tucking it into his pocket.

Eli and Kadmiel burst out of the sorcerers' hideout, leaving the door ajar as they coughed and gasped for clean air. Eli slumped to the ground, dizzy from the smoke. His head was spinning from what they had seen.

"We still... don't understand... what we're up against," said Eli between fits of coughing.

Kadmiel sat next to him, then pulled the scroll out from his pocket and began to examine it. It was gold and green on the outside and had intricate carvings on the rods. He flipped it over and saw a name inscribed on the outside.

"Look," said Kadmiel.

"'Eli,'" Eli read aloud.

They looked at each other quizzically. Kadmiel paused for a moment then shrugged and went to open the scroll. But it remained tightly sealed, no matter how hard he attempted to pry it open.

"Magic," said Eli, shaking his head.

"Give it a try."

Eli took the scroll and gripped both ends, preparing to use all his strength, but it unraveled effortlessly for him. His apprehension grew, but his curiosity at the document's contents was greater.

Inside was a small amount of parchment, with a single line of text written in flowing calligraphy. It read: *'Your people have been imprisoned at the Inner Kingdom, while your enemies take up residence at the corners of the Tetrad Union.'*

At that moment the sorcerers' meeting house collapsed inward, and a great cloud of smoke billowed upward from the wreckage.

Eli barely noticed the structure falling, as his attention

was rapt on the scroll. *'Your people have been imprisoned at the Inner Kingdom...'* He kept reading it over and over while his mind raced with more questions than before they had entered the strange house. Could this scroll be trusted? Who wrote it? Why was it addressed to him?

He closed his eyes and rested his chin on his knees. They lived in the village of the Southern Shores, one of four parts of the Tetrad Union. The union was also home to the Western Plains, the Eastern Peaks and the Northern Marshes. The four regions formed a sort of diamond shape, not unlike the shape of the four-pointed star they had seen on the sorcerers' floor, Eli noted. In the center of these four territories was the Inner Kingdom, where the High King used to rule and watch over the Tetrad Union from his throne.

"There're three of them," said Eli. "And they've wiped out the Southern Shores. That leaves one sorcerer to take over each of the other three regions, so they can rule without fear of defenses rising from any surrounding royal allies."

Kadmiel's eyes widened. "You really think they're after the throne?"

"It's the only thing that makes sense to me. They can't commit murder and take hostages and get away with it while the government is intact. No, I think this was the first phase of a larger power play."

The two swordsmen thought in silence about their next move.

Kadmiel spoke up. "I'm just wondering how something concerning you came into the possession of those men..." He gave up on the conundrum and stood to his feet. "In any case, we should be off. We've explored their hideout and done our best to gather information on our enemies. Now there is no time to waste."

Eli rose and shut the scroll, pocketing it. "I agree. We have to get to the Inner Kingdom and take our people back, before the Warlocks' plan advances."

Kadmiel hesitated, then spoke slowly. "I, too, am glad that we found information on their whereabouts—if the scroll is to be believed—and I count it even more fortunate that the sorcerers are not accompanying them in their captivity. But, Eli, I don't think invading the Inner Kingdom first would be wise. It's easily defensible—surrounded by our enemies in each region."

He didn't want to hear what Kadmiel was suggesting, but his point rang true. Eli pawed at the ground with his boot, then conceded. "And even if we were to free our villagers, they could be overthrown and retaken by the sorcerers."

Kadmiel nodded. "As long as they live, they are a threat to us and our people. And the best chance we have at fighting them are while they are separated, spread out around the Union."

Eli sighed. "Yes, we need to challenge them individually. Besides, there's a chance we can help the other inhabitants of the Union if we make it to them in time."

With their minds made up, the swordsmen turned from the sorcerers' ruined building. The town was eerily still and quiet, like they had never seen before. No fisherman, no merchants, no children—no one.

Eli tried to think of what they might need for a potentially long and assuredly dangerous journey ahead. One thing was fortunate: they were already outfitted in strong sets of armor due to being interrupted during the Championship of Warriors. *It doesn't hurt to be thankful for the small things,* Eli thought.

Kadmiel started rattling off a short list. "Food. Waterskins. Money. Bedrolls. Pots, pans. As much as you can carry without overly inhibiting your speed. Meet me back here as soon as you can."

They set off, and Kadmiel stopped at the entrance of a home a few paces away.

"I didn't know that's where you lived, Kadmiel."

"It isn't," he said. "But I don't think the owners will be needing their supplies anytime soon. Let's get moving."

Chapter 3: **STEPS**

E li and Kadmiel met back with their packs full of provisions and supplies. Eli felt guilty about taking things from their neighbors' homes until he realized their food might well go bad during the villagers' absence, and other supplies could be returned in the event that their mission was successful. One thing he couldn't bring himself to take was money, but Kadmiel had arrived with a pouch of coins.

"Kadmiel... what *is* our mission?" Eli asked.

He scoffed. "Rescue our people, avenge the warriors along the way."

"They must think we're dead."

"Who?" asked Kadmiel. "The sorcerers or the villagers?"

"Both, I suppose," said Eli. "Fathi, Edric, and Barid were killing all the championship competitors in sight—anyone who could pose a threat to them. Then they tried to kill us. I bet everyone thinks they were successful."

"You're right!" said Kadmiel, sounding almost excited for the first time. "That's one advantage we have. And we need to keep that advantage. We shouldn't reveal our identities when we confront the sorcerers—they could use our families as leverage over us."

Eli nodded. "We'll grab our helmets and keep the visors down when we need to. Hold on!"

He returned a few minutes later carrying two helmets, and handed one to Kadmiel. They stored them in their packs along with their excess armor.

"I think that's it, then—we're finally ready," said Eli. He turned and took one last gaze in the direction of his home, and a lump formed in his throat. He had to look away, and that was when he realized that the sorcerers had stolen or slaughtered every horse in town. They would need to travel on foot. He couldn't believe just how much had changed over the course of a single day.

They set off through the town's gates and stopped at the fork in the road. The path to the left led to the Western Plains, and the one on their right would take them to the Eastern Peaks.

Eli sighed. "I almost think we should split up."

"Not a chance," said Kadmiel. "Our odds of defeating a sorcerer are slim enough as it is. Dividing ourselves would be suicide. No, we choose a direction and we will see it through together."

Eli looked from east to west. The sorcerers either had a significant head start, or they were enhancing their traveling speed by supernatural means.

"Well, I suppose there's no wrong decision here," Eli said, and he took the first few steps toward the Western Plains. Kadmiel followed.

"You know," Kadmiel said after a few moments, "it's quite a shame how today turned out. I was really looking forward to defeating you and taking that championship title."

Eli smiled in return, thankful that he was not alone on this journey. Maybe together they would have an actual chance at defeating the sorcerers.

The swordsmen fell into a comfortable pace side by side. They did not speak much, but opted to save their breath and not strain their lungs. They were traveling quickly considering the size of their packs; they were on a mission.

"Tell me more about yourself, Kadmiel."

A long pause followed. "What do you want to know?"

He thought for a moment. "What family do you have? What do you do for a living?"

Kadmiel frowned. "My father is dead, I take care of my mother, and I have no siblings. I hunt for our food, mostly."

Eli frowned. "How did your father pass?"

"He was in the service of King Zaan, a royal guard. Died on his night watch trying to stop some petty thieves. Just a risk of the profession."

Eli felt that a change of subject was in order. "Speaking of the High King, what do you think of him? Where do you think he's been all these years?"

Kadmiel shook his head. "I think he's dead. We just passed the twenty-fifth anniversary of his departure from the throne—were you aware of that? I think a new king should have been appointed long ago."

"But don't you think that the citizens of the Tetrad Union have done just fine, observing the laws that he established and being looked after by the High King's next-in-command subjects?" asked Eli. "I mean, Zaan has been missing since before I was born, and things haven't been bad."

"Things *are* bad now, Eli," said Kadmiel. "Three sorcerers are on their way to overthrow the kingdom. People want a ruler—someone on the throne they can look to, plead with. Someone to blame besides themselves when things go wrong in the world."

Eli contemplated that idea. "My father always told me, 'The High King has departed and promised to return plenty of times before, and he never broke his word.' My family has always believed he is still out there."

"Well if he is," said Kadmiel, "now would be a great time to show up and help us fight."

They continued plodding over the dirt road, west of their home. No one was in sight.

Their odds of victory were heavy on Eli's mind.

"There are three sorcerers, so we are outnumbered in that regard. They can use magic, which we don't know how to combat, and they could be capable of anything. They slaughtered dozens of warriors in the arena without breaking a sweat...

Kadmiel, how are we going to do this? What's our plan? Is there anyone that can help us?"

"I never said that this was going to be easy. I think the only way we stand a chance is through the element of surprise. We need to kill these men before they see us coming. If the scroll you read is to be believed, the sorcerers have split up, so we won't be truly outnumbered. We just need to arrive, lie in wait, set a smart trap, and strike at the right moment. They may be able to use sorcery, but they are still only men," said Kadmiel.

Eli nodded. "You do have some experience with this kind of thing."

Kadmiel raised an eyebrow.

"Hunting," said Eli. "You were starting to sound like a hunter, sneaking up on prey."

Kadmiel smirked. "If only our enemies were as fierce as deer."

Silence fell over the duo as they continued their journey. They must have walked for half the day before weariness overtook them. The sun had long since set, and their legs were stiff and tired.

"Let's rest for the night," suggested Eli.

Kadmiel shrugged off his pack with a sigh. The two swordsmen dragged their belongings a few yards off the dirt road and unrolled their bedrolls on a flat portion of ground nearby.

Eli's bones ached, compounded from his brutal duel with Wade, being knocked unconscious in his competitors' tent, and a full day of traveling. He was hungry and thirsty. Eli took a long drink from his waterskin and then passed it to Kadmiel, who nodded his gratefulness. Eli was too tired to satiate his hunger; food would have to wait for the morning.

Eli dreamed of his family. He dreamt of his little sister's birthday, of his mother and father's anniversary, which they had recently celebrated, and of seeing his loved ones supporting him from the Championship of Warriors' grandstands.

Chapter 3: STEPS

Then violent flashbacks of the sorcerers' attacks filled his mind's eye and caused him to toss and turn on his bedroll. He jumped and awoke with a start.

For a few moments, he thought the whole experience had been just a nightmare. But when Eli opened his eyes and saw the distant waves of the Southern Shores, the dirt road a few yards away, and Kadmiel's empty bedroll next to him, the painful reality of what had happened began to set in all over again. He slowly sat up, his body still aching. He felt like he had experienced no sleep at all, as restless as the night had been.

Where's Kadmiel? Eli blinked around blearily, but there was no sign of him. A great sense of isolation pressed in. While normally he would wake up in a warm home to the sounds of his family downstairs, he now found himself on the side of a road, and the only other free man of the Southern Shores was nowhere to be seen.

Eli shook his head, stood up, and stretched. He started digging through his pack, looking for the scroll from the sorcerers' hideout. Eli wanted to read its message again, the only remaining connection he had to his family. He grasped the scroll, pulled it out of the bag, and gripped both sides, but it wouldn't budge. The document was locked tight. Eli flipped it over and examined the backside.

The parchment no longer bore his name on it, but instead the fine script read: *Idella.* Eli's jaw dropped. He had a whole new respect for the object in his hands. After marveling at it for a few more moments and trying unsuccessfully to open it again, he placed the scroll back into his pack and started gathering the necessary wood and tinder to start a fire. His stomach was protesting loudly about the amount of time it had been since he last ate.

Kadmiel stepped out from the trees and into the clearing, bearing game slung over his shoulder, which he dropped heavily in front of the fire that Eli had prepared.

"You look all right," said Eli. "Sleep well?"

"I did," he answered. "Don't worry, Eli. We'll get them."

He nodded. As Kadmiel began to skin the deer, Eli told him about the sorcerers' scroll.

"It *changed* names?" Kadmiel asked. He showed him, and Kadmiel shook his head. "What does it say inside?"

"I can't open it, just like you couldn't when my name was written on it." Eli shrugged. "It must only open for who it's addressed to."

Kadmiel sighed. "I suppose these are the kinds of things we need to be expecting from our enemies—all sorts of inexplicable happenings and trickery."

Eli fixed a soup, and, before long, Kadmiel had the meat ready. They ate in silence, contemplating what the day would bring.

Finishing their bowls, they packed what could be saved for the coming days.

Eli thanked Kadmiel for the deer. "You're a good hunter."

Kadmiel smiled. "Thanks. With my father gone, I had to be."

"How did you learn to hunt—did your father teach you?"

"No," said Kadmiel. "I was too young before he died. My family barely survived for two years after my father's passing, then I decided to step up and make the provisions come instead of waiting for them to come. I learned how to hunt by hunting."

Eli waited for him to expound.

"I didn't allow myself to come home until I brought something with me," Kadmiel finished.

The next two days passed much the same way. The road to the Western Plains was long, and Eli and Kadmiel fell into a reliable rhythm of traveling, making camp, cooking, hunting, and setting off once again. The trail they followed was straight, for the most part, and oddly vacant. Where they expected to cross paths with caravans of merchants and traders, instead they met no one. It was like the sorcerers were completely shutting down the economy of the Tetrad Union, freezing all activity as they established their control. A greater sense of dread settled into the pit of Eli's stomach the closer they got to an inevitable confrontation with a sorcerer.

Periodically, Eli glanced at the scroll he carried to see if anything had changed. The name *Idella* remained written on the back, and the paper stayed decidedly unopenable. Eli concluded that it would be that way until he discovered who Idella was and delivered the scroll to him or her. Just then a terrifying thought gripped him.

"Kadmiel, what if it's a trap?" He gestured to the name on the parchment. "It tells us where our people are located, then gives me the name of someone we have no idea if we can trust."

Kadmiel half-shrugged. "While that is a fair point, Eli, think about it—could we possibly be in any *more* danger? And besides, I don't think that it's a trap. The sorcerers believe us to be dead, which is to our advantage. They haven't set a trap for us because they think we're been taken care of—along with the rest of the warriors that they killed."

Eli and Kadmiel then devoted themselves to discussing strategies for combatting their enemies. At their disposal were Eli's and Kadmiel's skill with the sword, Kadmiel's proficiency with a bow and arrow, and other, more devious means of victory involving knives in the night.

No matter the course of action, Eli didn't like their odds. However, knowing that they were doing the right thing and believing that they embodied the only hope for the inhabitants of the Southern Shores, and maybe even the Tetrad Union, helped him push past his fear and keep marching toward the goal.

One day out from their destination, Eli decided to forgo sleep a bit longer than usual and drew his sword, challenging Kadmiel to a sparring match. They donned some of their armor from the Championship of Warriors, but kept their loads light-weight and agreed to hedge their intensity.

Kadmiel proved to be as formidable an opponent as ever, his height lending him an advantage. Their swords were a blur, weaving in and out of each other's defenses and clashing without pause. They would have drawn a crowd if the area was not so desolate. Both swordsmen worked the other into submission and called for another round multiple times. Eli appreciated the opportunity to refine his combat skills and prepare for what was to come. Before they expended all of their energy and collected too many bruises, Kadmiel called the sparring off, and they collapsed onto their bedrolls for the night.

Just after dawn, when the Western Plains finally came into sight, it became clear that the situation was far worse than they had imagined. The area was known for its agriculture, but no farmers were in sight. Empty fields stretched for miles. The ground was scorched; where crops had been, burnt stalks were strewn. Trees were uprooted and lain across the ground. Sparse cattle wandered aimlessly through the fields. It was a lot to take in at one time.

"Kadmiel... how? How could a sorcerer arrive here so much faster than us and wreak this much destruction?" Eli's voice was hoarse. "We've been traveling every waking moment... We went as fast as we could..."

Kadmiel rested a hand on his shoulder as the pair continued to survey the landscape. As soon as the first tear left Eli's eye, his sadness melted into rage and he shook off his pack, reaching in to retrieve the two helmets that they had taken from the Southern Shores. Kadmiel took his apprehensively, saying, "The sorcerers lived around us—they might recognize the work of the smith from our hometown."

Chapter 3: STEPS

Eli placed the helmet over his head and secured the strap beneath his chin. "I think we'll give him a bit more to worry about," he said determinedly.

The two swordsmen buckled on the remaining portions of their armor, steeling themselves. Last, they donned cloaks to conceal their weapons and draw less attention.

"There's no turning back from this point," said Kadmiel.

Eli grunted. "There's nothing to turn back to. They've taken everything from us, and they're showing no signs of ending this madness. This is it, Kadmiel."

Fully outfitted, Kadmiel grabbed their packs and stowed them beneath one of the few trees that were left standing outside of the town proper. Sweating and with cold resolve, Eli and Kadmiel stepped foot into the Western Plains, gripping the pommels of their swords tightly, watching closely for any sign of movement.

The swordsmen were midway down the main street when they realized that they had been very wrong about the town. Eli spotted something unusual in a window—there, pressed up against the glass, was the tanned face of a townsperson, with wide eyes fixed on Eli and Kadmiel. The farmer looked scared and did not move an inch as he watched them. Eli tapped Kadmiel on the arm and pointed out that they were not completely alone.

As they traversed deeper into the town, they kept seeing glimpses of life—all hidden, and all terrified. Trembling fingers pulled back curtains slightly, mouths opened in shock at the sight of them. Kadmiel pulled Eli off the road, and they ducked behind the cover of a wooden porch. Whispering, they discussed what to do.

"The sorcerer is here, no question," said Kadmiel.

"Yes," agreed Eli, "and he's spared the locals, but intimidated them."

Kadmiel's temper flared. "Why kill and destroy our village, and not this one? I can't figure out why the sorcerers targeted our home."

Eli leaned his head back on the porch, pondering Kadmiel's question in his mind. A steady gust of wind picked up over the Western Plains, swirling up the dirt on the roads. The town was eerily quiet.

"Don't take it personally, Kadmiel. If Fathi, Barid, and Edric wish to overthrow the government of the Tetrad Union, and they decided to subdue three of the locations, one for each sorcerer, that left—" Eli paused, choking on the memory. "That left one town too many. One to destroy for fear of an uprising."

"Perhaps," Kadmiel agreed grimly. "However," he said, standing to his feet and offering a hand to Eli, "the sorcerers will have their uprising yet."

Chapter 4: **CONTINGENT**

E li and Kadmiel marched carefully but confidently down the dirt roads of the Western Plains, alert for any sign of the sorcerer. Eli did his best to ignore the fearful and inquisitive stares of the frightened onlookers hiding inside their homes. His heart beat wildly and his knuckles were white on the hilt of his sword. Kadmiel followed closely behind him, watching their flanks.

Twice Eli thought he heard footsteps approaching and they stopped their advance, searching behind objects and around every nearby corner for enemies.

They were nearing the town center when Eli heard it again. He stopped dead, glancing about. Seeing nothing, he looked to Kadmiel, who gestured for him to continue. Eli took a few tentative steps forward, eager to locate the sorcerer and begin their confrontation.

Suddenly Eli's head was snapped back, and his helmet pulled off from behind. He lost balance and reached out for help, and Kadmiel caught his arm. "What in the—"

Kadmiel stowed their helmets beneath his cloak and looked at Eli earnestly, as if begging him to remain quiet.

"WHO GOES THERE?"

Eli's gaze fell upon two armored men who had just rounded the bend in the road and revealed themselves from behind a log house. They wore full warriors' suits and were armed with swords on their belts, bows on their backs, and knives around their thighs. Their cruel eyes were locked on Eli and Kadmiel's faces, with teeth bared in a snarl.

"Sorry, sir," spoke Kadmiel.

What is Kadmiel playing at? Eli wondered, disoriented and confused.

The armored men made no threatening movements, but studied the swordsmen closely. Eli tried to remain collected and follow Kadmiel's lead.

"Ha, I told you that we weren't supposed to be out here," said Eli, giving Kadmiel what he hoped appeared to be a playful shove.

One of the guards gave a deep sigh and shook his head. The other pointed an accusing finger at Eli and Kadmiel, saying, "The Gathering's not for another two hours, so GET BACK INSIDE!"

Eli and Kadmiel needed no further instructions. They turned on their heels and retreated down the dirt road. It was at that moment that Eli realized how fortunate he and Kadmiel were for having their cloaks drawn around them so as to conceal the sheaths of their swords, preventing them from arousing even more suspicion. They passed a handful of houses until spotting one with its door hanging ajar. They bounded up the porch and stepped through the doorway, trying to look familiar with their "home" as the armored guards scrutinized them from the road. Eli regretted giving them one more backward glance, and a chill ran down his spine as he met their steely gazes.

Kadmiel shut the door behind them, and they took stock of their new surroundings. It was a home that looked as if it was once warm and comfortable, but had recently been ravaged. Sheets of parchment lay strewn across the floor, and there were a number of holes in the walls.

"No, not this time, scum!" called a brave-sounding voice from the kitchen. A man covered in knotted muscles and scars stepped around the corner into the living room holding a butcher knife at the ready, a deep scowl set in his brow. Other wrinkles in his face betrayed the age that his physique did not.

Chapter 4: CONTINGENT

Eli and Kadmiel raised their hands in a gesture that showed they meant no harm.

The knife-wielding man lowered his weapon and gave a weary sigh. "Oh. I thought you were the Enforcers again... What are you doing in here?"

"We're seeking refuge," said Eli. "Three sorcerers have attacked our village, and we believe they are spreading out to take over the rest of the Tetrad Union."

The man in the kitchen doorway looked shocked, and studied them for a moment. "Where are you from?"

"Southern Shores," said Kadmiel. "They killed our friends and stole our families. We don't know what's been done with them. Tell us: is one of the sorcerers here?"

"Oh yes," he said darkly. "He is here. Barid is his name—follow me."

He led Eli and Kadmiel into a dining room, which was also in poor condition. Broken dishes were everywhere. Eli tried not to step on any shards of plates and bowls, but their host paid no heed to the pieces on the ground as they crunched loudly beneath his boots. He seated himself at the dining room table, joining a haggard-looking group of two men and three women.

"My name is Valdon," said the man who had confronted them in the living room. "And this is the Uprising of the Western Plains." He spoke with a sort of faux grandeur, and the men and women seated around the table gave off a round of chuckles.

"And the rest of you are...?" asked Eli.

"No names," said an impatient-looking woman who was constantly bouncing her knee and tapping her fingers upon the table. "No time, no need."

Eli glanced at Kadmiel, wondering if they could be trusted. Kadmiel seemed to catch his meaning and gave a small nod.

"We are Eli and Kadmiel," said Eli. "Swordsmen of the Southern Shores. We are here to destroy the sorcerer that has invaded your village."

"Welcome, Eli and Kadmiel. We share the same goal," said an older woman at the table who spoke slowly and confidently. "How do you plan on accomplishing this?"

There was an uncomfortable silence that fell between them for a few moments.

"We know that our chances are slight," said Kadmiel slowly. "But... the strength of our will won't allow us to fail. We are determined to put an end to this threat and rescue our people."

"Kadmiel and I have experience in battle," said Eli. "Unfortunately, most of the other warriors in the Union were killed a few days ago, when they were gathered at the Championship of Warriors." The assembled Uprising moaned and lowered their heads. "That is when the sorcerers struck," finished Eli.

The Western Plains villagers had a moment of silence for the deceased, then lifted their heads with renewed resolve and determination.

"We share in your tribulations, swordsmen," stated one of the Uprising, a large man with a gray beard. "We have avoided trouble with the sorcerer Barid and his Enforcers here—for the most part," he said, gesturing around the kitchen at the broken dishes and general disarray of the room.

"What happened?" Eli asked.

"A mere warning," the man continued. "The Enforcers suspected that we were forming a rebellion, and they came in here to rough us up. Removed the locks from the doors. Told us to mind ourselves."

"Who are they?" Kadmiel inquired.

"The Enforcers are our countrymen who have proved loyal to Barid—whether by choice or by force, we do not know. We think he may have some kind of leverage over them."

"Bartering chips, per se," added a young woman seated across from Valdon. "Hostages from their families, perhaps."

Chapter 4: CONTINGENT

Eli's eyes widened slowly as a realization dawned on him. "We never should have come here. The Enforcers saw us enter this home..." He trailed off, considering the implications.

The woman with the bouncing knee shrugged. "Everything is coming to a head anyway. We won't be remaining concealed much longer."

"Tell us more about the situation here," said Kadmiel. "Why is everyone holed up in their homes?"

Valdon gave a long sigh, and the wrinkles in his face seemed to deepen. He looked weary. "The Western Plains has been home to our peaceful farming village for decades. We provided for ourselves, for the most part, and traded for some supplies from the other cities of the Union. We were content and, ultimately, very unprepared for the attack that was sprung on us." Valdon shook his head slowly. "The sorcerer Barid entered our village and established his dominance like that," he said, snapping his fingers. "He made an example out of the High King's subjects of our region and a few of the people that tried to stand up against him. He spoke to everyone else with an unnaturally amplified voice, telling us that he was in control now. Telling us to obey him and we would be spared. We lost friends and family members that day..."

The gathered villagers' eyes were glazed over, all remembering the terrors they had experienced just earlier that week.

Valdon continued. "Everyone who tried attacking Barid was killed. Everyone who attempted to exit the village and flee would drop dead. And now, anyone who shows open opposition to the sorcerer is struck down by the Enforcers."

"The Enforcers are a nuisance," said the bearded man, "but Barid is the real threat. He is a terrifying force to contend with. He is constantly uttering spells as if talking to himself—causing people to burst into flames, suffocate, or become bound in place while he walks up to them and takes their life."

Eli could feel his pulse quickening—both for fear of the sorcerer, and also for a growing desire of revenge upon his enemies. Eli looked at Kadmiel, who appeared to be equally determined.

"What is this 'Gathering' that will be taking place?" asked Kadmiel.

"We're unsure," stated Valdon. "Since Barid invaded our village, we have been commanded to stay in our homes. The Gathering takes place at high noon and will be the first time he plans to address us all."

"We think," said the old woman, "that Barid has far larger plans than ruling the Western Plains. We expect that he intends to use us, the citizens of the Plains, to advance whatever the next phase of his plan is."

"We are going to help you," said Eli. "So then, what is your plan?"

"Barid is currently residing in our city hall," said Valdon. "And we have a man on the inside who is working for him."

A smile broke across Eli's face. *That's the best news I've heard in a long time!*

Valdon grinned as well. "He owns our town's brewery, and he is loyal to our cause. He has informed us that the sorcerer is extremely troubled—he is on edge, constantly upset, sweating, having trouble sleeping... We are told that he has taken a great liking to our friend the brewer and his drinks."

Kadmiel raised an eyebrow. "What exactly is our strategy?"

"We will poison the sorcerer, of course," said Valdon, with a mischievous glint in his eye.

Eli was skeptical. "Valdon... I'm happy to hear that there is an ally in close contact with the sorcerer, but... is Barid really going to be *drinking* this morning, before the Gathering?"

The villagers all looked taken aback.

"Oh, yes. Certainly. He really hasn't stopped drinking since his arrival," said Valdon.

Eli was encouraged by Valdon's confidence but not entirely convinced.

Chapter 4: CONTINGENT

"And this poison," said Kadmiel. "What will it do?"

"We are not certain," said the older woman. "It would kill you or me, but it might take more to stop a sorcerer. We aren't experts on these things, you know. We were not assassins before this whole ordeal." She smiled sadly.

Eli was moved with compassion for these men and women. *I'm sure they want nothing more than to live normal lives, yet here they are, sitting in a destroyed kitchen, hiding and plotting, trying restlessly to take back their village from an evil that has invaded, interrupted, and upended their lives.*

"Barid may be unconscious, asleep, weakened, drunk, or killed," said Valdon. "We do not know the extent to which he will be affected by the concoction, but we are confident that he will consume it in his chambers before the Gathering. The brewer will let us in to confront Barid once and for all."

Chapter 5: **UNSEEN**

"How can we help?" asked Eli. "We wish to see this sorcerer fall as badly as you."

Valdon smiled, looking optimistic for the first time. "You managed to get a pair of swords into the village. Your aid will be invaluable."

"It's time to move," said the hurried lady, rising from the kitchen table. "Barid should be given the poison any minute. By the time we are in position, the effects will have set in. Everyone, grab a—"

Her words were lost in a tremendous crash coming from the entrance of the home. The sound of soldiers' feet marching through the doorway was heard next, and someone called out, "Rebels, you are under arrest! Show yourselves!"

The Uprising scrambled to arm themselves, grabbing nearby kitchen knives, furnace pokers, even shards of broken glass. For a brief moment, Eli almost found the sight of the ragtag rebellion amusing. Then the gravity of the situation set in, and he prepared himself to contend with the Enforcers.

Valdon grabbed Eli and Kadmiel by the collars and drew them in close, whispering quickly, "Get out. Back door. Go to the city hall—west end of town. Complete the mission."

"But—" Eli started.

Valdon shoved them in the direction of the back door and turned away without a backward glance. Eli hesitated, but Kadmiel shook his head and pulled on Eli's arm, steering them toward the back of the house. Out of the reach of the kitchen's lights, they were shrouded in darkness. They could hear the clashes of swords and makeshift weapons behind them, and Eli desperately wanted to come to the aid of their new allies.

But he knew that the mission was more important.

Groping around in the darkness, Eli finally reached the back door of what was a storage room at the end of the house. He gave a push on the swinging doors, which budged slightly but did not open.

"Locked! From the outside... Kadmiel, we're trapped," said Eli.

Kadmiel grunted and stepped back a few paces, then took off running full speed toward the swinging doors. He crashed into them, and with a loud bang they broke open. The doors hung askew on the ruined hinges and the lock lay on the ground, torn from the wooden doors. Kadmiel's momentum had carried him out of the storage room and onto the dirt ground.

"Well done, Kad—"

Eli halted at the sight of two Enforcers standing outside, guarding the back exit. They looked as if they were just having a good laugh when Kadmiel came bursting through the doors, and their expressions quickly changed to ones of surprise.

Eli acted quickly and stepped forward, unsheathing his sword and slamming its pommel into one of the guard's temples in one motion, felling the man before he could react. The other Enforcer drew his sword and launched himself at Eli, hacking at him furiously. Eli was on the defensive, trying to stay light on his feet as he backed away from the attacker slowly, focusing on blocking every strike. His enemy was a brute, with imposing physical strength and a rage that lent his blows an element of unpredictability. Eli ducked under a ferocious horizontal swing that could have split him in half, then spun and kicked the Enforcer in the chest. The sorcerer's guard stumbled backward into Kadmiel's range, who had just stood to his feet and drawn his sword. Kadmiel finished their second opponent before the Enforcer could regain his balance.

The swordsmen caught their breath and attempted to slow their heart rate down in the sudden silence that followed. All that could be heard were the distant sounds of the clash between the Uprising and the Enforcers.

Kadmiel mostly recovered from their bout and walked to

the body of one of the soldiers, and bent down to grab it by the boots. Eli caught his intention and did so with the second body, and they dragged the fallen warriors through the busted doors and into the concealment of the storage room.

Kadmiel nodded. "Thanks for covering me. You did well, Eli."

Eli barely heard him. "We better move—the soldiers inside may have heard us!"

The skirmish from inside the villagers' house seemed to have died down. For better or for worse, they did not know, but they would have to find out later. Eli and Kadmiel set their course for the city hall.

As the two swordsmen traversed the streets again, the uncanny feeling of being watched returned. This time, they didn't stop to return the glances of the peering eyes in the houses. There was no time.

They treaded silently and kept alert for any sounds of the Enforcers, but none were to be found. They drew up to the city hall and hid themselves behind the corner of a home that had a good view of its entrance. There they waited for a handful of minutes that felt like a lifetime. The town was utterly still except for the wind that swept up the dirt roads.

Eli's heart leapt when someone came into view, approaching the entrance to the city hall. He bore a serving platter with a goblet and two elegant bottles. The brewer, for that is who Eli realized he was, balanced the platter on one hand while retrieving a large key from his breast pocket, then opened the door. Stepping inside, the man shut the door behind him.

Kadmiel listened intently for a moment. "He didn't lock it."

"That's our cue," said Eli.

They gathered their wits and then approached the entrance to the city hall in Western Plains, to meet Barid the Sorcerer.

Eli's hand trembled as he softly shut the door behind himself and Kadmiel. They were standing inside the city hall, quickly taking in their new surroundings. The building was unlike the modest homes in the vicinity, but was constructed with stone and marble, and the tall ceiling was supported by imposing pillars. Artwork adorned the walls, and statues resided in the corners. The air smelled clean, and it looked like precautions had been made to keep the Western Plains' dirt and dust on the outside. Echoes bounced off the walls from the Enforcers' boots as they rushed back and forth; they appeared to be preoccupied with the Gathering that was about to take place.

While they were distracted, Eli grabbed Kadmiel and they ducked behind what must have been a mascot for the farming town, a statue of a scarecrow, which provided them with cover from the bustling Enforcers. Peeking from behind their hiding place, they saw him.

At the end of the long hallway, the sorcerer Barid was seated on a tall chair, which partially made up for his short stature. He wore long blue robes and held a goblet in his hand. The man was a blur of activity himself, as he was constantly pointing and barking orders, sometimes beckoning Enforcers to him for instructions. Other times he appeared to Eli to be issuing commands to empty places in the room.

They watched as the brewer delivered a glass to the sorcerer and filled it from the bottle. The member of the Uprising bowed slightly to Barid while balancing the contents of the platter that he carried, and left the building through another exit.

As the swordsmen continued to observe from their vantage point, they noted that Barid already looked fairly tipsy. His eyelids were only half open, and his speech seemed to be slowing, judging by the movements of his lips. Indeed, three empty goblets lay strewn on the floor.

Just then, the cups began to move seemingly of their own accord. Barid was shouting something that they were too far away to hear, and then the three goblets were scooped up by nothing and floated away from the sorcerer, out of sight.

The sight of magic unnerved Eli. Growing up after the High King Zaan had outlawed sorcery in order to prevent its abuse, he had not encountered magic before the events at the arena. While he had seen this very same sorcerer strike down friends and companions with magic, even a menial use like this set him on edge.

"No one has noticed us yet," said Kadmiel in a whispered tone. "What do you think we should do?"

"We wait just a bit longer," said Eli. "We need to make sure that the brewer's poison is—"

Eli was cut off by a scream of rage. They whipped their heads up to see Barid rising from his chair (although not gaining any height) and dropping his goblet on the ground, spilling the contents that the brewer had delivered.

No! Eli almost shouted, hoping that the sorcerer had consumed enough of the drought.

Barid appeared upset at an Enforcer, pointing accusingly at the man in armor. The sorcerer yelled so loudly that Eli and Kadmiel could hear him clearly from across the corridor.

"You're a fool! You won't make that mistake again," said Barid. He turned away and growled, "Burn him."

Eli expected to see Enforcers carrying out his order and issuing their comrade's punishment, but none of them made a move. Then a flame sprang to life around the offending Enforcer's feet. Soon, a pillar of flame engulfed the soldier, cooking him in his own armor. His cries of anguish died out, and his suit collapsed to the ground with a loud crash.

"It is time!" announced Barid. "Gather the inhabitants of the Western Plains, and I will address them shortly." He retook his seat with a huff, then added, "AND GET THAT BREWER BACK HERE!"

The Enforcers completed their preparations with renewed urgency and then began marching out of the city hall's exit.

Eli and Kadmiel pressed themselves between the wall and the scarecrow statue so as not to be seen.

The brewer stepped up to Barid and appeared to take another drink order, then pivoted on his heel and made his leave. Near the exit he turned and met eyes with Eli and Kadmiel and held up a fist, wishing them strength. Eli gave him as much of a smile he could muster while Kadmiel nodded back.

Helmets! They had almost forgotten. Eli undid the knot on his belt where the helmets were tied, donning his and handing Kadmiel's to him.

Taking another look back at the sorcerer, they saw that he was leaning forward in his chair, gripping the armrests angrily, glaring at the last spilled goblet on the floor. But this time he was getting frustrated, and the cup wasn't moving. Eli's heart leapt. *This is our chance.*

Before Eli could fully think through what was happening, he was on his feet and sprinting directly at the sorcerer. Barid looked up from the mess on the ground with a look of shock and a growl. He attempted to stand up on short, untrustworthy legs.

Tunnel vision enveloped Eli; all he could see was his enemy in front of him. Sprinting at full speed, he drew his sword and quickly crossed the hallway, closing in.

Eli threw himself toward the sorcerer. Barid's eyes narrowed and he lashed out, batting the weapon aside, but the swordsman's momentum carried him, and he slammed into Barid. The sorcerer was knocked back onto his throne and his head met the hard wooden chair with a crack, dazing the man.

Eli reached for the sorcerer's arms, attempting to restrain them. Barid was a stout man, wrestling beneath his grip and trying to break free.

"GUARDS!" Barid screamed. "ENFORCERS! REPORT TO ME IMME—"

Eli let go of Barid's left arm and slammed his forearm underneath the sorcerer's throat, cutting off his sentence and his oxygen. The man's breath was heavy with the smell of alcohol, causing Eli's eyes to water.

"K—" Eli started to say, almost fumbling and using Kadmiel's name in front of the sorcerer. "Help!" he said simply.

"Blocking the entrances," said Kadmiel. Indeed, he was securing the doors just in time—Enforcers could be heard banging on the doors, but for now, the locks were holding.

Eli tightened his choke on Barid, but the man had one free arm and began to pummel his side. Finally, the sorcerer landed a blow on Eli's ribs that made him double over, buckling under the pain. Barid kicked Eli away from him and gasped, taking in breaths. Kadmiel rushed to his aid and helped him off the floor, Eli clutching his side.

The sorcerer had drawn a short sword with an emerald pommel from a sheath hidden in his robes, but he made no advance with it. Instead he pointed at the two swordsmen and began muttering, "Bind them! Burn them!"

Eli felt his ankles slam together, and there was nothing he could do to counteract it. Try as he might, his feet would not move.

Kadmiel was in the same situation, and heat began to rise until a flame sprung up around where they were standing. Eli's heart sank. *We can't be defeated already!*

"Who are you?" demanded Barid. He looked sick and was wobbling unsteadily on his feet. "Remove their helmets," he added, to whomever he was uttering.

Kadmiel's feet were stuck like Eli's, but his hands appeared to be free. He grabbed the bow from his back and an arrow in one swift motion, then nocked it.

"No, protect me—PROTECT ME!" cried Barid.

Immediately, the pressure around Eli's ankles alleviated, although the flames did not disappear. Eli leapt out of the fire and dropped to the ground, rolling and patting at his singed breeches. Kadmiel sidestepped the fire and let an arrow loose at Barid. The projectile came to a halt a mere two feet in front

45

of the sorcerer, clattering to the ground. Kadmiel persisted with his attack, nocking arrow after arrow and launching them toward their enemy. At least for the time being, Barid was on the defensive, and his sorcery seemed to be focused on self-protection. It was Eli's time to take action.

He approached the sorcerer quickly and raised his sword high over his head, then swung downward with all his might. Intending to strike Barid's head, he was surprised when his sword came to a dead halt above the man, jarring his arms. Eli lost his grip on the blade, then Barid gave him a backhanded slap to the chest that sent him sprawling against the wall; it was too powerful a blow for any normal human. For the moment, Eli watched limply from the floor as the battle continued.

Barid staggered about, fending off Kadmiel's attacks. The drunken sorcerer attempted to bark out his enchanted orders, but his speaking was slurred and often had no effect. Kadmiel was not faring much better than Eli; he was out of arrows and had drawn his sword, but every swing was stopped by an invisible presence. Kadmiel held his sword tightly with both hands so as not to lose his weapon, striking blow after blow upon the sorcerer's protections.

Barid laughed at the attempts, but Kadmiel didn't seem to notice. He was focused on his anger against the sorcerer.

"Who are you fools, to come after me with your homemade weapons and armor from the Southern Shores?" Barid chuckled. "You must be upset about what I and the other Warlocks did to that town. Poor boys," he mocked. "The Tetrad Union has come under new management, and the South has no part in our plan. Nor do the two of you," he said angrily.

Eli slowly pushed himself off the ground, his body trembling from his injuries. He quietly circled behind the sorcerer and Kadmiel, and positioned himself in front of a large pillar in the center of the room.

"Why haven't you killed us already?" demanded Eli, spitting

the words through his helmet. "Don't you have somewhere to be? You're leaving the people of the Western Plains waiting. I'm sure they're very interested to hear your great plan for the Tetrad Union."

Barid whirled toward Eli in rage, looking up at him with a fierce glare. "Crush the boy!" shouted the sorcerer.

The scarecrow statue stirred in the corner of the city hall. The area around the statue shook and cracked, then the statue floated a few inches above the ground.

Kadmiel seemed to understand what Eli's strategy was, and began battering the sorcerer's defenses with renewed energy. Barid blocked the blows, but Kadmiel advanced step by step, pushing the short man backward toward Eli.

"His defenses are weakened!" shouted Kadmiel. "He can't keep up all of his enchantments at once!"

The scarecrow statue suddenly hurtled through the air, turning to point its huge mass directly at Eli. It passed the dueling swordsman and sorcerer and was mere feet from smashing into him.

Eli mustered all his strength and leapt at the last moment, diving out of the way and hitting the ground hard. He groaned as his wrist twisted beneath him. There was an enormous boom that drowned out every other sound, and Eli and Kadmiel stared as the center column of the city hall began to give way. The statue had collided with the pillar and taken out a huge portion of the support. A crack spread up the column, and the whole structure crumbled when it reached the ceiling. The roof began to cave in, and Barid stood beneath it, his mouth agape.

Eli and Kadmiel scrambled away, trying to avoid the falling pieces of the building. Then the center of the city hall's roof gave out and collapsed inward.

The rubble and the dust settled. Eli and Kadmiel were hit by pieces of the falling structure, but nothing as serious as what

Barid experienced. The sorcerer had been standing next to the center column when it was destroyed, leaving him underneath the weakest part of the building when it collapsed.

Eli and Kadmiel stood shakily on their feet, observing the ruined surroundings. The destruction of the city hall was immense; light from outside poured in through the gaping hole in the roof, shining directly down onto the rubble piled where Barid the Sorcerer had stood.

Suddenly, to Eli and Kadmiel's utter dismay, the debris stirred. They looked at each other with dread, and then together slowly approached the rubble.

A few pieces went flying, and then Barid came into view; he had punched a hole in the stone tomb that was enveloping him. He laid flat against the floor, his head turned to see them. He had survived. The piled-up rubble rested a few inches above the man, short of crushing him.

Kadmiel drew his sword quickly and knelt down next to the sorcerer, looking eager to end their confrontation. Barid's eyes were wide with terror.

"Kill them!" rasped the sorcerer. As soon as he had given the command, the hundreds of pounds of rocks above him started to shake loose and fall downward. "WAIT! COME BACK! Protect me!" he pleaded. The rocks were then contained but Eli felt no attack, and Kadmiel appeared unharmed.

"That's it," said Eli. "You are out of tricks, Barid. For all your power, you can't escape this time."

The sorcerer just growled and shook his head back and forth with anger. He again addressed the invisible forces at his command: "Push harder, you worthless souls! Get this stone off of me!"

But the weight appeared to be too much; it moved but a fraction. After more growling and thrashing about, Barid finally quieted himself and appeared to accept the fact that he was at the mercy of the two swordsmen standing over him.

Chapter 5: UNSEEN

"I hope you know," he spat, "that you are making a grave mistake in killing me. You are fools. You all wait for the *High King* Zaan to reclaim the throne, but myself and the Warlocks have seen the truth. There's no use waiting for a dead king to come back; he's gone for good."

"I suppose you and the Warlocks think that you are fit to rule the Tetrad Union in his stead?" asked Eli.

Barid smiled. "No doubt. We do this out of our enormous respect for Lilith, she who was the greatest of us all."

Eli didn't know that name, but a deep chill ran over his body at the sound of it.

"I've heard enough," said Kadmiel. "I'm sure Lilith thinks your efforts are very sweet, Barid. But your time is up."

Kadmiel drove his sword into the sorcerer, who was unable to stop the attack without letting himself be crushed.

Just as Eli was about to celebrate their victory, a huge shockwave exploded outward from the slain sorcerer. The swordsmen were thrown into the air and landed on their backs, then they were pelted by falling fragments of stone. Eli lay flat on his back, stunned by the explosive energy, and then his vision faded to black and he lost consciousness.

Eli awoke to Kadmiel shaking his shoulders. "Eli, wake up!"

His eyelids were heavy, and his body ached like never before. Both of their helmets lay apart from them, removed by the force of the blast. Kadmiel did not look like he was in the best shape either.

"What was that?" Eli shouted.

"I have no idea. The last of Barid's tricks, I suppose."

"Are you all right?" asked Eli.

Kadmiel gave a deep sigh and then shrugged, wincing. A few moments passed and then he answered, "He's dead." A grin spread across his face.

A rush of excitement gripped Eli, and he returned the smile.

"Good work, Kadmiel!"

"That was not easy," he said.

"Well," started Eli slowly, "I suppose now is as good a time as any to get up."

They picked themselves up off the ground gently and stood in the ruined city hall of the Western Plains. The explosion from Barid's lifeless body had scattered the rubble across the room.

Kadmiel observed the caved-in ceilings and broken objects strewn about, then said simply, "Oops."

This caused Eli to give into a short fit of laughter, which was painful with the injuries he sustained.

"Come on," said Kadmiel. "There is still work to be done."

Eli scooped up their helmets and tied them to the back of his belt, ignoring the protests of his hurt wrist. No longer needing to conceal their identities, the two swordsmen armed themselves once more and exited the city hall.

Gathered outside was a mass of people, the assembled inhabitants of the Western Plains along with Enforcers, who had evidently given up on trying to enter the building and resorted to keeping the Gathering orderly. Everyone was wide-eyed and looked as if they had been watching the town hall anxiously, curious about what was happening. Then a look of relief spread through the crowd when they saw that they were not Barid, and Eli began to choke with emotion. While he certainly had personal reasons to seek revenge and justice upon the Warlocks, the feeling of setting these people free was an unexpected joy. For a moment, Eli forgot his wounds and his bodily aches, and he met eyes with all the survivors and fighters in the crowd, identifying with them as brothers and sisters.

"People of the Western Plains," said Kadmiel, "you are free! Enforcers, your sorcerer is dead. You are released from any magic or trickery that may have bound you to Barid. If you attempt to harm these citizens, then... you will be killed."

All eyes turned to the various Enforcers. Some leapt for joy, some wept for what they had been forced to do, and still others opted to flee the Gathering and head for the exit out of town.

This caused some villagers to give chase to the fleeing Enforcers, but Eli discouraged them. "Go ahead and let them run—enough blood has been shed today. Now it is a day of rejoicing and rebuilding!"

The crowd answered in a round of cheers.

"Go on!" said Eli.

Some of the villagers remained to thank them. Eli and Kadmiel appreciated their gratefulness, but they were tired. Soon the swordsmen seated themselves and shook hands with the villagers as they passed by and stated their thanks.

Someone even brought them water, which Kadmiel was desperate for.

A seemingly endless line of people passed in front of them, gripping the swordsmen's hands and telling them how thankful they were. Eli only felt half-present, though, because he realized that Valdon and the other Uprising allies were not among the crowd.

At last, there was a break in the throng of people. Eli and Kadmiel rose and, by unspoken agreement, angled down the road in the direction of the Uprising hideout. They located the house and Eli pushed the door inward, only it didn't swing open all the way. It stopped with a *clang* when it hit the armor on an Enforcer's dead body.

The swordsmen squeezed through the narrow entryway and surveyed the destruction all over the house.

Bodies covered the floor. The Enforcers were so many that Eli imagined they must have called for backup. The bodies of every member of the Uprising were also present. A tear dropped from his eye as Eli imagined the fierce fight these brave villagers put up while he and Kadmiel advanced on the city hall.

Kadmiel chuckled. Eli shot him a questioning look.

"I can't help it. Look at them!" he said, gesturing to the

fallen heroes. "Kitchen knives, broken pottery, furnace pokers. Look at what's in their hands. And they killed all of these attackers? This may have been the most fearsome group in all of the Tetrad Union."

Eli smiled sadly as he gazed on their fallen comrades. "Kadmiel," said Eli, "look at them. They are all *dead*. Look at us. We barely escaped with our lives. Barid could easily have destroyed us, had he not been poisoned. We cannot expect to have the same advantage over the other sorcerers, or Warlocks, as he referred to them."

"You're right," said Kadmiel. "We got lucky this time, but we still have a monumental task in front of us. We need more help."

"Should we—hang on," said Eli. He took one last look of respect at the deceased and then stepped out from the carnage onto the porch, where he could think much clearer.

Kadmiel joined him and said, "Hmm?"

"Do you think we should recruit some assistance from the village here?" continued Eli.

Kadmiel sighed and looked out at the Western Plains before them. "I don't think so. Each member that we add to our party makes us more vulnerable, less stealthy. All the warriors from this village were at our championships and were killed. I don't think I shook one able-bodied person's hand in that whole crowd, and I don't want to be responsible for their deaths."

Eli knew he was right. "We need people with some training in combat or tactics to really help us. In that case it would be worth the risks of expanding our party. But who can we possibly turn to?" he asked.

"There may be no one." Kadmiel shrugged. "But, hey... did you honestly think we would make it this far?" he asked with a sheepish grin.

Eli chuckled. "One Warlock down," he said.

"One down," Kadmiel agreed.

And the two swordsmen embraced, grateful for one another and glad to be alive.

Chapter 6: **PRISONERS**

The surviving villagers in the Western Plains were very accommodating to the swordsmen, assisting Eli and Kadmiel in acquiring food, refilling their waterskins, and applying bandages to their more serious wounds. Soon, they were prepared and on their way.

Upon exiting the town they stopped at the tree where their packs were stowed, and retrieved them. Eli untied their helmets from his belt and tucked them away inside their packs. Then they shouldered their bags full of belongings and set out on the road once more, this time heading north toward the marshes.

The Northern Marshes were said to be a dangerous place. Few opted to travel there, because people were known to get lost along the way if not familiar with the path. There were safe ways to navigate the marshes without getting yourself stuck, but that was something Eli's family never had a reason to do.

"Kadmiel, have you ever visited Northern?" asked Eli.

Kadmiel shook his head. "I haven't—never needed to. I always used a midway merchant in the Western Plains."

Eli nodded. A midway merchant was someone who made a living carrying goods between two of the neighboring locations within the Tetrad Union. The products they carried and sold had some markup, of course, but it did save time and travel for the buyer.

The two swordsmen were keeping up a good pace down the dirt road, perhaps even faster than their approach to the Western Plains. Their encounter with Barid reminded them just how serious this mission was, and that time was of the essence. Every moment they spent in the Plains was another moment that their friends and family had to survive on dwindling hope.

53

"We fought pretty well against Barid, wouldn't you agree?" asked Eli.

"Yes," answered Kadmiel. "Fairly well. I think that we need to try to work better together as a team, though—too often we were split up."

"That's true," said Eli. "I think that he was intentionally trying to keep us apart. Not only that, but fighting as a team is brand new to me. I've been a solo swordfighter all of my life."

"Maybe once all of this is over," said Kadmiel, "we'll start up a new Championship of Warriors with team competitions. It's fun."

"*Fun?*" asked Eli. "That was your experience with confronting Barid?"

"I was only joking," said Kadmiel.

"Ah, sometimes I can't tell. Your voice—it doesn't change much."

"Just keeping you on your toes." Kadmiel smirked.

I think that I still have a lot to learn about Kadmiel, thought Eli.

Their discussion paused briefly as they focused on keeping up their pace. The scenery was slowly becoming more lush, green, and mossy. More and more moisture was appearing along the way.

"So, who are you doing this for?" asked Kadmiel.

"What do you mean?" asked Eli.

"Your parents, of course," said Kadmiel.

"Yes, Abner and Lana," said Eli. "And then there's my sister Gabbi," he added faintly. It made him anxious to think about his sister. His parents could handle themselves, but Gabbi was so young...

"What about a woman?" asked Kadmiel.

"Lana and Gabbi are girls," Eli retorted quickly.

"You *know* what I mean."

Eli chuckled. "Well, there's someone from the Southern Shores named Tabitha. Did you know her?"

Kadmiel shook his head then raised an eyebrow.

"No, no," said Eli. "She's my best friend. Spunky and positive. Always fun to be around."

Kadmiel kept staring at him expectantly.

"As a friend!" added Eli. There was silence for a handful of steps, and he felt awkward.

"Why?" asked Kadmiel.

That single question gave Eli some pause. "I'm not certain," he said after a while.

"Do your parents dislike her?" asked Kadmiel.

"Not at all. Quite the opposite. I don't know, Kadmiel. I think that she's the best friend I could ask for, but that doesn't mean that I should marry her."

"You don't want to marry your best friend?"

"Okay!" said Eli, flustered. "What about you? Any—uh—love interests?" he asked halfheartedly.

Kadmiel laughed. "No."

"Just 'no'?"

"Never really had time for women. No one from Southern Shores that I'd like to be with for the rest of my life," said Kadmiel.

"Well then, maybe we'll find someone in our travels for you," suggested Eli. "I'll keep my eyes open."

The two swordsmen traveled for miles. They often walked in silence, admiring the scenery around them, never having been so far north. Slowly but surely, the dry landscape was left far behind and gave way to greenery. The sky took on a deeper tone of blue.

An hour after the sun had set, they had walked about as much as they felt their legs could carry them, and the companions stopped for the night.

Kadmiel strung his bow and stepped off the path into the trees while Eli prepared the fire and their sleeping area. It was a wonderful relief just to remove the heavy pack off of his shoulders. Eli stretched and yawned, then continued looking for firewood in the surrounding area. This task was more difficult than it had been in their camps along the way to the Western Plains, where the trees and dead branches had been much more dry.

Eli made do with what he could find and sat down next to the fire supplies, two sticks in hand to get the flame started. He began rubbing them together rapidly. His stomach growled, and he hoped Kadmiel was having luck hunting.

There was a noise, and Eli dropped the sticks. *What was that sound?*

Someone or something was nearby. Eli stood and rushed to his sword belt, strapping it on as he looked in each direction around their camp. Then he stood absolutely still and silent to listen for the sound again.

Nothing.

Eli tried to relax and return to his work on the fire, but he kept his sword with him this time.

Try as he might to think about anything else, his mind kept drifting back to the confrontation with Barid. They had encountered so many strange things in their battle with him; sorcery was a frightening thing.

Who was he constantly shouting orders at? Why were his magical abilities limited—was it the effects of the poison? Will the other Warlocks have the same amount of power, or could they be stronger?

Eli was still hurt from their battle with the sorcerer. His side, where Barid had struck him, especially stung.

Suddenly, there was the sound again. Eli stood up and threw down the materials he was working with, frustrated now.

"Kad, that you?" he asked.

No answer.

Eli drew his sword and circled the perimeter of the camp, checking for anything hiding behind trees or the large boulders in the area.

Chapter 6: PRISONERS

Then Kadmiel emerged from the opposite side of the trees, carrying a pair of geese by the neck.

"You're back!" said Eli.

"Missed me, or are you just starving?" asked Kadmiel.

"Both," Eli admitted honestly. "But I kept hearing a sound like I was being snuck up on."

Kadmiel dropped the fowl and immediately went to work with his knife.

"Try not to be on edge. Honestly, it's about time we ran into some travelers between cities. There *must* be people that the Warlocks haven't gotten ahold of yet. We're bound to encounter someone out here."

Eli shook his head. "What's the point of ruling the Tetrad Union if everyone despises you?"

"I suppose they just want power," said Kadmiel. "And they don't care how they acquire it."

"It makes no sense," asserted Eli.

"True, but I tend to think we are a bit more level-headed than these crazy, old sorcerers... Your sword is still drawn, Eli."

"Right," he said, sheathing his sword and attempting to relax. He focused on the fire and finally got it blazing, and then he helped Kadmiel with the remaining preparations.

Both swordsmen ate more than they thought possible. Not only were they ravenous from a full day of traveling, but they also weren't sure if they would be stopping again before reaching the Northern Marshes. Their destination was not yet in sight, but their view of the horizon was obstructed by the distant trees. The city could be close enough to reach before the sun set again.

They filled their stomachs and soon had eyelids too heavy to keep open. Eli and Kadmiel congratulated each other once more on what they had done in the Western Plains, and then retired to their beds. Eli thought that he heard a mysterious sound once more as he laid down, so he kept his sword nearby, and then his dreams took him away from the campsite and back home to the Southern Shores.

Eli woke abruptly. Something had startled him awake, but his mind still felt fuzzy from sleep. He opened his eyes, but his vision remained pitch black. Suddenly, he was being lifted by the shoulders, off his bedroll, and onto his feet. He tried calling out for Kadmiel, but found that his mouth was gagged.

Everything seemed to be happening so quickly, but his reaction time felt slow. He attempted to struggle against his captors, but it was too late. He was loaded roughly onto what felt like the back of a wagon, and then heard a *thump* beside him. Eli assumed that Kadmiel was in the same situation as him. Eli's hands and feet were then tied together, and he was rolled onto his stomach. The wagon began to move, and he heard the sound of horse's hooves pulling them.

Eli wanted to make contact with Kadmiel, so he tried to squirm in his companion's direction. Then a woman's voice sounded above and behind him saying, "Ah-ah-ah." At the same time, he felt a pointed boot collide with his shoulder. Painful, but nothing more than a warning.

Eli's heart sank at the revelation that he and Kadmiel were being watched over even in their transport. That left no hope of escape.

Resolving himself to that fact, Eli set his mind to figuring out what was going on. *Who are these people? What could they want from us? There are no women Warlocks. Were they hired by the sorcerers to capture us? Are they taking us to Fathi or Edric? Did the Warlocks already find out that we killed Barid?*

His thoughts turned over slowly. Eli felt as if he could fall asleep, which was unthinkable in the midst of his current predicament. Despite himself, his mind faded into quietness and he slept there in the captivity of unknown enemies.

Chapter 6: PRISONERS

*
**

Eli's blindfold was torn off without warning. He was sitting on a rough wooden chair in the center of a tent. All of his armor and possessions had been removed. Across from him, a woman stared at him with a scrutiny so intense and piercing that it chilled Eli. He sat there, meeting her gaze for a long, uncomfortable minute.

"Could you maybe put that blindfold back on for me?" he asked.

His captor was not amused. Not in the slightest. She bored her eyes into Eli even harder, and gave no indication that she intended to answer him.

Eli took the opportunity to study his surroundings. Coarse rope had been used to secure his hands and feet to the center pole of the tent and to the chair on which he sat. The chair itself, he discovered with dismay, was *also* tied to the pole.

"Wow," said Eli. "You've really gone to great lengths to keep me here. I'm flattered."

There was nothing else in the tent. The woman across from him used no chair, but towered above him with a perfect, even stance. She appeared to be in her early forties, her physique was toned and she wore her black hair in a braid. Eli noticed the protrusions of several hidden weapons on her body, but she held none. Her hands were clasped together behind her back as she studied Eli.

Another minute passed with no exchange, and Eli grew impatient. "Where is Kadmiel?" he demanded.

"So that's his name," she said flatly.

Eli's head fell against the pole behind him. *I blew it,* he thought. *Within seconds I've given away information.* At that point, he decided that there was no use telling anything but the truth.

"Yes," he replied. "My companion's name is Kadmiel, and mine is Eli. We have no quarrel with you, unless you are sympathizers of the tyrant Warlocks, in which case... I don't think we'll get along very well."

The woman straightened her spine even taller. "We are no friends of sorcerers, Eli."

"Then what are we doing here?" asked Eli. "You have no business interfering with our mission. We're going to stop the sorcerers from taking over the Tetrad Union and destroying more than they already have. Every second you delay us puts more people in jeopardy."

His captor raised a single eyebrow and continued to study him from head to toe. Eli sighed, exasperated. "Who are you?!"

The woman drew close to Eli and knelt to speak to him, eye to eye. "You will not receive any information from me but this: myself and my convoy serve the High King, and no amount of deception will benefit you here. You would do well to cooperate with us." She stood and turned on her heel, her back facing Eli. "We will not tolerate lies. You have no option but to tell us the truth, and you are completely at our mercy." She eyed him over her shoulder. "Do you understand?"

"Yes," replied Eli, downcast. "But this is a misunderstanding and a waste of time. I have been honest with you."

"We will see," she responded, then crossed the length of the large tent and snapped her fingers. A rustle of armor could be heard from outside the entrance as two guards stepped to either side, allowing her to open the flap and step through. Eli heard the guards secure the tent flap and retake their positions.

What is going on? Eli wondered, feeling bewildered and hopeless.

Similar interrogations followed. The imposing woman would enter Eli's tent, study him quietly, and then proceed to demand answers from him about himself and Kadmiel.

Chapter 6: PRISONERS

Eli told her everything truthfully, to the best of his ability. However, he seemed to be earning none of her trust, and no progress seemed to be made after several of these interactions throughout the day.

Mercifully, the first break came that night, when Eli was completely famished. He braced himself when he heard the tent flap rustling, but when a women entered, it was not the one he had spoken with before.

It was a younger girl with the same dark black hair as the first, but she had a much kinder and softer appearance. Rather than an orderly braid, she wore her long hair down and had a white lace headband. She carried with her a plate of food, and Eli found it hard to study the girl when his eyes kept darting to what she was holding.

"Hello, Eli," she said.

The girl set the plate before him, and Eli grew suspicious that it was going to be used as some kind of bargain for information. He was surprised then, when she immediately circled around him and began working on the knots restraining him to the chair and tent pole.

Within a few minutes, he was free of the bonds.

"There you go," she said. "Eat up."

Eli rolled his shoulders and popped his neck, then rubbed the raw skin where the thick ropes had rubbed against his wrists all day. He looked at the girl quizzically and then did his best to examine the food for any signs of poison, but he couldn't be sure what was done to the roast beef and vegetables before him.

And... I don't really know the first thing about poison, he thought sheepishly.

The girl seemed to notice Eli's hesitation and said simply, "It's safe." Then she surprised him by taking a bite of the food to prove her point. Eli saw no reason not to trust her now, so he ate the whole plate rather quickly while the girl watched him with a look of what he thought might be amusement.

Finished, he set the plate aside and thanked the girl. She nodded politely. Eli wondered what was supposed to happen next. He held his arms out behind him in expectation of being tied up once more, but the girl just laughed.

"You probably have to relieve yourself, I would think."

"That would be nice," admitted Eli, taken aback by the girl's consideration.

She extended a hand and helped him stand up, then led him out of the tent. At the entrance she snapped like the first woman had, and outside Eli saw two armored guards. They appeared to be men behind the full metal suit and helmets. One held a spear and the other a broadsword.

Free of bonds and blindfolds, Eli walked beside the girl. He looked around the camp they were in, which was mostly comprised of tents like his, with a large fire in the middle. Eli could not perceive from the outside which tent contained Kadmiel—or other prisoners—and which belonged to their captors.

I'm sure their own tents are more comfortable on the inside, though, he thought bitterly.

"What's your name?" Eli asked the girl.

She smiled but did not answer him. "If only you knew," she seemed to tease.

Eli was guided by the kind young woman to the designated area for relieving oneself; she turned her back and gave him a generous amount of space. He finished and then walked up beside her, and then she led him back to his tent.

Eli was baffled by the experience. He felt as if he could have run away at any time—this girl kept only a loose watch on him. Yet... he never felt compelled to do so. He also would not have wanted this girl to get in trouble if he escaped. There was something intriguing about her.

The tent guards nodded to her and let them pass back into Eli's quarters.

"Am I supposed to sleep like this?" Eli asked her, gesturing to the wooden chair with the pile of ropes around it.

The girl frowned. "No, that would be ridiculous, don't you think? I'll be right back."

She left him standing there in the tent while she went to retrieve something. Eli could hardly believe what was happening. *She just left me unattended! I could storm out of this tent now and I would just need to get past the guards... I have no weapon, but with the element of surprise...* Then a contrary thought occurred to him. *Maybe they're testing my trustworthiness right now.*

Either way, he doubted that Kadmiel had earned this much wiggle room. *He doesn't mess around,* thought Eli, chuckling. He hoped his friend was all right.

Eli's tent flap was pushed aside and the young lady returned, carrying a bed mat and a blanket.

"That's for me?" asked Eli.

"Yes. I want you to get an actual night's sleep."

"You are far more understanding than the other woman— what's her issue?"

The girl crossed the tent and started laying out the bedding. "Don't speak badly of her," she warned. "That's my sister."

Aha, thought Eli. They did have a resemblance, especially in their light skin and dark hair color.

"I just mean to say that you are very kind," said Eli. "And I think that your sister is wrong about Kadmiel and I. We serve a noble cause."

The girl finished laying out Eli's bedding and straightened up, turning to study him closely.

"I'm starting to agree with you," she said.

Eli couldn't help but smile. "Thank you. Our village in the Southern Shores was attacked by the sorcerers that call themselves the Warlocks. They stole our families and our friends, then they spread out to attack the other regions. We've made it our mission to free the Tetrad Union from the oppression of the sorcerers, and we've already succeeded at the Western Plains! You can ask the townspeople there—they will tell you that we helped them. And we *need* to continue our travels and do the same for the Northern Marshes. There are people there that need us."

She listened intently to his story, giving him a sad smile at the end.

"You may not be bad people, but neither are we. My sister, myself, and the rest of our convoy, we are compelled by duty just as you are. We have done what we believe to be right."

Eli's stomach sank. "That's what your sister said—that you serve the High King. But Zaan outlawed the use of sorcery. Don't you think that Kadmiel and I are acting in service to the king by protecting his kingdom from the abuse of sorcery?"

She nodded in consent but also shrugged. "I'm not in charge here, Eli, but I will see what I can do. Get some rest, all right?"

Weariness overtook Eli, and he did not argue with the girl. He stepped over to the bed and collapsed onto it.

"I should at least tie your ankles," she said apologetically.

Eli didn't mind. *I suppose that's reasonable for being in captivity.*

By the time she was finished with her knots, Eli was almost asleep. As she rose and walked toward the exit of the tent, he noticed that her scent, which smelled of lilacs, did not leave but stayed with the bedding.

Are these her own things that she gave me? he wondered. The girl looked backward at him and gave him one more smile.

"My name is Idella," she said. Then she walked out into the blackness of the night, and the tent closed behind her.

Eli slept fitfully and woke with a start. His eyes snapped open, and one word echoed in his mind with immense clarity: *Idella.*

Chapter 6: PRISONERS

It was the name that the mysterious scroll bore on the outside after Eli had read the prophecy. Eli still carried apprehension about the artifact they found in the Warlocks' hideout, not knowing if it could be trusted. In any case, the item was most likely in his captors' custody, along with all of his and Kadmiel's belongings, which he had not seen since being unloaded out of the caravan. Curiosity gripped Eli as he wondered what message the prophecy scroll contained for Idella. He also wondered many things about Idella herself.

His questions would have to wait, however. The kind young girl did not visit him that day, but a middle-aged man did who remained completely silent. Eli was brought breakfast and then placed back in the uncomfortable wooden chair. Two more meals were delivered over the course of the day, and he did not manage to get a single response out of the tight-lipped man. After hours of excruciating boredom and silence, Eli was allowed to transfer to the bedroll again, with the male captor tying his ankles to the tent pole once more, rather more roughly than Idella had. While Eli had never considered trying to make an escape when under Idella's supervision, he didn't know how much more he could take of the other imprisoners.

An entire precious day has slipped away, and no progress has been made here... I wonder how Kadmiel fares, thought Eli, drifting to sleep once more.

Fortunately, Idella came to see him the next morning. She went to work untying Eli, and he thanked her again for the bedding. She accepted the gratitude absentmindedly.

"You seem troubled," said Eli. "What's going on?"

Idella sighed deeply. "This whole ordeal is about to get interesting. My sister will be here shortly, and she has agreed with me to give you another chance—a fair shot at hearing your story and trying to find the truth."

"Idella... have you, by chance, seen the scroll that was taken from my possession?"

"I have," she said. "It is one of the reasons that my sister is more open to what you have to say."

Eli suddenly became hopeful. "You read it! What did it say?"

Idella knelt next to him and folded her hands in her lap. "Well..."

Uh-oh, he thought.

"It said, *'If you choose to set your prisoners free and aid them in their quest, great danger awaits you.'*"

Eli's heart sank, and he leaned his head back against the tent pole in frustration. "Perfect," he said.

Idella smiled sadly. "It's not exactly good news, but I think it does help your case somewhat. This scroll we speak of has a storied history of aiding those who serve the High King. We'll discuss everything with my sister, but I think we will get her to see your point of view."

Eli's emotions swelled at the young woman's words. "It means so much, really, that you're doing this."

She dipped her head in acknowledgment.

"Is Kadmiel going to join us for this discussion?" asked Eli.

"I don't think so. He has been... less cooperative."

Oh, Kadmiel, thought Eli.

The tent flap flew open, and the stern woman walked through. She crossed the tent with long strides, and Idella and Eli rose to meet her.

The older sister cast a disapproving look at the bedding on the floor, then locked eyes with Eli.

"How are you?" she asked.

Eli was taken off guard. He considered her question for a moment, then answered, "I'm glad that we will soon put this misunderstanding behind us. Thank you for agreeing to hear me."

The woman jerked her chin in a stiff nod and placed her hands on her hips. The stance already looked familiar to him.

"It's not out of the kindness of my heart, believe me," she said.

Chapter 6: PRISONERS

Eli did believe her. "My name is Mikaiya. You've met my sister, Idella," she continued. "We are part of the Royal Search Party, and I am the leader of the group. Have you heard of us?"

"No," answered Eli.

"Good," Mikaiya replied. "That means we are doing our mission well."

"And what is your mission?" asked Eli.

Idella answered, "Ever since Zaan disappeared twenty-five years ago, his royal subjects have done their best to keep the peace in his absence. The stewards of the Union have taken on the responsibilities of the High King, and have continued to enforce his laws throughout the land. Zaan stated that he would one day return, and everyone in his service believed him."

"And still do believe him," added Mikaiya.

Idella nodded, and Eli listened patiently as the sisters covered history that he was already familiar with.

"I was in the Inner Kingdom Guard itself at the time of the king's disappearance," Mikaiya continued. "I was the youngest member back then. After a handful of years passed with no sightings of the king, the Guard was going to be downsized. I proposed that a search party be formed to try and locate the High King, and assist him in his return if necessary."

Now this was new information. *A search party was formed a couple of decades ago, and they've been looking for the High King ever since?*

"What?" asked Idella to Eli, noticing his look of surprise.

"It's just... amazing. You've dedicated your lives to finding Zaan, and you look for him, day after day, all these years later?"

"Yes," said Mikaiya blankly.

"I had only just been born when my sister formed the Search Party," said Idella. "I grew up wanting to be like her, and I joined her and the other members a couple of years ago."

Eli hadn't noticed how much of an age difference was between these two sisters. *Mikaiya must stay very fit to retain such a strong and youthful appearance—she's old enough to be Idella's mother!* he mused.

"Have you ever seen him? King Zaan?" asked Eli excitedly.

Mikaiya answered slowly. "I'm still not sure..."

Eli felt her eyes boring into him, searching him for anything he might be hiding. Her gaze unsettled him and made him nervous, even though he had no cause to be.

"There's something I'm not understanding," said Eli, interrupting her stare. "What business do you have apprehending me and my companion when there is a war going on? Shouldn't you be helping, or locating Zaan?"

"There is another piece of this puzzle that you must understand," stated Mikaiya.

"Lilith," said her sister.

Lilith. The name rang within Eli's mind and made his skin crawl. The sorcerer Barid had spoken that name.

"Who is she?" Eli asked.

"Lilith introduced the dark art of sorcery to our kingdom," answered Mikaiya. "She was a dreadful, evil woman who abused her abilities for her own gain. She cared not who she hurt or what she destroyed in her lust for power."

"How does it work?" asked Eli. "Sorcery. What is it?"

Both sisters eyed him with caution, seemingly unwilling to broach the topic.

Eli spoke confidently. "Please. Similar to your mission, I have dedicated my life to a cause, and mine is to destroy the Warlocks and free my people. But I need to understand what I'm up against—Kadmiel and I barely escaped the Western Plains with our lives."

Mikaiya hesitated, but acquiesced. "Sorcery is no magic trick—it is communicating with the spirit realm and commanding them to do one's bidding."

Understanding suddenly came over Eli. *That's why Barid was constantly shouting at the unseen, giving orders.*

Chapter 6: PRISONERS

Shortly after that revelation sank in, a host of other questions came to mind.

"What is the spirit realm?" asked Eli.

"We think that it is the dwelling place of the deceased," said Idella. "Lilith was known for settling old debts and exacting revenge on enemies of the dead. She seemed to gain the spirits' loyalty that way, and her power grew accordingly as more and more spirits joined her command."

This Lilith sounded like the most vile person Eli could possibly imagine. "What ended up happening to her?" he asked.

"As she abused her power over the spirits, Zaan issued a decree that sorcery was banned throughout the entire land. It did nothing to deter her. Some of the mightiest warriors in the kingdom were sent to stop Lilith, but—" Mikaiya then seemed to choke up. It was the first real emotion that Eli had witnessed from the woman.

"It was no use," finished Idella, looking sadly upon her sister and placing a hand on her shoulder.

Mikaiya wiped an eye and then continued. "Lilith was working ruthlessly toward a singular goal. So intoxicated was she with her strength and her command over the dead, she wanted to destroy the barrier between the physical world and the spiritual world entirely. She wanted the two realities to become one."

Eli's eyes widened. "How is that possible? What would happen if she succeeded?"

Mikaiya shook her head. "It would certainly imbalance this world, but to what end, we do not know. The High King wanted to personally ensure an end to Lilith's destruction, and so he left his throne to confront her. The sorceress has never been seen since, nor has the king. We know not their fate, but we search for both of them." Mikaiya finished recounting her story and grew very still and quiet.

Eli leaned back and tried to take in all the information that had just been divulged.

After a few moments, Idella broke the silence. "You're probably wondering what all of this has to do with you," she said.

Eli smiled faintly.

"Zaan and Lilith are the two most powerful beings to have ever lived," said Mikaiya. "We do not practice sorcery but we *have* studied it, and we also know how to sense the measure of power within others. Yours"—she gestured at Eli—"and your companion's"—she pointed over her shoulder in what must have been Kadmiel's direction—"are exactly the type of energy surges that we have been looking for all these many years."

Eli was unsure what to think about that. "That's a compliment, right?"

*
**

Eli opened the entrance flap to Kadmiel's tent. It appeared to be an exact replica of his—bare floor with a pole in the middle, and a man tied to the pole.

Kadmiel looked haggard and was hunched over, his messy dark hair lying over his eyes.

"How are you, my friend?" Eli asked.

Kadmiel tried to bolt upright, but he was restrained to his wooden chair. "Eli!" he exclaimed. Kadmiel quickly lowered his voice and added, "You've escaped! Untie me—we're getting out of here!"

Idella stepped into the tent behind Eli, and Kadmiel's eyes narrowed.

"What is this?" he asked.

"We were apprehended by the group of scouts that call themselves the Royal Search Party. They have devoted their lives to locating King Zaan and his fiercest enemy, Lilith," explained Eli. "They saw that we were warriors of unmatched strength and took us in for questioning, to see if we were related to the ones they are looking for."

Kadmiel scoffed. "You must be joking! Do I look like the High King?"

Eli gestured for Kadmiel to calm down, which only served to further upset him.

"And tell me, Eli, which one of us is this *Lilith* woman?!"

Idella chuckled, which seemed to catch Kadmiel off guard.

"You're right, Kadmiel," she said. "It was a mistake to delay your journey, but we were only doing what we were charged with and what we believed to be right. With that behind us, myself and the rest of the Search Party would like to accompany you on your quest to defeat the Warlocks."

Kadmiel was listening now. Slowly, a smile spread across his face and then he shrugged. "So be it. Now untie me."

Eli and Kadmiel joined the rest of the members of the Royal Search Party in their main pavilion, used for strategizing. A map of the Tetrad Union was stretched out on the table that they were gathered around. Mikaiya and Idella were present, as well as the remaining members: three muscular and intimidating men who were introduced as Suvien, Elhart, and Marrick. They each seemed skeptical of partnering with Eli and Kadmiel, but once the swordsmen were given their weapons back and made no move to attack, the party began to relax.

"Tell us more about the sorcerers," said Elhart.

"We've already recounted the entirety of our battle with Barid," said Kadmiel. "And we don't know much more."

Mikaiya frowned. "The battle you described doesn't make sense, particularly the degree of sorcery that you witnessed—it should not be possible for any normal magic wielder. There's something we're missing..."

"You said you explored their hideout in the Southern Shores," said Idella. "What did you find?"

Eli recalled all that he could of the burning home of the sorcerers, from what brief time they had spent in it.

"The symbol on the ground," said Mikaiya. "Draw it."

The woman flipped over the map and gave Eli a bit of charcoal, which he used to make the intersecting diamonds that formed a four-pointed star. Eli drew a number of circles surrounding the shape, and a few other marks from what he could remember.

Kadmiel sighed. "Is this necessary? Why are we making drawings when there are captives to free?"

"Hold your tongue, Kadmiel," snapped Mikaiya. "I recognize this symbol."

"What is it?" asked Suvien.

Everyone gathered around the table looked up at Mikaiya anxiously, waiting for further explanation. She studied Eli's drawing carefully and then closed her eyes, as if examining her memories.

"This is similar to many of Lilith's attempts to break the barrier between the physical world and the spiritual world. This type of sorcery is not the completed act of darkness which she sought, but it does partially accomplish her goal. The evil ritual in which this symbol is invoked allows a spirit of the deceased to inhabit a living host. The spirit and the host become bonded, and an abomination is born."

"Why would anyone do that?" Eli inquired.

Mikaiya grimaced. "In housing a spirit in one's body, the host has a much stronger and more direct link to the spiritual realm, making the commanding of the deceased that much easier. It also allows the dead spirits a stronger control over the physical reality in proximity to the host, like what you experienced in your last confrontation."

"You're saying that Edric, Barid, and Fathi performed a ritual that summoned dead spirits into the physical realm, and they share their bodies?" asked Eli.

"So it would seem," said Mikaiya. "But not just the three Warlocks of which you are aware—there was a fourth."

Chapter 6: PRISONERS

Eli looked at Kadmiel with dread.

"A fourth!" Kadmiel exclaimed. "How are you certain?"

Mikaiya gestured to the recreated symbol of sorcery before them. "Four points to the star. This symbol was much bigger, yes?" she asked.

Eli nodded. "It was about twice the size, burned into the carpet."

Mikaiya shook her head. "As I feared. There the four sorcerers stood when the ritual was performed. There they stood when the dark beings entered them, binding them with the spirit world and taking them one step closer to accomplishing Lilith's ultimate goal."

A silent pause followed Mikaiya's revelation. Eli slid back into the chair behind him, considering the implications of all that had just been disclosed.

A fourth sorcerer is involved in this whole ordeal? Eli brooded silently, sitting on the edge of the Search Party's camp. *This series of events has just been one terrible thing after another.*

"What troubles you so?" It was Mikaiya. She joined Eli, taking a seat beside him and folding her hands. She then waited patiently for him to gather his thoughts.

Eli scowled. "It's like we haven't made any progress at all. We set out from the Southern Shores thinking that there were three Warlocks to kill, and now there are still three Warlocks to kill."

"Yes," said Mikaiya with a shrug. "But there were four Warlocks, and now you have eliminated a quarter of their ranks. You have already accomplished a great deal."

"But, Mikaiya," said Eli, exasperated, "what difference are we really making if the *dead* can be revived and brought back into this world? What are we actually accomplishing by killing these sorcerers?"

"You are sending their spirits, as well as the dark spirits which they host, to the realm of the dead, where they belong."

Eli recalled the unnatural explosion that had accompanied Barid's death. But he still had questions. "Couldn't another evil sorcerer just bring them back someday?"

"Not likely, Eli. The dark art of spirit-hosting hasn't been seen in this land since the time of Lilith—it takes many years to learn and many more years to perform. These Warlocks, they are radicals—admirers of Lilith, I'm afraid. Their kind is not common. They are an enormous threat to our kingdom and we must rise up against them now, or the world may never be the same. Your mission is of dire importance."

Eli didn't feel convinced, but Mikaiya placed a hand on his shoulder and added, "We are very fortunate to have met you and Kadmiel. You are two incredibly powerful warriors."

"Thank you," said Eli. "We feel the same about you—your assistance in our mission will make a great deal of difference."

"Have you thought about what you will do when this is all over?" asked Mikaiya.

Eli was taken aback. "No, I guess I haven't really considered living through this. I'm dealing with people much more powerful than I, and with forces beyond my sight and my control. Why do you ask, anyway?"

"I think that you would make a worthy addition to the Search Party," stated Mikaiya.

Eli's eyes grew wide. "I'm honored—"

They were interrupted by Kadmiel, who joined and said, "It's time we get on the move, and I have an idea."

"Let's hear it," said Mikaiya.

"We need to split up." Kadmiel looked grave and urgent in his suggestion. "The Warlocks destroyed the Southern Shores and kidnapped its inhabitants, leaving it bare. That left three regions of the Tetrad Union to overthrow: the Western Plains, Northern Marshes, and Eastern Peaks. Now, considering a fourth member joined their ranks, it's likely that he has been stationed at the Inner Kingdom to watch over the Shores captives."

Mikaiya was nodding slowly as Kadmiel spoke.

"After the... *delay* here," he continued. "We can't spare any more time. Eli and I will take one location while your warriors handle the other. All of us can meet back up at the Inner Kingdom and join forces against the last sorcerer."

Mikaiya considered Kadmiel's plan for a few minutes, but could come up with no better alternative. They then went to work making preparations for their separate journeys.

"I believe this is yours," said Idella. She came up behind Eli and held out her hand, which contained the prophecy scroll that had been confiscated.

"Thank you," said Eli, taking it from her. He turned the document over, eager to read the name written on the back. It was there, inscribed in flowing handwriting with dark, smooth ink: *Rayorden.*

Eli glanced from the scroll to Idella, but she already knew what he was about to ask.

"No, Eli, I am unfamiliar with any man named Rayorden. But you will find him when fate deems the time right, just as we met." She smiled.

"You're right," said Eli, pocketing the item and putting the question of Rayorden's identity out of his mind for the time being. "Say, I wanted to ask you about the bedding which you gave me."

"Yes?" she asked.

"Was that yours?"

Idella squared her shoulders and said, "Yes, as a matter of fact. The thing is, we were never prepared to have visitors."

Eli raised an eyebrow.

"All right, *captives*," said Idella. "The Search Party has looked all over the kingdom for the High King and his adversary for years upon years without finding them. We don't travel with extra tents or supplies, because we don't anticipate taking people into our camp. When we acquired you and Kadmiel, we had to improvise a bit." She chuckled.

"Well thank you," said Eli sincerely. "It was a very kind gesture."

"Don't mention it. Besides, you needed it more than I!" said Idella. "I wake up during the night and take turns on watch duty. That's what we do—always searching."

"Really!" Eli was surprised. "Your group stays active during the night?"

"Just on a rotation," answered Idella. "Mainly meditating and opening our feelings to the surges of power that would indicate a great warrior like the High King or a threat like the sorceress Lilith." She was silent for a moment. "I couldn't sense anything apart from the energy pouring out of your tent and Kadmiel's."

Eli did not know how to respond to that. "Can you teach me sometime, to be able to sense power like that?"

"I would love to."

Eli nodded. "I hope you are right about us," he said, weary of the task ahead.

"You and your friend will overcome," replied Idella. "You have the strength within that you need."

Eli's thoughts turned back to the scroll he carried. Not to the name of Rayorden, but to the prophecy which it gave to Idella. "I'm worried about you," said Eli.

Idella pursed her lips and drew herself up. "Because the scroll foretold danger?"

"Great danger."

"Well then, *great* danger. Thank you for your concern, Eli, but we will be okay. There are five of us. Besides, we did not choose this path in life for safety—we are just fulfilling our duty to the king."

Eli looked on the young woman with admiration, feeling that she was the bravest person he had ever met. They embraced.

Chapter 6: PRISONERS

"I'll see you at the entrance to the Inner Kingdom," said Eli.

"We'll be there," said Idella. "Don't take too long."

"You had best hurry—you have farther to travel to get to the Eastern Peaks."

Idella grinned. "But we have horses."

"Unfair," Eli teased.

Chapter 7: **HOLLOW**

Eli and Kadmiel set out from what had been the Royal Search Party's camp. The tents were collapsed, fires covered up, and everything packed onto the horses which they rode. No signs of the camp remained. It was a wonder to Eli that a group of their size, operating for so many years, could travel in complete secrecy.

The Search Party had apprehended them on the route between the Plains and the Marshes, and taken them off the road some distance to the west. The swordsmen would first reunite with the path and then continue their journey north.

"So what do you think?" Eli inquired.

"About what?" asked Kadmiel.

"Everything. The king's Search Party, the workings of sorcery, the fourth Warlock..." Eli trailed off.

Kadmiel was silent for a moment. "It's a lot to take in. Most of all I think that fate has a funny way of working things out."

"What do you mean?" asked Eli.

"Sending us the help that we needed in the strangest way."
Eli nodded.

"Think about it," Kadmiel continued. "Here we thought that we were the only free warriors left in the kingdom—and we need help, badly—then we discover this group of traveling fighters that have trained their whole lives to assist the High King if necessary."

"Right," said Eli. "Sure, they slowed our progress for a few days, but now they have joined forces with us, and together we are covering much more distance at once. I'm glad to count them as friends."

A smirk appeared on Kadmiel's face.

"Don't start," warned Eli.

Kadmiel did start. "Idella—"

Eli punched his arm, hurting his knuckles on Kadmiel's armor. "Have you ever heard of Rayorden?" he asked, changing the subject.

"I have not. Oh!" he exclaimed. "Is that whose name appeared on the scroll?"

"Indeed," said Eli, handing him the prophecy.

Kadmiel examined the name, and then tugged on the handles. Try as hard as he might, the document remained decidedly sealed. He grunted in defeat and handed it back to Eli.

"Aren't you a bit worried about that thing?" asked Kadmiel. "Kept closed by magical means, found in the Warlocks' hideout. It could be some kind of dark relic."

"That's possible," admitted Eli. "But I'm starting to trust it. This scroll follows those that serve the king—at least, that's what Idella told me."

Kadmiel gave him a knowing look once more, and Eli became agitated.

"This is serious, Kadmiel! The prophecy it revealed to her said they would be in great danger if they chose to help us. Do you think they will be all right?"

Kadmiel shrugged. "Honestly, think about it. The entire kingdom of the Tetrad Union is in great danger at the moment. But if anyone the sorcerers haven't killed has a chance of turning this state of events around, it would be ourselves and the Search Party."

"You're right, Kad. I'm glad we found them, or... glad they found us."

"Mmm."

After a few hours, the main road was in sight on the horizon. They were relieved to see something familiar again.

Once back upon the path, two days passed uneventfully. The swordsmen trudged onward at a quick pace, but the

Chapter 7: HOLLOW

hard-packed dirt road grew wetter and eventually turned to mud. This slowed their progress considerably, and traversing through the mud caused them to need more frequent breaks for rest.

On one such respite, Eli and Kadmiel sat down next to a river. They draped their legs over the bank, washing their boots free of muck in the slow-moving water.

The swordsmen lingered there a bit, enjoying the refreshment. They were surrounded by rushes and reeds everywhere—a very different environment from the shores and salty air that they were accustomed to.

"I've never seen a flower like this," said Eli, indicating a pink flower with drooping petals and purple splashes of colors.

"The animals here are different as well," said Kadmiel.

"What animals?" asked Eli.

"You haven't seen them?"

"No," he admitted.

"You should learn to be more attentive to your surroundings then," warned Kadmiel. "Aren't you concerned about what we will eat today?"

"That's your job," said Eli with a grin.

Kadmiel gave a mock sigh. "What ever would you do without me?"

Eli laughed. "Starve, I suppose."

"That's exactly right."

A breeze lazily blew along the river, making the reeds sway gently.

"Speaking of starving," said Eli, "I am really hungry."

Kadmiel made no move to get up from the river. "I think it's your turn to go hunting," he said.

"My *turn?*"

Kadmiel unbuckled his bow and arrows, holding them out for Eli to grab.

"I don't believe this. Don't you want to eat before sundown?"

Kadmiel smiled slightly, still extending the weapon expectantly.

Eli turned away defiantly, so Kadmiel stood up and dropped the bow and arrows in his lap.

"You're serious?" Eli asked.

"Why not? You have to know how to survive, too."

Eli looked down at the bow as if it were something foreign. He had never hunted before.

"Will you help me?"

Kadmiel appeared shocked by the question. "You mean to say that the great Champion of Warriors needs my help?"

Eli rolled his eyes.

"It would be my utmost honor," said Kadmiel, bowing and sweeping his arms in an exaggerated gesture. "Come, champion, let us learn the ways of the archer."

A few unnecessary hours of hunting later, the two swordsmen sat around their campfire and devoured a meal of rabbit meat. Eli had fared decently, catching on quickly to the stealth and tracking aspects of hunting. He would need much more practice with the bow itself, though—lining up the shot while accounting for distance and wind.

He had not taken to the challenge with the best attitude, and he reflected on the experience while he ate. Finally, feeling full and relaxed, he thanked Kadmiel for the opportunity to learn a new skill. Kadmiel graciously smiled and dipped his head.

"Maybe you should continue acting as our designated hunter," said Eli. "Until this is all over."

"What about learning to survive without me?" asked Kadmiel.

"I don't have my own bow," Eli pointed out.

Kadmiel tilted his head. "Should I fall in battle, you would only need to—"

"No," Eli cut in. "Perhaps I can acquire one at some point once we reach the city of the Northern Marshes. But either way, I would enjoy continuing my training with you once we're back home."

Kadmiel paused, gazing into the crackling fire between them. "I don't know if things will ever go back to normal."

Eli frowned. "Why? Is that not exactly what we are trying to do—right wrongs and restore what was?"

Kadmiel gave no response. After a moment, Eli joined him on the opposite side of the fire, sitting beside him on a log.

"We're doing it," said Eli. "We're nearly halfway there. We are going to destroy the Warlocks and free the people of the Tetrad Union."

Kadmiel nodded slowly, seeming distant.

"You know the single thing that gives me the most hope?" continued Eli. "It's what the sorcerers did back at the Championship of Warriors."

Kadmiel raised his eyebrows. "Slaughtering our comrades?"

"Sparing our families," said Eli. "If the sorcerers wanted to kill them, they would have done so right there in the arena along with all the warriors they murdered. They didn't. They left our families alive and took them."

"Which tells you what?"

"That the sorcerers have a purpose for them—that they're *alive*. The thought of seeing my parents, my sweet little sister, and my friend Tabitha again gives me new hope each morning to rise to the occasion."

"Mm," acknowledged Kadmiel. "Thank you, Eli. You're right. They must be alive." He smiled.

Eli got up quietly and doused their fire, and then set out his and Kadmiel's bedrolls. They laid down in the chill of the night, cold in the absence of the flames but entranced by the brightness of the beaming stars above.

The next morning, Eli and Kadmiel woke and packed up the camp wordlessly, eager to be off. They gathered their things and did their best to upturn the ground where they had made footprints and bury the signs of the previous night's fire, covering up their tracks.

Eli wasn't sure if the precautions were necessary, because they still had yet to encounter any travelers. He shook his head absentmindedly. *How can three—four—men cause this much of an upheaval? This has to come to an end, and soon, or else our people may never bounce back.*

They found their way from the site of their camp back to the muddy trail that led from the Western Plains to the Northern Marshes, which they took immediately, angling north.

"Ouch," said Kadmiel.

"You feel it too?" Eli's legs were sore from the repeated motion of lifting his leg and pulling his foot out of the sticky mud. It was going to be a long day.

Eli's thoughts turned to the most troubling news that he had received lately—the workings of sorcery. "What do you think about what Mikaiya told us, about how the Warlocks' power works?"

"It's scary," said Kadmiel. "But not as scary as the unknown. Before, we didn't know what we were seeing when we watched the sorcerers round everyone up in the stadiums and kill warriors with the flick of a wrist. Now we know. They command dead spirits—it finally makes sense. Barid wasn't as crazy as he seemed when he was yelling at people that we couldn't see."

"So you are more confident now, knowing what we are fighting?" asked Eli.

"It helps," said Kadmiel.

"But there's still so much we don't know. Like why can dead spirits interact with things within the physical reality? How can they pick up statues and throw them at us?"

"It's like Mikaiya said: The Warlocks are working toward Lilith's goal of removing the barrier between the physical and spiritual world. Right now the contact a spirit can have with our world seems to be limited and frail; I imagine the Warlocks would like to do away with those limitations."

"We have to kill them before they completely imbalance our world," said Eli.

"We have to free our families before *they* become dead spirits," finished Kadmiel.

The swordsmen subconsciously quickened their pace, slogging through the mud of the Marshes. It was a cold and damp day, with gray skies and no sun in sight. A heavy mist hung over the green hills all around them.

Eli shivered. Their discussion about magic made him want to be done with this whole calamity as fast as possible. He imagined what his parents and sister must be going through, imprisoned and helpless, and he felt his resolve further harden. *I will rescue you. Stay strong. Wait for me,* he willed them.

***

"*Eli!*" Kadmiel hissed.

His eyes snapped open. The sun was up. *How late did I sleep?* Eli wondered.

Kadmiel whispered his name again. He hastily rubbed his eyes and looked around. Eli saw that Kadmiel was on his bedroll, lying flat on his belly. He didn't appear to be resting— no, Kadmiel was wide awake, and his attention was fixated on a point in the distance.

Eli rolled onto his stomach and propped himself up on his elbows, matching Kadmiel's posture.

"Stay down!" urged Kadmiel.

"What are you looking at?" Eli whispered back.

Kadmiel's face was grim. "Soldiers."

Eli tried to focus in on the place where Kadmiel was pointing, at the extent of his vision. He could make out the gleaming reflections of what could be the soldiers' armor, but the sight was faint.

"Do you think they're looking for us?" asked Eli.

"Yes, probably."

"What's our plan, Kad?"

"What are our options?" responded Kadmiel.

Eli thought for a moment. "Hide, let them pass us. Wait, let them fall asleep and spring an attack. Bow, pick them off from a distance. Charge at them with swords, probably die."

Kadmiel chuckled. "I count five, maybe six, men. We need to be very careful."

"Could you shoot them from here?" asked Eli hopefully.

"Oh, you were serious," said Kadmiel, surprised. "No."

Eli waited for an explanation.

He sighed. "I would have to get a lot closer—close enough for them to notice our presence. I also don't know the weak points in their armor—I could just be bouncing arrows off of them while drawing attention to our position. I liked your other ideas better."

"Even charging at them with our swords drawn?" Eli asked.

Kadmiel paused. "You're right, I'm not fond of that idea either."

Eli was unsure how much time passed in the following standstill, but neither party moved and it felt like they were there all morning. He was growing impatient. And stiff.

"We're wasting daylight," he stated.

Kadmiel pursed his lips.

"We can take them," said Eli.

"Oh?" asked Kadmiel. "With which brilliant strategy?"

Eli racked his brain for the proper tactic to defeat a group of men that was two to three times larger than their party. Then it struck him.

"They're all suited up. We can outrun them if need be," said Eli.

"If need be?"

"Well," he continued, "we don't even know their intent.

86

I think that we should approach the soldiers nonchalantly and maybe ask for directions. They might *not* be after us. They might not be under a sorcerer's command—they could be escaping the city to keep their freedom!"

Kadmiel was silent for a few moments and then conceded, "You could be right."

The two swordsmen rose up into the full view of the distant soldiers, attempting to appear natural and relaxed. They kept their swords sheathed at their sides and strapped their shields onto their backs, trying not to stare at the gleaming armored men ahead while casually walking in their direction.

Despite their course of action being Eli's own idea, his heart still pounded and he could feel his palms getting sweaty.

Leaving their camp behind them, Eli and Kadmiel approached the group of soldiers at a moderate pace.

"Say it comes to running," said Kadmiel. "They will fire at us with bows."

"That's what the shields on our backs are for," said Eli.

"Ah."

Eli was unnerved that the group of soldiers had yet to move an inch. The group of men were sitting unnaturally still around their camp, as if frozen in time by the sorcery of a Warlock. None of them seemed to notice him or Kadmiel drawing closer; they made no move to greet or intercept them.

After traversing a few dozen yards of muddy terrain, Eli called out, "Beautiful morning!" and raised an arm to salute the soldiers.

No response.

"There's something very odd about this," said Kadmiel in a hushed tone.

The swordsmen closed the distance to the soldiers' camp and stopped in front of them.

Suddenly, all of the soldiers stood up in perfect unison, turned to face them, and drew their weapons in one smooth motion. Their movements were quick and unhuman-like, causing the hairs on the back of Eli's neck to stand on end.

It was then that he and Kadmiel could see the true nature of the "soldiers." They were but empty suits of armor, moving of their own accord.

There were no eyes behind the helmets' face guards; there were no bodies within the chest plates, no arms within the greaves, and no feet within the boots.

Eli stole a sideways glance at Kadmiel, who was staring in shock.

"Still think we can outrun them?" inquired Kadmiel.

He was not given an opportunity to answer; the suits of armor sprung into the offensive.

They both stumbled backward and drew their weapons, attempting to stay out of reach of the attacks of the suits pressing in on them. One soldier had leapt toward each of the swordsmen, and Eli could see the remaining three enemies circling behind him and Kadmiel, attempting to flank them.

Eli turned his full attention to his attacker, a suit of armor wielding a long, thick blade. They exchanged a few blows, with Eli staying mostly on the defensive. *I don't know what I'm aiming for—how do you kill a suit of armor?*

The armored soldier's quick movements were jerky and unpredictable.

"They are weak!" cried Kadmiel. "Destroy them before we are overrun!"

Eli heard Kadmiel's sword tear into his opponent's armor, and then there was the sound of metal crashing to the ground.

Eli lunged with his sword, invigorated by Kadmiel's victory. He plunged the blade into his attacker and then twisted the handle of his sword, causing the armored soldier to fall apart piece by piece.

"Eli!" Kadmiel screamed.

He instinctively ducked then heard the rushing sound of a sword inches above his head. He whirled to see another armored soldier behind him, while Kadmiel was fending off the last two at once. Eli stretched out his leg and swept the feet out from underneath his enemy, causing the entire suit of armor, held together by an unknown force, to crash to the ground. Eli sprung up and stepped on the soldier's sword-glove, then stabbed mercilessly into the breastplate and helmet of the enemy until it stopped moving. Dark tendrils of wispy smoke emanated from the punctures in the armor.

Eli's eyes snapped up, searching around the camp to see Kadmiel and the status of his battle. His companion was doing his best to defend himself from two attacking suits of armor, but had just taken a nasty slice on the cheekbone from one of the enemies.

Eli growled and sprinted to his friend's aid, unstrapping the shield from his back. Eli engaged with one of the soldiers, battering it with quick blows. The suit of armor was on the retreat, blocking his advances as it continually stepped backward. After a massive sword strike that the armor intercepted on its gauntlet, Eli drew back and hurled his shield at the enemy. The shield hit its target soundly, knocking the armor's helmet from its shoulders. Eli walked up to the metallic suit and gave it a hard kick in the chest, scattering the rest of the pieces to the ground. Eli turned to see that Kadmiel had taken the final armor suit's sword and with two blades rent the enemy in half. The camp became still and silent.

Eli's wide eyes met Kadmiel's and they shook their heads in unison, panting from exertion.

"What *was* that?" asked Kadmiel.

"Magic," stated Eli.

Kadmiel dropped to his knees and examined one of the fallen suits of armor. "I gathered that much."

Eli joined him and saw that his companion was placing his hand within the armor, as if checking it for something. "What are you doing?"

"Trying to discover the nature of our enemy," Kadmiel stated. "Invisible men? No, this armor is hollow. What was that dark matter that they released?"

Eli examined the air around them, but the smoky substance had completely dissipated. "Their movement was too strange and halting to be that of men, invisible or otherwise," said Eli. "I think what we have here are simply suits of armor under the control of a sorcerer..." Eli frowned. "You're bleeding," he added.

Kadmiel took no notice of his wound or of Eli's words, but continued to study the broken parts.

"And what makes this armor unfit to control any longer?" asked Kadmiel.

He had a good point. "I suppose it's too damaged now? Look!" Eli exclaimed, gesturing around the camp at the scattered pieces of torn metal. "We really took care of them, didn't we?"

Kadmiel smiled absentmindedly as he began gathering up the nearby pieces of armor.

"What's your plan?" asked Eli.

"Burn it all. Melt it down," answered Kadmiel, dumping the armor into a pile and picking up more.

Eli assisted him, and soon all of the destroyed suits were heaped into the center of the camp.

"I'm hungry," said Eli with his hands on his hips.

Kadmiel retrieved the bow that was strapped to his back and offered it to Eli. He smirked and pushed the bow back toward Kadmiel and said, "I'll get to work on the fire. Let's stick to our areas of expertise for now."

Kadmiel nodded. "While I'm gone, if anything... starts to move, shout for me."

Eli took a few steps back from the gathered pieces of armor and began to look for firewood as Kadmiel ventured out to hunt. Eli continually glanced over his shoulder, but the pile remained still.

Chapter 7: HOLLOW

Kadmiel returned an hour later with a catch. He looked disappointed that only a small flame had been started.

"Turns out, the marshes aren't the best place to find firewood," said Eli defensively. "And by the way, armor isn't the most flammable substance, either."

After they had eaten, the swordsmen gathered up their belongings from their camp across the way while they left the pile of armor to melt.

"It could prove to be unwise to leave such a large fire behind, with evidence of our rebellion against the sorcerers," warned Eli.

Kadmiel considered that for a moment, but countered with, "It would also be unwise to leave behind parts of armor that could be reanimated to attack us along the way, and that might also contain memories of our identities."

"Memories?" asked Eli.

Kadmiel lifted his palms and shrugged. "You never know."

Eli couldn't help himself. He laughed at the notion of the pieces of armor remembering what they looked like.

Kadmiel shook his head. "It's a weird world we live in now, Eli. You just never know."

Chapter 8: **BREACH**

"I didn't think the mud could get any muddier," said Eli.
"Or the marsh any marshier," added Kadmiel.
"We were very wrong indeed."

The swordsmen trudged through the sticky terrain as the city of the Northern Marshes loomed before them. Beyond a large gate with a drawbridge, they could just begin to make out the details of a busy network of buildings. The city had been on the horizon for hours, but their progress seemed slow.

"The city inhabitants—they must have some kind of special boot made for this mush," Kadmiel said wishfully.

"If I see a pair, I'll borrow them right off of someone's feet," said Eli.

The repeated motion of unsticking their legs from the mud had caused the swordsmen's limbs to become sore—not the ideal condition for confronting a sorcerer.

"Which Warlock do you think we will encounter here?" asked Eli.

"Not Barid," said Kadmiel with a grin.

"That leaves Edric, Fathi, and an unknown fourth sorcerer."

"I'll go with Fathi, the crazy old man."

"I'll place my bet on Edric, the well-dressed one," said Eli with a chuckle.

The companions were doing a decent job at keeping their conversations light and their morale high as they approached the city and drew ever nearer to the drawbridge entrance.

"And what exactly is this bet?" inquired Kadmiel.

"Let's say..." said Eli, thinking aloud. "The loser of the bet has to take first watch tonight, while the winner sleeps blissfully and forgets the troubles of the day and the pains of the body. Fair?"

"Fair," agreed Kadmiel, and they shook hands. "And if neither of our bets are correct?"

"You can go ahead and take the first watch," said Eli.

Kadmiel scoffed.

Up ahead, the large drawbridge was raised, which was the main access to the city of the Northern Marshes. Beneath it was the city's sewer canal, a wide bank that would discourage anyone from attempting to infiltrate the city.

"I've never seen defenses like this," muttered Eli.

They stopped a hundred yards from the city's entrance and remained concealed behind a tree so as not to be seen by any sentries.

"We need a plan to get in," said Eli.

Kadmiel grunted, already scanning the area and squinting to see within the city, looking for anything that might help them get inside.

"It looks locked down," he said. "Just like the Western Plains—it seems these Warlocks have no intention of letting people live their daily lives. I see no activity."

"And if the Warlock has taken over the city and put all of the inhabitants within captivity," said Eli, "I would assume that no one is allowed passage in or out."

"I would assume you are correct."

A gentle breeze was all that stirred, swaying the plants and the tops of trees that stuck out of the marsh's muddy waters.

"This is bad." Eli sighed.

"Come now," said Kadmiel. "Let's not expect anything to be too easy, all right?"

Eli grinned slightly and assisted in searching their surroundings for anything that might help them gain entrance to the shut-down city.

"The drawbridge must be lowered at *some* point—otherwise they would run out of supplies," said Eli.

Kadmiel shrugged. "Maybe the Warlocks can conjure up food from nothing."

He shook his head. "I don't think it works that way, exactly. We learned that sorcery is nothing more than commanding dead spirits to do your dirty work, so I suppose what we would see is food and supplies hovering through the air toward the city—now that would be a sight."

After a few moments of silence, Kadmiel frowned. "I see no weaknesses on this side. Shall we circle around and have a look for other entrances?"

Just then, the sounds of approaching footsteps became audible in the distance along with the clanking of armor. Eli pressed his back up against a tree and slowly glanced around the trunk to see what was coming.

"It's the hollow soldiers," he said with dread.

Kadmiel instinctively reached for the pommel of his sword, but Eli held up a hand. "They can get us in," he whispered.

A look of understanding crossed Kadmiel's face, and he nodded. Eli glanced back at the approaching enemies, whose footsteps were growing louder. Their count was formidable.

"They're coming right this way—we need to move," said Eli. He started looking around desperately, but every bush and tree looked small compared to the group of marching suits of armor drawing nearer.

"Kad, help!"

"I'm looking!"

Have we been seen yet? He kept glancing over his shoulder, wasting precious time. Frustrated, he gave up the search for proper concealment and turned to face the suits of armor.

"Fine, maybe we will have to confront—"

Kadmiel grabbed him by the collar and pulled him downward, into the marsh. With a splash, Eli and Kadmiel were submerged in the murky, muddy depths. With the suits of armor nearly upon them now, the swordsmen broke the surface of the water once more.

"Breathe," said Kadmiel.

Eli gasped, and then they dove deep into the dark waters. Eli bumped into a tree root near the muddy floor of the marsh and held himself firmly to it, keeping still and trying not to disturb the waters and draw attention. He tried opening his eyes to glance at Kadmiel, but the stinging sensation that followed was so great that he clamped his lids firmly shut. Eli knew that in the best of conditions, he could hold his breath for no longer than two minutes. He just hoped that the convoy of armor suits passed quickly.

At the same time... *If we stay submerged for too long, we could miss our window of opportunity... if the soldiers are indeed entering the city.*

Eli's lungs burned and he was beginning to feel claustro-phobic, with the dark, heavy waters pressing in on him, and without any sound or indication of the passage of time.

He let go of the tree root and began to swim toward the surface, but someone's hand reached out and held him in place. It must have been Kadmiel, implying that they needed more time. Eli didn't know how much longer he could take—each second felt like the one where his lungs might burst. Finally, Kadmiel released him and the two companions swam to the surface, raising their heads above the marsh as quietly as possible. They gasped for air.

Eli couldn't see anything. His eyelids were covered in mud, and trying to wipe them with his hand only smeared more dirty water onto his face. He was anxious to see where the armor soldiers were—they could be crossing the drawbridge now into the Northern Marshes, or they could be surrounding him and Kadmiel in this murky lake with swords drawn.

Arms outstretched, Eli felt a patch of grass nearby and used it to wipe the muck off of his hands before clearing his vision. He could see that Kadmiel had done similarly on the other side of the pond.

But more importantly, he could see that their dive into the marsh had worked; they had escaped the soldiers' notice and remained under the water long enough for the entire group of armor suits to pass them. There looked to be about ten of the mysterious enemies marching in sync toward the city drawbridge. The entrance to the Northern Marshes was just starting to be lowered, but by whom Eli could not see.

"This is it," he whispered.

Kadmiel nodded, looking grave. "Sure, we just walk in right behind them... without them noticing we're there."

Eli shrugged. *What other choice do we have?* "Come on."

The swordsmen sidled up to the edge of the trees which sprawled before the clearing in front of the city's defenses. The drawbridge settled into place, and the armor soldiers continued their march across it.

"I don't know about this," said Kadmiel cautiously.

"Any other ideas?" Eli asked.

Kadmiel pursed his lips.

Just as the suits of armor had crossed the joining midsection of the drawbridge, Eli rose and forced himself to run toward the city. Kadmiel followed behind, and the companions found that they could not run as fast as normal. The mud from the marsh was heavy and clung to their clothes, weighing them down and slowing their progress.

They were in the clearing now, plainly visible to any sentries that the Warlock may have posted. *I still don't see anyone inside the city, though,* Eli noted.

The last soldier had just stepped off of the drawbridge when Eli's and Kadmiel's feet hit the wooden planks. The swordsmen attempted to tread quietly, but so far the suits of armor had not taken notice of them and continued to march north.

"Come on, almost there!" said Eli, possibly too loud.

A great creaking sound emitted from what must have been nearby gears, and then the drawbridge started to move.

Eli's feet wobbled beneath him, and he reached out to grip the rails on either side. *Have we been seen?*

"Eli, don't stop!" said Kadmiel, giving him a shove in the back.

Eli willed himself to keep climbing as it slowly tilted upward. Heights were not his thing.

I have to get to the other side before it's too late.

Eli found that it helped to not look down, and he closed the distance to the top of the first bridge, each step becoming more difficult as it was drawn more and more vertical. At the top, his muddy boot slipped and kicked the top of Kadmiel's head, who grunted but otherwise ignored the accident.

"Jump now," said Kadmiel through clenched teeth.

Eli looked at the other half of the drawbridge and the growing gap between them. He knew that this may be their only chance to get into the city before it was closed off. Then without stopping to think, Eli crouched low, teetered over the city's moat, and jumped toward the second half of the bridge. For a brief moment, he hung in the air with an incredible view of the Northern Marshes.

Eli cleared the edge of the second bridge and began to slide down the other side. He reached out and grabbed the rails to slow his descent, but the bridge was getting steeper by the second. Soon, he would be hanging at a ninety-degree angle.

There was an impact above him; the structure shook and its gears groaned. Eli looked up and saw Kadmiel's hands gripping the top of the bridge as he dangled on the upright underside of the structure. Eli used the side rails to climb up and reach the top where he could help Kadmiel, who was calling for him.

"I'm here," said Eli, extending his hand. "Don't let go."

"I need to let go... to grab your hand."

Eli rolled his eyes. *Sarcasm, at a time like this?*

The drawbridge creaked into place and completed its transition. Eli and Kadmiel were hanging on opposite sides, fifteen feet above the entrance to the Northern Marshes.

"Let's get you on this side, where we can both use the railings to let ourselves down into the city," said Eli.

"You sure you want to go into the city? How's the soldier situation?"

Eli's heart sank. He had forgotten about the soldiers. He slowly turned his head, forcing himself to look and see that they were surrounded by suits of armor below.

"Yeah, Kadmiel... They noticed us."

He heard a *thump* that he assumed was Kadmiel's forehead.

"We'll worry about that in a minute, when you're not hanging over Sewage River and when we've got feet on the ground, all right?"

Eli propped himself up against the bridge, squared his boots on the beams supporting the handrails, and planted his elbow as if getting ready for an arm wrestle. Kadmiel locked eyes on Eli's hand and squared his jaw, mustering up the courage needed to release his grip.

Kadmiel took one hand off and dove forward to grab Eli's hand. Their grip was muddy and slippery, but the swordsmen held on to each other with all of their might. Eli leaned backward dangerously far, attempting to pull Kadmiel up and over the lip of the bridge. The burden of Kadmiel's weight was causing Eli's arm socket to burn.

Finally, Kadmiel was able to swing a leg over, and the weight that Eli was bearing decreased instantly. He had to lean forward into the bridge and regain his balance before momentum took him tumbling off the side. Chests heaving, the companions tried to catch their breath.

"Thanks," Kadmiel said. But Eli had already turned away to look again at the suits of armor gathered at the foot of the drawbridge.

The soldiers stood still, with weapons drawn and helmets upturned to face them.

With a quick glance at the city beyond the entrance, Eli determined that no one else seemed to be watching.

"Eli, was this the whole group of soldiers that entered the city?"

He shrugged, uncertain.

"If we can dispatch them, and none of them have already broken rank to inform anyone of our arrival, we still may have the element of surprise against the Warlock here."

"Good point," said Eli. "All we have to do is get down and kill ten or so suits of armor."

"Right," Kadmiel agreed.

"*Can* suits of armor *tell* anyone of our presence?" inquired Eli.

"Your guess is as good as mine," said Kadmiel.

"Hey!" shouted Eli. "Can you guys talk?"

Silence.

"All right, then... Kadmiel, let's see what these soldiers are made of."

The swordsmen lowered themselves partially down the sheer side of the bridge, just to where they were out of the soldiers' reach. Then as one, the swordsmen leapt down into the waiting soldiers' midst, drawing their blades in the air.

Eli landed on one suit of armor, instantly pressing it into the ground. From the sound of it, Kadmiel had done the same immediately behind Eli. By unspoken consent, the swordsmen took up defensive positions with their backs pressed firmly against one another. While severely outnumbered, they could leave no opportunity for the enemy to find their backs open. Together, Eli and Kadmiel scuffled to one side a ways so that their footing would be on solid ground.

Then the battle began in earnest.

Four soldiers closed in on Eli while an equal amount drew toward Kadmiel. They were surrounded. The two flattened suits of armor scraped against the ground as they picked themselves up.

Chapter 8: BREACH

Eli's sword arm was put to immediate work, flying to intercept the stabs and swipes of four enemies at once. He had fought human swordsmen his whole life, but he had such little experience with these servants of sorcerers. The hollow suits of armor were fast, but they were not strong. Little weight carried their blows, and the attacks that Eli could not block were not strong enough to incapacitate him on their own. He focused on guarding his neck and his vital organs, while absorbing some hits on his bracers and shield.

The non-human movement of the armor was unnerving and twitchy. Eli was having a difficult time predicting their attacks. *I can be unpredictable, too.*

Eli took a fierce lunge toward the suit of armor on his far left, the one that he was having the most difficulty blocking with his sword arm. His blade pierced the enemy's breastplate and made a screeching sound of metal on metal. Eli twisted and tugged on the hilt of his sword, but it was stuck. Gripping his weapon with both hands, he grunted and swept his sword to the right, the suit of armor on the end in tow. The skewered enemy crashed into another suit of armor and shook free, both enemies tumbling in pieces to the ground.

Before Eli could resume his defensive stance, another soldier had drawn its sword back and then swung forward with a deadly horizontal slice toward Eli's throat. He ducked instinctively and watched as the sword passed an inch over his head... and collided into Kadmiel's left shoulder.

"Agh!" he yelled. "What are you doing, Eli?"

"Sorry," Eli groaned.

"We duck together," Kadmiel grunted.

Eli shook his head, clearing his frustration, and focused again on the combat at hand.

The enemy that Eli had jumped onto when entering the fray had now collected itself and joined the battle. With only three enemies to contend with now, he found defending himself to be easier and was able to remain on the offensive more often. Fighting back-to-back with Kadmiel presented one challenge: it limited the swordsmen's mobility. Whereas they would normally incorporate more sidestepping, advancing thrusts, and generally more footwork into their individual battle styles, their movement was limited when attempting to cover each other.

But suddenly, Eli was surprised when he could no longer feel Kadmiel's back behind him. "Are you all right?"

Kadmiel appeared beside him with a grin. "Of course, why do you ask?" He interjected himself into Eli's battle, drawing an opponent away from him and attacking it fiercely.

"Did you already defeat the other *five?*" asked Eli, incredulous.

"I did," Kadmiel responded. "What have you been doing over here?"

It was a matter of pride now. Eli glared at the suits of armor before him and launched into a furious series of stabs and slices. He cut one soldier down and then whirled on the other. In his haste, he left himself open to an attack on his forearm, causing him to drop his sword.

The suit of armor may have expected Eli to try and retrieve it off the ground or retreat behind Kadmiel, who was making short work of the other remaining soldier, but Eli took neither of those options and instead switched his shield to his strong arm and threw himself at the suit of armor. Eli grabbed onto the enemy's sword hilt and grappled with the soldier as he battered it with his shield. He landed blow after blow, pounding against its helmet, breastplate, and limbs. The soldier disassembled before him, leaving only the gauntlet and sword that Eli was holding. He threw the remains of the enemy onto the ground and kicked the hollow helmet away.

Eli turned to see that Kadmiel was finished with his skirmish as well, and was sheathing his sword with an eyebrow raised.

"Everything okay?"

Chapter 8: BREACH

Eli took a moment to consider the various aches and pains in his body, but there was nothing life-threatening. "I'm well. I just want to know how you so severely outclassed me; I wasn't expecting you to defeat your half of the soldiers and then help with mine."

"I didn't know you were keeping count so precisely," Kadmiel teased. "Let me show you something."

Kadmiel turned back toward the drawbridge from where they had entered the city. Eli followed him but plugged his nose as they neared the mote, full of the city's sewage. Kadmiel led him to the very edge and peered over the side. There, flailing pathetically, were five empty suits of armor, barely recognizable in the muck that covered their once-shining armor.

"The bewitched suits are light and easy to push," said Kadmiel. "I was covering your back and facing this direction, so I decided to fight smart and find an easy way to contend with our enemies. You didn't have an advantage like this, so don't give yourself too hard of a time."

Eli shook his head in bewilderment at the sight of the suits of armor clawing at the side of the moat.

"Although," Kadmiel continued, "I could still defeat five soldiers before you, regardless of the terrain."

Eli smirked. "I'm sure we'll get the opportunity to test that theory. We need to get moving into this city, and there's a good chance someone has been alerted to our presence by now. Helmets?"

"Helmets," agreed Kadmiel, rummaging through Eli's pack and retrieving their disguises.

For the first time since they arrived at the Northern Marshes, Eli was able to look around and get a good view of the city.

It was an astonishing sight to behold. The city was built in the treetops, which were just above the high waterline. A sprawling network of bridges connected the homes and shops and various other buildings, allowing travel through the city without coming into contact with the marsh. Large platforms were scattered throughout, connecting multiple paths like a series of hubs. Tied to many of those platforms were rafts with paddles that could be used to bypass the network of bridges and travel by water. Altogether the city was very impressive in its construction and immensity.

"Just look at this," Eli said with awe.

"It's amazing," said Kadmiel. "When it's not trying to kill you."

Eli gave a sad smile. "It's not this place's fault. I can imagine what it was like only a week ago—children playing on the rafts, a bustling marketplace, the bridges full of people..."

"Didn't you say we should get moving?" asked Kadmiel.

He nodded silently. Sighing, he broke his gaze from the sprawling city and looked at his companion. "Where to?"

Kadmiel paused. "I've been contemplating our options— and we don't have many. There are three things that we can be sure this city contains: more soldiers, a sorcerer, and captives. Which do we try to find?"

Eli contemplated for a moment. "Perhaps we look for the captives; they could tell us more about the sorcerer we're up against, and we could even find some that are willing to help us fight—that worked out well in the Plains."

"It didn't work out so well for them," Kadmiel pointed out.

"All the same, we can't be the only ones eager to dethrone these madmen," said Eli.

"I agree. Now, where do we look for the Marshes' inhabitants? Holed up inside their own homes like Barid had them?"

"I don't think so," said Eli. "Barid had plans to centralize the captives and put them to work, but we arrived soon enough to interrupt his agenda. The Warlock here has had more time, and probably has some plot in motion for the townspeople."

Chapter 8: BREACH

"I bet you're right," agreed Kadmiel. "Now, where do we find a city's worth of people hidden within a city?"

"Let's explore," suggested Eli. "And stay alert."

They were soon lost. The network of hubs and bridges was disorienting and difficult to navigate without a map or any experience. The swordsmen may have traversed the same areas multiple times, but they were unsure. While at first they treaded cautiously, after an hour with no sightings of captives, soldiers, or sorcerers, they quickened their pace and heeded not the danger of being seen in open areas.

"Maybe it's just us here, Eli—it's a ghost town."

"Wait," said Eli, holding up a hand. "Do you hear that?"

Kadmiel paused and listened closely. "I hear the wind and the swaying of the leaves and reeds—the same marsh sounds I've been hearing for the last couple of days."

"Not that," snapped Eli. He listened for a few more moments and then grabbed Kadmiel's arm. "This way."

They crossed three more bridges and then stepped onto a raft, which acted as a shortcut to the hub in the direction that he was trying to take them. Kadmiel paddled while Eli kept his ear turned to the sound he was following. The raft moved sluggishly in the thick, mucky water.

Arriving at a large hub platform, Eli motioned for silence again. "There it is," he said.

"I can hear it now," said Kadmiel. "The sounds of a forge."

"You're right! That's what it sounds like. Let's go!"

"We're not looking for a forge," said Kadmiel.

Eli spun to face him but kept walking backward. "Maybe we are. At this point, we're just looking for anyone at all."

Chapter 9: **RANKS**

The pounding sounds of metal on metal grew in volume and intensity as the swordsmen angled toward the tallest building in sight, an imposing structure supported by four great trees, one on each corner. The light of a flickering flame could be seen through the window facing them.

"Look how far we've come," said Kadmiel, pointing behind them. The drawbridge entrance was no longer within eyesight.

"Who knew the Tetrad Union was so big?" said Eli.

"I have a feeling this world is much larger than we know," said Kadmiel. "Think about it—what lies outside of the Tetrad Union?"

"Nothing," replied Eli quickly. "At least, that's what I've always thought."

"I doubt it," said Kadmiel.

"Well... if there are other people and places out there, what if they could help us defeat the Warlocks?"

"I doubt it," Kadmiel said again. "Besides, we have no time to lose. We don't know if there are people living outside of the Union, if we could find them in time, or if they would help us overthrow the Warlocks."

Eli grunted. "I suppose you're right. Alone again, as usual," he said with a sad smile.

"We're not entirely alone," said Kadmiel.

"True, we did find the Search Party. I hope they're doing well."

Kadmiel clapped Eli on the shoulder as they crossed the final bridge leading to the huge building from which the noises of a forge were coming.

Standing this close to the source of the sounds, the swordsmen discovered that it was not the noise of one smith working his craft, but multiple sets of tools in use.

"We have to take a look, but be on guard," warned Eli. "Whoever they are, they outnumber us."

"Wait," said Kadmiel, listening closely. "Something's not quite right."

Eli agreed. "The forging, it sounds... frenzied. Something is wrong inside this building."

Kadmiel took a deep breath and shook his helmeted head. "Did we sign up for all of this?"

"I suppose so," said Eli, swinging open the door to the forge.

The sound of a hundred gasps came from inside the building. Eli cautiously stepped in with his hand on the hilt of his sheathed sword.

"He's early!" someone cried in dismay. Others wailed aloud. All pounding of metal ceased at once.

The room was overcrowded and full of villagers, tools, fires and, most surprisingly, suits of armor. Kadmiel stepped in behind Eli and shut the door.

"Who's this?" said a large man accusingly, pointing a pair of tongs in their direction. "Someone else to hand out punishments for you, eh?"

Seeing that there was no sorcerer present, only frightened captives, Eli removed his helmet. Kadmiel hesitated, but then followed suit.

Eli witnessed a great wave of relief spread over the room as the inhabitants of the Northern Marshes saw that he and Kadmiel were not who they had been expecting, or dreading.

The people breathed a collective sigh of relief and then immediately went back to work, turning away from them to face their forges or polishing and sharpening stations. Frantic noises surrounded them once more as men, women, and even a few children all labored to produce weapons and suits of armor.

"What's going on?" shouted Kadmiel above the din. No one responded or acknowledged his question.

Chapter 9: RANKS

"This is very odd, Kad," Eli commented, unnerved at the collective villagers' drastic change of focus.

Kadmiel nodded, looking concerned as he watched the captives work as if a slave driver commanded them. "Someone needs to talk," he stated.

Eli and Kadmiel tried to approach the workers individually, asking who they were, what the situation was, and why they were creating armor. Each person brushed them away, pursed their lips, or shook their head adamantly.

Eli came to a woman with two small children who sat by her feet as she pounded vigorously at what was shaping up to be a breastplate. The mother had tears in her eyes.

"What is wrong, woman?" said Eli, lightly touching her shoulder.

She cringed at the contact and let out a sob, but then clutched at his arms and leaned into an embrace. Eli held her, uncomfortable but compassionate to her plight.

"What has been done?" Kadmiel asked her.

The woman continued to cry, her body trembling as if she had stored up her emotions for weeks and was only now letting them out. "Who are you?" she managed to whisper.

"We're here to help you," said Eli.

"You are going to lose if you talk to them!" shouted a man who was working a grindstone to the mother's left. He shook his head in disgust and turned away, focusing on the sword he was sharpening.

"What does he mean, lose?" asked Kadmiel.

The mother locked her eyes on her children as more tears pooled up in her gaze. "The sorcerer," she gasped. "Every day he visits us... and he... *kills* whoever has produced the least armor." She buried her face in her hands. "I've just been trying to keep my children alive... It's been so hard to keep up!"

Eli looked at Kadmiel in disbelief as he comforted the woman, patting her back as she sobbed.

"Do you know his name?" asked Kadmiel.

"It's Edric. He's a monster," she said.

"We'll do everything we can," said Eli.

"You're just two people—what do you think you can do?" she asked despairingly.

Eli and Kadmiel were silent, neither knowing what to say.

"I need to get back to my work," she said, turning to her station and picking up her mallet.

Eli touched the woman on the shoulder once more and took a few steps to meet the person who had warned her about speaking to them.

"Will you answer us?" asked Eli.

The man grunted and then jerked his head in the approximation of a nod. "But I won't stop working. Be quick."

"How many of you are there?" asked Eli.

"Few hundred," he said shortly. "There were more, but the sorcerer's been at his sick game for a while now."

"Weren't there more inhabitants of the Northern Marshes before Edric arrived?" asked Kadmiel.

"There were," he replied. "There are other groups of us, other captives on different duties. Gathering metal for us to forge with, making firewood, that kind of thing."

"Does Edric—" Eli hesitated. "Does he have them on the same kind of *arrangement?*"

"He does," said the man gravely, shaking his head. "Of course he does."

Eli's gaze fell. *What a terrible fate to have befallen the people of the Northern Marshes.* He turned and grabbed his friend's elbow.

"Kad, what if the sorcerers have our people doing something like this?"

Kadmiel frowned. "There's a good chance of that, Eli. We'll worry about that once we've found them. For now, what can we do to help all of these people?"

Chapter 9: RANKS

Eli looked around the room, watching suits of armor being made before his eyes as the captives sweated and cried. The sight was a lot to take in.

"Sir, tell us more about the sorcerer. He visits daily to see who has produced the least armor, and what does he do with all of it?"

The gray-haired man spat on the ground. "The fiend bewitches the armor, creating his *spirit soldiers*. They answer to him—patrolling the city, chasing down escapees, executing whomever he pleases."

"Escapees?" Kadmiel inquired.

"A few have attempted," he said with disdain. "Their bodies were returned to this room by the spirit soldiers—by the very armor we created."

"That's madness!" exclaimed Eli. "What if you all made an agreement to not produce any armor, stopped competing against yourselves, and stopped providing the enemy with weapons?"

Against his word, the man did stop his work. In one swift motion he slapped the sword he was sharpening down on the table next to him and grabbed Eli by the collar.

"Hey!" shouted Kadmiel.

He held a hand up to Kadmiel without breaking his gaze from Eli's eyes. "You think we haven't tried that, boy? We had that idea the first day the sorcerer scum arrived. We thought we found a clever loophole in his plan. He killed *half* of us that night."

Eli didn't feel threatened by the captive. He felt compassion for him. Edric was the threat.

"When does he come?" asked Eli calmly.

The man released him suddenly and returned to his labor. "Sundown. Get out of here."

Eli watched him straighten his shoulders and sigh, as if he was clearing his mind and pretending that he and Kadmiel had never visited.

"How much time, Kadmiel, until sundown?"

Kadmiel sprinted back to the building entrance, ducked outside, and returned with haste. "Only a couple of hours," he reported.

"Are you thinking what I'm thinking?"

"I have no idea. Probably not?"

Eli grinned. "A revolt. We help these captives fight back, take their land, and rid the world of one more Warlock."

Kadmiel shrugged. "All in a day's work."

He nodded, satisfied. "Let's tell them what we intend to do."

Kadmiel pointed to an empty table, where someone had probably worked days ago. But evidently not fast enough.

Eli made his way to the table and jumped atop it. Trying his best to shout for the entire room to hear him over the sounds of the forge, he said, "Friends! Your work is completed. No more armor will be crafted today for the wicked sorcerer Edric. I repeat, NO MORE armor or weapons!"

Most of the captives ignored Eli but a few glanced up at him, at least curious as to who he was and what was happening. Kadmiel walked about the room, trying to still the workers and point their attention toward Eli.

"You may be wondering who my friend and I are. We are Eli and Kadmiel of the Southern Shores, and we are leading a rebellion against the Warlocks who have ensnared this land!"

"Where is this rebellion?" one woman demanded.

Eli smiled, trying to appear confident. "We have already confronted one sorcerer, in the Western Plains, and we've sent him and the evil soul that he hosted back to the spirit realm."

Finally, most of the inhabitants of the Northern Marshes were attentive. The cacophony died down, and Eli could address them all at once.

"We have defeated one sorcerer and we can do it again, with your help. Don't keep working for this evil man—you are supplying him with the army that he needs to completely take over the Tetrad Union and fortify his defenses for years to come! We will not stand for that. What right does Edric have to our land? What right does Edric have to rule over us? What right does Edric have to lock you up in a forge and work you like slaves every single day?"

At this point, Eli started to hear the crashing sounds of workers throwing their tools down onto the ground or the tables beside them. *I'm getting through to them!* he thought. His heart was pounding in his chest—he had never spoken to as large of a crowd.

Eli gestured for Kadmiel to come over and join him, and Kadmiel hopped up onto the table beside him and placed a hand on his shoulder.

"Kadmiel and I are swordsmen, victors from the Championship of Warriors. We will lead you into battle, *tonight,* because we will not allow this injustice to continue for one more day!"

Cheers arose from the crowd.

After the noise died down, Kadmiel spoke softly but determinedly. "We ask every one of you that is able: join us in the fight. We will be doing battle not just with Edric but with the army of spirit soldiers which you have crafted. I see that many of you are proficient armor and weapons makers, so I imagine that Edric's army has become sizeable. We need all of your help. But if it is any encouragement, I am happy to report to you that Eli and I have already put over a dozen spirit soldiers to the sword, and they fell before us, just like they will fall before our collective strength!"

Eli observed the crowd and saw a mixture of emotions: excitement, fear, awe, terror, determination, skepticism, and, perhaps the most powerful of all, hope. Hope was the feeling Eli wanted to take, to enhance, and to spread.

"No longer will you die in droves at the hand of this wicked man. Edric will pay for the lives that he has stolen from this city.

We will be prepared for his arrival by nightfall. Now! Craft *yourself* the armor that you need to do war! Make it the best armor that you have created yet. Take up arms. Prepare yourselves. A reckoning is at hand—who will join us?"

The forge roared with the sounds of inspired men and women. A lump welled up in Eli's throat at the sight he had just beheld: hundreds of people's countenances transformed by hope.

Kadmiel smiled and looked him in the eyes. "We're doing this, Eli."

They couldn't help but laugh.

Being inexperienced with metalworking, Eli was unaware of the length of time needed to create a full suit of armor, and it turned out to be taking longer than the few hours they had. Fortunately, the captives were making do with what was already finished, outfitting themselves and performing the adjustments necessary for a suitable fit.

Eli and Kadmiel would use their own armor which they traveled with, but they did take the opportunity to sharpen their swords before devoting themselves to strategizing and planning the attack.

One of the metalworkers had the suggestion of staining their armor in order to stand apart from the spirit soldiers that they would be fighting. The group collectively added an icon to their breastplates: painted in red, circles that represented the four points of the Tetrad Union were connected by one large ring. The symbol stood for strength in unity, and Eli could think of nothing better to represent their rebellion. He and Kadmiel partook as well, adding the stain to their Southern Shores armor.

"Should anyone have information on Edric," said Kadmiel, standing and shouting from the empty table, "please bring it forward! We're interested in which entrance he uses to the city, how many guards he usually has—things of that nature."

Chapter 9: RANKS

A woman piped up from the crowd: "We think he stays in the royal chambers, where the king's subjects live—or... lived."

"Have you seen the king's subjects since Edric's arrival?"

"No," someone murmured from within the gathered villagers. Eli frowned. An older man, bald with a goatee, approached them.

"Thank you, sir, what information do you have?" asked Kadmiel.

"I have no information for you." The man scowled. "But I have something more valuable: a warning." He drew close to Kadmiel and Eli, and placed a hand on each of their chests. "You have no idea what you are up against... Edric is ruthless—he kills, indiscriminate of age or gender... He slaughters anyone who disappoints him or stands in his way You've roused my people with your fancy words, and now you intend to lead them to their deaths with no good plan of attack."

Kadmiel pushed the man's arm away and Eli took a step backward, uncomfortable and stung by his words.

"What's your name?" asked Kadmiel.

"Elmund," he responded.

"Well, Elmund, I do appreciate your concern," said Kadmiel. "But we have precious little time left and we fully intend to free your people, not lead them to their deaths."

"We need time to plan," said Eli, then he added pointedly, "You're wasting that time."

A shadow crossed over Elmund's face, and the lines in his forehead grew deeper. "You are fools! Fools, I say!"

"We are no such thing," Kadmiel insisted. "We have slain the sorcerer Barid, and we are here to ensure that Edric meets the same fate."

"What would you have us do?" asked Eli, feeling his temper rising. "What would you have your people do? Continue making suits of armor for the sorcerer, so that they can be used to incite chaos all over the Tetrad Union? Look at them!"

Elmund did not move but glared at Eli unblinkingly.

He took Elmund by the shoulders and turned him around. "Observe your people," said Eli. "Have you seen them working with such determination and purpose? Have you seen hope and happiness in their countenance?"

Elmund turned slowly back to face Eli and Kadmiel and he leaned in close, inches from their faces. "I have not; you've hoodwinked them with a false hope. Their smiles will soon fade when they step foot outside of this forge and see the thousands of suits of armor they must face in battle. For the past weeks I have seen only one of my people die each day—today I must bid farewell to all of them."

Nearby workers were starting to pause and watch the argument. Eli tried to quiet Kadmiel and Elmund down, but they weren't listening.

Kadmiel scowled. "You speak nonsense! You have no better solution, no hope for the Northern Marshes. You are but a coward, too afraid of the notion of confronting a sorcerer! You lack a spine, old man. If you were content with living as a slave to Edric, then I'm sorry for disturbing you, but as for the rest of the captives here, Eli and I are proud to lead them into battle!"

There was a flash of anger in Elmund's eyes, and his right hand darted in and out of his tunic as he lunged forward. Kadmiel was prepared and snatched the man's wrist in the air, then punched him in the gut. He crumpled to the floor, holding a knife in one hand and clutching his stomach with the other.

There was a collective gasp from the onlookers. Elmund stayed on the floor, staring straight ahead with his teeth bared, rasping to regain his breath.

Eli began to kneel down and reach for the man's knife, but Kadmiel held him back.

"He's been humiliated, Eli. He won't bother us again."

As Kadmiel said, Elmund picked himself up off the ground, brushed his clothes off, and strode across the room to his forging station in a corner, where he remained with his head downturned. Onlookers from the crowd groaned and offered some knowing glances before returning to the task at hand.

Eli stared blankly, saddened and confused.

"What's wrong?" asked Kadmiel.

"Perhaps he's right," Eli muttered. "We don't have any idea what we're up against. We've never fought Edric, we don't know this city's layout, we don't know how many spirit soldiers there are..." He trailed off, feeling hopeless.

Kadmiel looked unfazed. "This has always been the mission, my friend, to defeat the Warlocks, and we set out on this quest without knowing any information other than this: they declared war on our homeland."

"Yes, Kadmiel. But we are about to be responsible for everyone in this room. Look around! Hundreds of people that are about to follow us, to victory or to death. We've *never* led an army before. How can we presume to command them? Are we prepared to have their blood on our hands?"

"I am not leading Elmund into battle," said Kadmiel. "And there will be others, of course, who wish to stay behind. That is their choice. We are not forcing anyone to follow us—that's what the Warlocks do, and that's the great difference between them and us."

Eli shook his head. "I didn't mean to upset anyone like this."

Kadmiel shrugged. "It happens, Eli. We can't expect every single person to be on board with our mission. Most of them are, though. Look, they're working excitedly. They can't wait to be free."

"I am looking at them, Kad. I see that. But I also see plenty of women, some children, and a few people that look too old to be taking up arms. We can't lead them into battle with a clean conscience!"

Kadmiel considered this as he looked about the large room. "Are you telling me that you think Elmund was correct?"

"No," said Eli. "No, just that he had a point. You did the right thing, Kad."

Kadmiel placed his hands on his hips. "Well, I agree that there must be some kind of compromise. I have an idea, but we must hurry—time is of the essence for our preparations before Edric arrives."

Eli agreed.

Kadmiel once again assumed his place atop the empty table, where everyone in the forge could see him. "Attention, all! I hope you are making good progress on your armor. Please see to it that you are outfitted and armed in the next few minutes. We will soon be drawing out a plan of attack and making tactical assignments—divide yourselves into groups of twenty and assign one representative to meet with Eli and I to receive your orders.

"Now, there are some of you that may wish to not enter the battle, for whatever reason. You may have small children, some kind of infirmity, or you may despise the very sight of us," continued Kadmiel, with a nod toward Elmund's turned back. "We want to accommodate you. Anyone who cannot or will not join us in battle with the sorcerer Edric and his army may stay within this forge. We will protect this building by setting a full guard around it—this will be the safest place for you. And when we are victorious over our enemy, you are welcome to enjoy your freedom."

Nervous laughter sounded from the crowd.

"By show of hands," Kadmiel continued, "how many intend to take this offer?"

Only a handful. *Good,* thought Eli. *We may have a chance yet.*

The swordsmen spent their remaining time conferring with each of the group representatives, of which there were nine. After learning as much as possible about the city's different gates, bridge networks, and other details the leaders found relevant, they assigned the battle units to different areas on a crudely drawn map. The group crowded around the plans were buzzing with excitement, eager to begin.

Eli and Kadmiel hadn't eaten in far too long, and they were relieved when rations were served, which the unit leaders graciously shared with them. And then it was time.

Eli addressed the people of the forge. "Kadmiel and I thank you for joining our cause. We are honored to fight alongside you and help win your freedom and your land back. The Warlocks are going to learn an important lesson today—no one steals from us and gets away with it! The people of the Northern Marshes are not to be trifled with."

The people roared their agreement.

"And I hope that when this is done, when the entire Tetrad Union is free, it brings us closer together and stronger as a whole. Perhaps we can arrange a Union Gathering and throw a feast to celebrate our freedom, yes?"

The idea garnered raucous applause.

Eli waited a few moments before broaching a more serious topic. "Look around you—your fellow countrymen outfitted in armor, swords at their sides. Your friends and family are going to war now, and you are not guaranteed to see any of them again."

The people became solemn at his words and embraced those next to them.

"May the High King look favorably upon us for defending his throne today," said Eli. "We fight not for revenge but for justice. For the future of the next generation..." Eli looked into the wide, frightened eyes of the few children that were present. "For the Northern Marshes!" he concluded.

"For the Northern Marshes!" the warriors echoed back.

Eli hopped down to the ground and went to Kadmiel, who smiled approvingly.

"Nicely done, my friend," he said.

119

"Thanks," Eli answered sheepishly.

"You know, I think if the whole Champion of Warriors career doesn't work out, you could always go around stirring up wars," said Kadmiel with a grin. "You've got a knack."

"You flatter me, O Sarcastic One," said Eli.

Chapter 10: **WAR**

Eli saw him—Edric the Warlock—approaching the Northern Marshes' main gate. Immediately, he felt his pulse quicken and his hands start to sweat. Eli looked at Kadmiel, who squared his jaw and gave him a firm, confident nod. The swordsmen were fully outfitted in armor, weapons at their sides.

What was Edric doing outside the city? Eli wondered. *Probably tending to the other groups of captives. Many will be freed this night.*

As the people of the forge had warned, Edric was surrounded by an entourage of marching suits of armor. He was still only a speck in the distance, but there was no mistaking him as the one traveling among the spirit soldiers.

Eli turned around and motioned to the various commanders throughout the city, signaling them to prepare their groups for attack. The time had come. Eli made eye contact with the lead guard named Jay outside of the forge, and held up a fist as a signal to stay strong.

"Do you think they'll be okay, Kad?"

"The people inside of the forge?"

"Yeah. They must be terrified right now."

Kadmiel did not take his eyes off Edric as he spoke. "They are safe—we posted some great warriors there."

Eli couldn't shake the feeling that they were making a mistake. "Something's not right," he muttered.

Kadmiel shook his head. "Let it go. We've done everything we can to protect them."

"No," said Eli, quietly. He pulled on Kadmiel's arm, spinning him around to see. "Look. Notice anything conspicuous?"

Kadmiel appeared confused for a moment, then a look of understanding came over his face. "The refuge is too obvious," he stated.

"Right!" Eli exclaimed.

"All right—fix that, but hurry back. I'd like to be alongside you when the fight begins. Go!"

Eli didn't waste any time; he sprinted to the lead guard in front of the forge as fast as his armor would allow.

"You're going to need to move," said Eli, out of breath.

Jay appeared intensely focused, with piercing blue eyes and furrowed brows. "But, sir," he said, "you told us to not abandon our post for anything."

"Right, good," said Eli. "But Edric is almost here, and it occurred to me—what will the sorcerer think when he looks at the forge and sees twenty armed men surrounding it?"

Jay thought for a moment. "Probably that we are hiding something, sir."

"Exactly," Eli agreed. "Have your men spread out for now. If the time comes to defend the forge, by all means, regroup and protect those inside of it. But for now, don't draw any attention to the building. Edric might as well assume that it's been completely vacated."

"Yes, sir!" said Jay. The lead guard immediately set out to deliver new orders for his team.

Satisfied, Eli turned back toward the north entrance. Edric and his spirit soldiers were nearly upon the city. Kadmiel stood on a large central hub with bridges extending off of it in every direction. The eight other warrior units were stationed around the city, facing the advancing Warlock.

This is it. Nothing more we can do to prepare. It's finally time to win the city back and rid the world of one more sorcerer.

Eli sprinted back to Kadmiel's side just as the north gate swung open, held by two armor soldiers for Edric to pass through. His hollow guards followed behind him.

"Go," said Kadmiel, drawing his bow and knocking an arrow. "I'll cover you."

Eli nodded without taking his eyes off the man. He couldn't break his focus; confidence was paramount. Lowering the visor on his helmet, Eli approached the sorcerer and his personal guard of spirit soldiers that had followed him through the city's entrance. Edric appeared to be well aware by now of the confrontation about to happen—with an armed swordsman approaching, someone pointing a drawn bow at him, and several units of armored villagers posted around the city.

The plan was to ask Edric to surrender. Eli was tempted to scrap that plan now and tell Kadmiel to release his arrow—but no. *I must take heart. For Abner and Lana. For Gabbi and Tabitha. I will confront the evil that has befallen our land.*

Eli sized up the sorcerer, who had stopped a few yards past the city entrance and was observing him with a slightly amused expression. Edric was tall, slender, and middle-aged but surprisingly handsome. He wore robes that stopped at his ankles, and his most prominent feature was his facial hair, with a mustache and pointed goatee. Surprisingly, the sorcerer did not appear to wield any type of a weapon, which encouraged Eli that their plan may yet succeed. However, the Warlock's guard of spirit soldiers was large, and they stood behind Edric on either side with swords at the ready.

Eli drew up to a mere ten feet from his enemy, and suddenly his fear was displaced by a stronger emotion: anger. Anger toward the man that robbed him of his family and his home.

"Edric," said Eli, with as much venom in his voice as he could muster, "the city of the Northern Marshes has been taken from your despicable rule and given back to the people to whom it belongs."

The sorcerer regarded Eli with his eyebrows raised and then looked past him, observing the city and taking note of each unit of warriors. "I see," replied the man. "What do you intend to do now?"

"We would like to make you an offer," said Eli. "In exchange for your immediate disbanding of the spirit soldiers and volunteering yourself for imprisonment."

"What have you to bargain with, boy?" asked Edric.

"Your life."

The sorcerer's face lit up with glee, and then he let out a deep, rich laugh. "Well done, very well done. You, a stranger, have more heart in you than anyone from the Northern Marshes. Their spirits broke quickly." He stroked his short beard as he pondered a thought. "You must be involved with the destruction of my suits of armor outside the city..."

Eli felt his stomach sink. He wanted to keep this conversation focused on the sorcerer and off of himself.

But Edric continued. "Who are you? Where do you come from? How did you get in here?" He gestured to the assembled warriors throughout the city. "Why do the people follow you? We have so much to catch up on." He drew closer to Eli, and the way he spoke was smooth, even enticing. The man had a charisma that was impossible to deny.

"Will you take our offer or not?" Eli asked hesitantly, shuffling backward.

The enemy halted his approach and wrinkled his nose. "In regard to your bargain, young warrior, I thoroughly and adamantly refuse... but I am very interested in you. Perhaps I will make an offer of my own."

Eli drew his sword and pointed it at the man's face. "I won't hear it. I won't listen to you for another moment."

Edric frowned deeply and folded his hands behind his back. He was much less attractive when he was upset.

"We've already won!" taunted Eli. "The people are united against you! They are outfitted for battle and are prepared to defeat you and your hollow suits of armor. You have made a grave mistake, sorcerer, when you set yourself against the Tetrad Union."

Chapter 10: WAR

"The mistake is yours, foolish boy," said Edric. The sorcerer turned his back on Eli and walked past his guard of spirit soldiers so that ten suits of armor stood between them. "I bid you farewell, and I hope you've enjoyed your visit to the Northern Marshes. It's a beautiful place, isn't it? A fine place to die, indeed."

Eli paused, confused. *This was the sorcerer's plan—only ten suits of armor?* He glanced back at Kadmiel, who gave a small shrug.

Then Edric spun on his heel to face Eli, standing on an incline slightly above the guards between them. There was a mad, evil look about him, and the sorcerer showed his teeth in a wicked grin. The man appeared possessed, which Eli remembered—he was. A cold touch of fear entered Eli as he locked eyes with the Warlock, unable to avert his gaze.

The sorcerer raised his hands above his head with fingers bent like claws and started to chant something under his breath. The very air felt as if it was reverberating with the sorcerer's words, coming to life at his command. The swamp waters all around started to slowly churn, and then with a deafening roar, the waters of the marsh exploded all around the city. Eli lowered his sword as he watched the murky waters rise high into the air and then come crashing back down to earth.

There, crawling out of the marsh on every strip of land throughout the city, were spirit soldiers. Covered in mud and rust from the waters, the enemies spanned as far as the eye could see in every direction. The city was overrun with the bewitched suits of armor.

Eli's eyes darted around furiously, trying to take in as much as he could. He saw Kadmiel loose his arrow into the helmet of a spirit soldier before stowing his bow and unsheathing his sword. He saw the warriors reeling from the shock of the ambush and struggling to maintain their formation and defend themselves.

Eli had mere moments before the spirit soldiers surrounding his platform reached him. He looked for Edric, but could catch no glimpse of the sorcerer. He was no longer hiding behind his personal guard, which was easy to locate, being the only suits of armor not dripping with the mud of the marsh.

The invading spirit soldiers were quickly making their way onto dry land, crossing between platforms and surrounding the city. They paid no heed to the moss and mud clinging to them, but drew their swords and advanced toward the villagers. Eli estimated hundreds, if not thousands, of soldiers.

Eli unsheathed his sword and readied his shield. *Today will see the war for the Northern Marshes after all*, he thought grimly.

The nearest suit of armor approached him. Eli used his shield to strike the armor's helmet off its shoulders, then smashed his sword's pommel into the enemy's breastplate with a backhanded swing. With a trail of thick, black mist flowing from the suit of armor, it reeled backward and swung its arms in an attempt to keep its balance. Eli kicked the decapitated spirit soldier, which collided with another behind it and sent both toppling back into the marsh.

Enemies were pressing in all around, and he could no longer see Kadmiel. "Kad!" he screamed above the noise of metallic boots pounding on the wooden platforms.

"I'm here!" came a distant voice.

Eli oriented himself toward Kadmiel's direction. He had to make it to him, or else their fight would be over all too quickly. Eli gritted his teeth, knowing his progress would be slow with the numerous enemies advancing toward him on every side. He forced himself to take a deep breath. He thought of Idella, and her image in his mind gave him strength.

He threw himself into a frenzy of offensive advances, striking down each enemy before him. He received numerous cuts from his opponents but he took not a moment to consider them, blocking anything of more consequence on his shield or on the guard of his sword. Eli was careful not to leave his back exposed for more than a few moments at a time, knowing that would be fatal. But still he pressed toward Kadmiel, putting all of his focus on getting to the bridge that separated them.

Eli fell into a comfortable groove in the battle, where he let his instincts largely take over for him, a benefit of long being a seasoned swordsman. This freed up his mind to consider the nature of his opponent, which often helped him focus or find an exploit against his enemy. But it frightened him to think of the spirit soldiers. It was easier to imagine the enemies as mere empty suits of armor, rather than vessels possessed by the forces of the dead that Edric had befriended. Eli shuddered, blocking a downward strike from above and attacking the armor's elbow joint with his shield. The armor broke and he was left with a gauntlet and sword in his arms, which he tossed aside and ignored as he pressed onward.

The going was slow but Eli finally felt his feet hit the bridge, which proved to be a much more defensible position, as the approaching enemies were bottlenecked.

"Kadmiel, meet me here!" he shouted.

Eli was given no response, but he could hear Kadmiel grunting as soldier after soldier clattered to the ground in pieces. The air was soon filled with shadowy matter released by the felled enemies.

The suits of armor did not make it easy for Eli; they learned to approach him from both ends of the bridge in unison. He often found himself needing to block two blows at once, utilizing his sword and shield, and then immediately retaliating with his own strikes. It took a great deal of concentration, and the enemies managed to land wounds on the unprotected sides of his limbs—enough to start slowing him down.

Eli felt fatigue setting in. Although there was no end in sight to the advancing of the spirit soldiers, he and Kadmiel were evidently thinning them out in their own vicinity, for at long last they were able to see one another. Eli whooped and Kadmiel smiled, and then they cut down another group of enemies until there was a clear enough path to join each other on the center of the bridge.

Eli briefly grabbed Kadmiel's forearm, and then another wave of spirit soldiers marched toward them. The two swordsmen pressed their backs against one another and bent their knees in a ready stance. They let the suits of armor approach them and, with their backs covered, were able to destroy their opponents with less difficulty.

"Are you all right?" Eli asked over his shoulder.

"I am," answered Kadmiel. "This is much better. I saw that you're cut."

Eli swept the legs out from underneath a soldier and stabbed it through the helmet. "Only minor injuries, nothing too serious."

"Take care that you don't bleed out," warned Kadmiel. "No single suit of armor will challenge our skill with the blade here today, but—" Kadmiel paused as he caught a soldier's "wrist" and twisted the attacker around, then stabbed it through the back and tossed the armor into the water. "But," he continued, "be careful not to die by a thousand cuts."

The spirit soldiers seemed to endlessly march forward, from every end of the city and from every hidden place in the marsh. The night was growing darker, which was presumably an advantage for the enemy, not requiring light to see. Lanterns hung in the tops of trees throughout the city, but they were unlit and would have to remain as such.

"We're making no progress here," growled Eli.

Kadmiel grunted, striking down a suit of armor with his shield and knocking its helmet off with his sword. "But are you alive? Because I'm still enjoying the land of the living."

Chapter 10: WAR

In the brief moments between the enemies' advances, Eli tried to glance at the units of warriors stationed throughout the city. They were frighteningly difficult to spot amongst the waves and waves of muddy spirit soldiers.

Eli's attention snapped back to the bridge when a giant impact made it shake and then sag lower toward the marsh below. He frantically looked around and saw that a suit of armor was hacking at the rope that tied the bridge to the platform on one side. The soldier had successfully untethered one cord and immediately went to work cutting another.

"Shoot him!" shouted Eli.

"Trade me spots," said Kadmiel.

The companions rotated, and Eli worked double time to defend his side as well as Kadmiel's so that he could retrieve his bow. Kadmiel nocked an arrow and crouched quickly, then loosed it at the suit of armor who was attacking the ropes. The missile penetrated its gauntlet, but the soldier did not slow down.

Eli received a cut on his shoulder and a bruise on his back while he was trying to defend Kadmiel's vulnerable position. He grunted and did his best to keep the area clear as Kadmiel released another arrow. This one entered the spirit soldier's fist, but to no avail. With its other hand, the soldier raised its sword high into the air and sliced it down across the ropes, causing the bridge to creak and bow downward toward the water. A final cord snapped, and all was confusion as the bridge and all the combatants on it toppled into the murky water below.

Eli was submerged before being able to take in a breath, but he managed to clench his eyes shut so as not to damage them in the mud. He felt the bridge sink beneath him and a spirit soldier fall on top of him. Eli received a kick to the head from a boot that he guessed was Kadmiel's, then he began to turn and flail, trying to twist out from underneath the weight pressing down on him.

Eli's own armor slowed him down and made him heavy in the water. He lost his sense of direction somewhere in the confusion and was unsure which way was up. Panicking and short of breath, he writhed in the marsh. Finally, he broke the surface and gasped for air. Eli removed his helmet so that he could wipe his face on a tuft of grass nearby and find Kadmiel.

"Behind you!" Kadmiel yelled from the other side of the pond.

Eli spun in the water and propelled himself away. Two spirit soldiers were approaching him, virtually unhindered by the marsh. His heart sank at the sight. *These empty suits of armor have the perfect advantage over us in the marsh: mobility. And they still outnumber us ten to one.* And then Eli realized that he had dropped his sword during the fall. There was no outrunning the spirit soldiers in the marsh, so Eli gritted his teeth and prepared himself for defense, shoving the helmet back over his head.

Reaching him, the soldiers appeared to have a dangerous strategy—one opted to stab toward Eli, which was difficult to evade in the muddy water, and the other soldier made sweeping slices for his neck while he was off-balance.

"I need help!" he cried.

"I'm coming!" answered Kadmiel. Fortunately, Kadmiel's sword was sheathed when the bridge was cut, so he was able to deal with his own attackers and then come to Eli's aid, dispatching the enemies threatening him.

The swordsmen's movements were slow, however, and the surrounding spirit soldiers looked as if they had no intention of letting them escape from the marsh onto dry land. Every platform and bridge nearby was surrounded by the enemy suits, which lowered themselves into the water one after another to join the attack.

At this pace, they would soon be overwhelmed.

Kadmiel stabbed through the helmet of a soldier and Eli dove for the armor's sword, retrieving it for himself. *This will have to do for now.*

Chapter 10: WAR

Reunited, Eli and Kadmiel pressed their soaked backs up against one another again and squared their shoulders, preparing for what could be endless hours of battle. The broken armor that they were rending began to pile up on the marsh floor, making it even more difficult to maneuver in the water.

The chill of the night and the cold of the lake started to seep into Eli's bones, and the clothes beneath his armor were weighed down by filthy water. Exhaustion was setting in. Eli watched as his reflexes slowed down, and his sword didn't travel through the air as quickly to block the incoming blows. His breathing became ragged. *Is this it?* he wondered.

Kadmiel must have been experiencing similar fatigue, for he grunted and clutched a bleeding cut on his wrist, and then smote the soldier responsible. Eli tried to see if he was all right, but let his guard down and received a deep slice on the shoulder, between his plates of armor.

Eli growled in frustration and renewed his vigor, attacking the oncoming soldiers with ferocity. How much longer he could maintain this pace, he dared not consider.

Just then, a great commotion could be heard from the main platform nearest them, and the suits of armor paused in their advance toward the two swordsmen. They had turned their attention to something approaching—something coming very quickly based on the sound of thundering footsteps. Suddenly, an entire unit of warriors burst into view with their swords raised above their heads, and the leader shouted a war cry as he sprinted in front of the line. The warriors collided with the suits of armor, sending some sprawling, crushing others, and tearing them to pieces. A few enemies closest to Eli and Kadmiel pivoted away from the disturbance and made haste toward them, but they too were intercepted by warriors who leapt fearlessly into the marsh and ran the suits of armor through with their blades, dumping the ruined armor parts into the water.

Eli had never been so happy to see anyone in his life. Looking around, he and Kadmiel were finally out of reach of the spirit soldiers for a brief moment. Eli let his arms drop to his sides to give his aching shoulders a rest. Kadmiel waded to the nearest bank and set his sword down, leaning against the edge of the pond and resting his head upon his forearm.

The warriors had destroyed every last spirit soldier that had been surrounding Eli and Kadmiel, and they cheered and hollered in their victory.

"You are amazing!" exclaimed Eli, looking up at the gathered warriors. "All of you, you're truly wonderful."

The villagers seemed to swell with pride at Eli's words.

Kadmiel nodded in agreement. "We can't thank you enough—we sorely needed that."

The lead warrior dipped his head, accepting the gratitude.

"What is your name?" asked Eli.

"Russell, sir."

"No need to call me sir. How goes the battle?"

Russell's eyes drifted past Eli, and his grin faded. "This is madness. We're so outnumbered, and to think... this is the army that we created." Russell shook his head sadly.

Kadmiel and Eli edged toward the warriors along the bank, wishing to join them and be out of the marsh at last.

"Well, let's go help them," said Kadmiel.

Russell blinked, surprised. "You two have done enough. You're bleeding. Shouldn't you—"

"No," asserted Eli. "This is our lot. This is our battle as much as it is yours."

"Very well," Russell said, kneeling down and grabbing Kadmiel by the forearms. The warrior heaved him out of the marsh and onto the platform above. Eli waded to the edge, tossed his borrowed sword over the side, and then reached for Kadmiel's extended hands. They grasped each other and

Chapter 10: WAR

Kadmiel started to pull, then Eli heard a splashing noise behind him and whirled to see what was approaching.

A suit of armor, damaged in the battle, had risen from the marsh. Its helmet was dented and one arm was missing, but its remaining hand held a sword that was pointed toward Eli's back. The soldier was mere feet away from Eli, who was pressed up against the bank with no weapon.

He flinched and tugged free of Kadmiel's grip. There was a blur of motion above Eli's head and another splash—he didn't seen what happened. Then the suit of armor rose out of the water once more, entangled with the warrior Russell, who had leapt down to defend him. The foes grappled with each other, and the lead warrior's muscles rippled as the suit of armor tried to escape his grip.

The struggle was intense, but quick. Russell subdued the soldier into a bear hug from behind, and Eli could hear the armor starting to creak and snap. Then the spirit soldier did something that no one could have predicted: with its one arm, it stabbed itself through the chest. Inky black smoke poured from the hole in the soldier's breastplate.

Russell's expression was one of shock, but the look never faded from his face. In a moment it became clear that the soldier's sword had been thrust through its own body and into Russell's. Slowly, both combatants slipped deeper into the marsh and moved no longer. The suit of armor had killed itself and Russell in one attack.

"No!" Eli screamed. He lunged toward the spot where Russell's body had begun to sink, willing the warrior to be alive. Eli removed Russell's blade from his cold grip and took the man's hand, but Kadmiel grabbed Eli by the collar and pulled him back toward the bank of the platform. He was shaking his head.

"There's no use. Russell's gone—we need to get you out of here."

Kadmiel helped him out of the water, but Eli couldn't take his eyes off the marsh. No bubbles broke the surface. The warrior had given his life to save him.

Eli raised Russell's sword and loosed a ragged growl, daring anyone to confront him in his grief. Three suits of armor nearby accepted the challenge and he cut them all down, spilling dark matter into the air.

Something touched him on the shoulder. Eli whirled around with his sword raised, but stopped his attack when he saw that it was his friend.

Kadmiel flinched and looked at Eli with unknowing eyes. "We need to get to the forge," he said. "Their defenses are falling."

Eli blinked and looked up at the building. Kadmiel was right. It was then that Eli realized the rest of Russell's unit looked to be awaiting orders from... him? He didn't know how to address them, and a lump kept forming in his throat. He nodded to Kadmiel.

"We cannot thank you enough for your help," Kadmiel said to the warriors. "We wouldn't still be here if not for you. You may have never guessed it of yourselves, but you all are fine warriors. Now, we must help Jay and his unit defend the forge—it's under attack and they're not holding up well."

The warriors of Russell's unit corralled themselves, perhaps not quite as enthusiastically as before but courageous nonetheless.

These are great men, thought Eli. *I'm fortunate to be fighting beside them. And I'm going to help them get their city back.*

Eli and Kadmiel led Russell's unit to join what was left of Jay's warriors at the forge. There were an unfortunate amount of bodies strewn across the ground in front of the keep where their women and children were staying. Suits of armor pressed inward, encroaching on their defenses.

"What happened?" Eli called out. "How did they know to attack the forge?"

Chapter 10: WAR

"I don't know," Jay replied breathlessly, fending off three spirit soldiers at once.

Eli rushed to his side and helped him dispatch the opponents.

"Maybe the sorcerer has an inside informant. Did you catch Edric?"

"No," Eli answered, shaking his head. "He got away. How many of your warriors have fallen?"

"Half of my unit," growled Jay through clenched teeth.

Eli winced.

The spirit soldiers advanced tirelessly, at a consistent pace. They did not slow or weaken. When one fell, another took its place immediately.

Kadmiel was having difficulty keeping up with the onslaught of soldiers nearby, and Eli attempted to assist him. That was when Jay began to get overrun again.

"You can't worry about me" said Jay. "We have to spread out around the forge. There's just not enough of us."

Eli heard a piercing scream coming from behind him—the direction of the building. He lunged, stabbed, and felled an opponent, then spun around to see the source of the noise. A wide-eyed boy, eight or nine years of age, had opened the slats on a window to peek outside.

Shouldn't have done that, thought Eli. "You'll be okay!" he called, but the child didn't seem to hear him. Eli sighed and sprinted toward the window, blocking the boy's entire field of view. He only had a handful of seconds until he would have to defend his section again.

"What's your name?" Eli asked then repeated again when the boy finally met his gaze.

"Jacob," he said quietly.

"Here's what I need you to do, Jacob. You can help us win this battle. Go get all the people you can and tell everyone inside to block the doors, all right? Pile stuff in front of it."

Jacob's mouth hung open, but he nodded slightly.

"You can do it!" said Eli. "Go!"

He saw Jacob hop down from the window and scurry off. Turning back to the battle, Eli realized that those moments had costed him. Now six spirit soldiers were upon him, and they were far too close to the forge. "Kadmiel!"

Eli lowered into a battle-ready stance and steeled himself. The soldiers fixed their eyeless gaze on him with unflinching determination and rushed him with their blades pointed at his heart. He had to exercise the use of his sword and shield simultaneously to defend himself. *I never knew that all the practice I put in for the Championship of Warriors would help this much.* It was the only thing keeping him alive.

There was a second scream, but this time from a man. Another Northern Marshes makeshift warrior falling in battle.

Kadmiel arrived just in time, cleaving two suits of armor in half with one horizontal swing.

Eli beheaded another and then propelled all his weight behind his shield into a fourth, which sprawled toward Kadmiel and met its end on his blade. The last two spirit soldiers fell quickly afterward.

Eli smiled. "Thanks."

Kadmiel just shook his head. "Eli, it's no use. There's no end in sight to the soldiers."

It was true. The suits of armor were visible to the horizon.

"I can't keep fighting for long," Kadmiel continued, still bleeding from the wound on his wrist and other cuts on his body.

Eli knew that Kadmiel was right, but didn't want to admit it. "We can't give up on the warriors. We led them here," he said, clenching his fist.

"Listen to him, Eli!" called Jay from a few yards in the distance. He ran over to join them momentarily. "You're just going to wear yourself out here. You should be looking for the sorcerer. Find Edric, and end all of this!" he said, grasping each of them on the shoulders and looking them in the eyes. "Kill him."

Eli hesitated, looking around the battlefield at the out-numbered inhabitants of the Northern Marshes.

"I *will* defend the forge," Jay asserted.

Eli dipped his head and finally agreed.

The lead guard started to back away. "Go!" he urged them, pointing toward the royal chambers.

It took Eli and Kadmiel a handful of precious minutes to weave through the thick of the battle and emerge on the other side, nearer the royal chambers. Tall, regal buildings lined the outskirts of the city, rising out of the marshes like monoliths connected by a web of bridges.

"Where?" asked Eli.

"Isn't that always the question?" Kadmiel grunted.

"Should we split up?" Eli proposed.

"You know that's a bad idea."

He smiled. "I was hoping you would say that."

"I'm going to need someone to hide behind if we fight another Warlock," said Kadmiel.

Eli surveyed the buildings before them. "I don't know what we're looking for."

The swordsmen stood on the bank of a platform sur-rounded by muddy water, with the sounds of the battle raging behind them. Time was of the essence.

"What about that?" asked Kadmiel. He had his hands over the visor of his helmet, blocking the sun.

Eli followed his gaze and saw what Kadmiel was indicating. There was one building with a severed bridge hanging limply in the water, which stirred slowly with the mild current.

"I'd say someone doesn't want our company," Eli stated. Kadmiel was already on the move.

"If Edric thinks *that* can keep us out," spoke Kadmiel over his shoulder, "wait until I explain how we entered the city."

Eli and Kadmiel soon understood why he had chosen this particular section of the royal chambers to retreat to—it had no direct connections from any other buildings around it. The building, which appeared to be a library upon closer inspection, had only one entrance: the recently severed bridge connecting it to the main hub for the royal chambers.

"Still no sign of soldiers," said Kadmiel hopefully.

"Stay vigilant," said Eli. "We know firsthand that they can be hidden well."

The swordsmen did their best to keep a distance from the marsh's waters, but there was little that could be done when crossing the many bridges along the way. Eli's hair stood on end as they approached the sorcerer's presumed hiding place. His body ached from the battle with the spirit soldiers, but his mind was occupied with the task of gaining entrance to the library.

"You're wasting your time," rasped a voice from above.

Eli and Kadmiel snapped their heads upward to see a pale and gaunt Edric, overlooking them from a balcony attached to the second story of the royal library.

Eli's hand instinctively grasped the hilt of his sheathed sword, but the Warlock was decidedly out of range. Kadmiel had his bow drawn in moments. "Should I?" he whispered.

"Do it!"

Kadmiel let loose the arrow, but it never met its target. The Warlock raised a vial full of liquid to his lips just as the arrow halted in midair mere feet from its mark. Gravity took the arrow, which fell insignificantly into the marshy waters below.

Edric closed his eyes as he drew upon the substance in the clear vial. Swallowing, he looked down at them with half-closed lids. "You have no business with me. Join your friends and die with honor before they are completely overrun."

Despite himself, Eli turned his gaze from the sorcerer to the clash of the soldiers and warriors in the city. All he could see was a blur of silver and rust—spirit soldier suits everywhere, like ants crawling over their nest. Kadmiel grabbed him and jerked his attention back to the sorcerer, who was sipping lazily from his flask.

Edric didn't look well, even compared to their confrontation at the gate only hours ago. His face seemed sunken in, his skin looked sickly, and sweat beaded his forehead.

If only we could reach him! thought Eli.

Kadmiel had not given up. He grabbed another arrow and fired, and another, and another, until his quiver was empty. But each missile bounced off of an invisible obstruction and tumbled helplessly away. Kadmiel growled and tossed his bow aside. Edric regarded them with a strange combination of boredom and disgust.

Eli shook his head as he stared at Edric. "You're a coward. A great, manipulative, power-hungry coward. You've invaded this city, enslaved its people, murdered their men, women, and children. And you relax upon your balcony comfortably while the armor of others' craftsmanship does your dirty work. I've never met a man like you," said Eli.

"That is because there are none like me," said Edric.

"Not even the other Warlocks?" asked Kadmiel.

He chuckled. "They are somewhat... *useful* to me, so I endure them—for now." Edric's eyes gleamed as he spoke.

"You may be interested to know that we killed Barid," Kadmiel uttered. "We will do the same to you."

Edric raised a brow then went for another drink and frowned deeply when the vial was empty. He slammed the container down on the railing of the balcony and shouted, "More!"

Within moments, Eli heard the door to the library balcony swing open, followed by quick footsteps likely belonging to a servant. Then a disheveled man came into view, who shifted his gaze nervously from the sorcerer that had summoned him to the battle raging within the city.

"More tonic," Edric repeated, dropping his flask into the man's hands. Scabs and bruises betrayed the fact that he had been mistreated, even more so than those in the forge. But what was most striking about the servant were the garments that he wore, which looked as if they had once been of regal status. The clothes were unclean and tattered, but it remained clear that they were once embroidered and crafted with care.

Then the servant noticed Eli and Kadmiel, and his eyes widened with shock.

"*Now,*" Edric added with venom in his voice.

The servant turned on his heel and exited the balcony. Edric gripped the railing tightly, looking lost without the liquid substance. He bared his teeth and tapped his fingers, waiting for the servant to return.

Eli felt helpless with the sorcerer being out of reach. Kadmiel fidgeted next to him, obviously feeling the same way. Eli flinched as the screams swelled from the battle raging behind them.

There was the sound of creaking hinges, followed by more footsteps as the servant returned bearing Edric's tonic. The Warlock released his grip on the balcony railing eagerly and turned to the servant, hands outstretched to receive the drink. The servant came into Eli's view over the railing, and he appeared nervous. He did not offer the vial to Edric immediately, but rather continued to hold onto it.

"Give it to me," hissed Edric impatiently.

A cold resolve seemed to overtake the man and he squared his shoulders, meeting Edric's steely gaze. "This has gone on for too long," he said simply.

The servant thrust the flask toward Edric, splashing the contents directly into the sorcerer's face. He reeled back and cursed, rubbing his eyes furiously on the back of his sleeve.

A thick, red substance dripped down the sorcerer's front, staining his beard and clothes. The servant wasted no time; he charged the Warlock, throwing all of his weight into a mighty shove that toppled Edric and pushed him over the balcony.

Eli could not believe what he was seeing. Edric hung over the railing for a moment then plummeted toward the earth. The sorcerer splashed into the swamp, and his cries were muted by the murky water.

The servant looked utterly conflicted, standing on the balcony with the empty vial still clutched in his hands. The look on his face was one of confusion: triumph and terror, pride and shock.

Just as Eli and Kadmiel had drawn their weapons, the marsh waters stirred. The arrows Kadmiel had fired hovered into the air, pointed toward the swordsmen, and then shot forward. Eli's visor was lowered, but he instinctively covered his face with a gauntlet before the arrows struck. His armor took the brunt of the attack, but he felt bruises forming beneath the metal. Kadmiel grunted beside him, hurt but not injured.

Edric had clawed his way out of the marsh and onto the platform where they stood with their swords raised. The sorcerer blinked hurriedly and spat, attempting to clear his vision from the thick tonic and the filthy water. Dripping wet and looking distraught, he turned slowly to the servant on the balcony and pointed an accusing finger at him. "I will kill you for that."

The man seemed to shudder at the sorcerer's words, and backed away slowly. But he did not retreat into the building, remaining outside where he could see.

We're his only hope, Eli realized. He tried to give the servant a confident nod, but the man's frightened eyes were fixed on Edric.

The Warlock turned his back to the balcony and spat on the ground. Then he reached within his wet robes and retrieved a weapon. It was a dagger with a ruby hilt.

"Let's get this over with," said Edric through clenched teeth. "I can't take much more of this."

Indeed, the sorcerer did not look well. Eli barely recognized him as the well-kept man that he had spoken with prior to the battle. He looked as if he had lost fifteen pounds along with all the color in his skin.

Eli took a deep breath and began to move. *There's no better time to defeat him. For whatever reason, he's weak.*

He advanced on the sorcerer. Kadmiel circled around Edric and approached his flank. The Warlock raised his hands, one hand holding his dagger and the other showing his palm. Instantly, Eli felt as if he ran into a brick wall; his momentum stopped immediately, and he hung with his feet dangling a few inches above the wooden floor beneath him.

Edric thrust his outstretched arms forward and both swordsmen fell onto their backs, slamming against the ground. Eli lost all breath in his lungs and slid backward on the platform before coming to a stop. The sorcerer growled and lunged toward Kadmiel, his dagger flashing through the air. Kadmiel jerked violently and spun away from the sorcerer, avoiding the sharp edge of the blade. But Kadmiel was out of space, and almost toppled into the marsh.

Eli sprang to his feet and dashed forward with his sword held over his head. Edric seemed to be muttering things under his breath that Eli could not hear over their own pounding steps upon the wooden planks. The sorcerer demonstrated another sweeping motion with his hands, and Eli felt himself lose his grip on the sword that he had taken from Russell's body. It clattered to the ground a few yards behind him. He did not stop to retrieve it, but collided with Edric and tackled him to the floor, away from Kadmiel.

Armed with no weapon, Eli pummeled the Warlock's jaw with his fists as Edric howled and attempted to buck him off. He refused to be thrown, channeling the entirety of his focus into making him pay for his actions.

Edric whispered another enchantment, then grabbed Eli around the neck. The sorcerer tightened his grip, but the true pain came as the rings upon Edric's fingers began to burn his skin. The jewelry had turned white-hot, unbearable to the touch. Eli yelped and disengaged from the Warlock, rolling backward as he clutched his neck.

Edric rose unsteadily, but Kadmiel leapt into action before the man could regain the offensive. The swordsman had retrieved Russell's blade that Eli lost and wielded it in addition to his own. Kadmiel executed a flurry of attacks that Edric seemed to catch with his bare hands, but the blades halted in mid-air just inches from the sorcerer.

Eli watched from his knees, still holding the burnt skin on his neck, unsure of how to help. Kadmiel was battling skillfully, but Edric's defenses were impenetrable.

The sorcerer, however, did not seem to be enjoying the upper hand. His visage was distressed, locked into a constant grimace. Suddenly, a fit of coughing overtook him, and Kadmiel landed a deep slice on the man's shoulder.

Edric fell to his knees and cried out, begging for mercy. "Please, make it stop, make it stop!"

But the sorcerer wasn't speaking to them, and his eyes were darting back and forth. In fact, he barely seemed aware of their presence at all.

Eli stood and went to Kadmiel's side, looking down upon the groveling sorcerer.

Edric crumpled to the ground and began to writhe wildly, clawing at his chest and his stomach. Eli glanced at the servant, still watching from the balcony, and he looked equally confused.

"What's going on, sorcerer?" Eli demanded.

Kadmiel handed Russell's sword back to him, and Eli pointed it threateningly toward Edric.

"It's—it's—it's," he stuttered through rasping breaths. "It's torturing me."

"What is?" asked Kadmiel.

"The spirit—the spirit inside me," Edric answered, with his gaze fixed somewhere on the horizon.

A chill ran down Eli's spine and he shuddered. "Why did you bring this upon yourself?"

Edric convulsed and barked a harsh laugh. "The Brotherhood of Warlocks will complete Lilith's great work. I wouldn't expect you to understand, whoever you two are."

"It's not looking too good for you," Kadmiel stated. "I would say you're running out of time to complete anything."

Eli saw tears appear on Edric's face, but his voice remained level. "It is in motion," the sorcerer uttered. Then the man's spine went rigid, and he resumed babbling. "Make it stop, make it stop!"

"Why's it torturing you?" asked Eli.

The Warlock turned his head and looked toward the battle of the spirit soldiers and the warriors of the Northern Marshes. He took a long time to answer, then said sadly, "It's furious with me, that I've led so many of its kind into battle, just for them to experience death all over again. They're dying in droves."

"You've failed," asserted Kadmiel. "You can't oppress these people forever. They will rise up against you and overpower you, no matter how many hollow suits of armor you command."

Edric shook his head repeatedly. "I've made a better world," he resolved. The sorcerer still thrashed with convulsions of pain, but his face took on a look of contentment.

"It's over, Edric," said Eli. "Let me help you out of this misery."

Kadmiel's mouth parted. The Warlock seemed to accept Eli's offer with expectancy, as if he knew that this must happen. He closed his eyes for a long moment, then nodded at Eli knowingly. "I will join the spirits in the land of the dead."

"Yes," Eli agreed, offering to help Edric up.

The sorcerer grabbed on with both of his hands, leaving his dagger on the ground. Eli bore his weight and pulled him up to stand at the edge of the platform. Edric never let go while the swordsman took Russell's blade and thrust it through the sorcerer's heart. Edric's grip loosened and he gasped. Eli gave a gentle push and his body toppled backward, over the edge and into the marsh below. Edric breathed his last breath, and a shockwave exploded outward from the body, which Eli now recognized as the death of a sorcerer and the destruction of the spirit which he hosted. The burst sent waves rippling through the water, and Edric's body began to slowly drift down the current.

"Your sword!" shouted Kadmiel.

Eli gazed at the body with a blank expression. "That's not my sword."

*
**

When Edric was killed, all the suits of armor that he had commanded instantaneously collapsed. As the armor clattered to the ground in a great din, the sounds of the Northern Marshes warriors celebrating their victory rumbled forth.

Eli and Kadmiel took the first opportunity that they had to sit down, right on the platform that acted as the main hub for the royal chambers. But against their will, they did not rest for long. Their work was not yet done.

The servant that pushed Edric off the balcony had watched the entire battle between the swordsmen and the sorcerer. Upon the Warlock's defeat, the man had dashed back inside the library, then emerged from the lower level with five others in tow. The royal officers looked underfed and abused, but overjoyed to escape their confines. Eli and Kadmiel ignored the protests of their aching bodies and immediately went to help the former prisoners repair the destroyed bridge.

Within the hour, the freed captives were able to cross over. Eli and Kadmiel received a blur of hugs, handshakes, thankyous, and blessings from the assembled royal officers.

145

"It's nothing, no problem," Eli assured someone for the third time. "Go and find something to eat."

"Won't you join us?" asked a kind aged woman.

Eli's stomach growled. "Soon," he said with a smile.

They seemed hesitant to leave Eli and Kadmiel, their new heroes.

"Go, go," said Kadmiel. "Celebrate with the warriors, the inhabitants of the Northern Marshes. Those are braver men and women than experienced sword fighters like us," said Kadmiel.

After a final round of gratitude, the freed prisoners turned and began to walk away.

Eli faced Kadmiel. "Shall we investigate Edric's living quarters? Do you think we could find anything useful, like information on the fourth Warlock?"

"I think—"

"Excuse me," someone interrupted.

The oldest member of the royal officers had paused before leaving and was looking at them with a questioning gaze.

"Yes, sir?" asked Eli.

The man hesitated. "My dear boy, are we acquainted?"

Eli glanced at Kadmiel, who shrugged.

"Surely not," answered Eli. "I am just a swordsman from the Southern Shores, the farthest point from your location in the Union. I don't think we've met."

But the royal officer was not convinced. He shook his head and muttered under his breath as he crossed the distance between them. He was short and stocky and had a long gray beard that was tied to a point at the bottom. Stopping just a few feet before Eli, the man studied his face with piercing eyes. "But you look so familiar..."

Eli felt slightly uncomfortable beneath the old man's scrutiny. "I don't think so," he said, shifting his weight. "I don't believe we've had the... pleasure."

"You said your name was Eli? Hmm... Eli..."

"What are *you* called?" Kadmiel interjected.

"My name is Rayorden."

Rayorden. The name was familiar. It tickled something in the back of Eli's mind, but he couldn't quite place it. Kadmiel shot him a questioning look, and then their eyes widened as the companions came to the same realization at once.

Eli reached within the pocket of his tunic and retrieved the prophecy scroll. There, inscribed on the sealed roll of parchment, was this man's name.

They had found him.

Chapter 11: **FORTIFY**

U pon seeing the scroll, Rayorden had insisted that they converse in private. He led them into the library in which he had just been held captive, but the man did not seem to mind.

Eli and Kadmiel entered a large reading room and sank into its lounge chairs eagerly. Rayorden took a seat in a rocking chair across from the companions, and he appeared to be in quite the hurry for a man of his age.

"We have a great deal to discuss," said Rayorden. "I've acquired your names in the process of thanking you for helping kill Edric and take back the Northern Marshes. I have gathered that you are extremely skilled with the blade. You said that you hail from the Southern Shores. Now, perhaps the most interesting thing remaining to learn about you is: how did you come by that scroll?"

Kadmiel was silent and looked at Eli expectantly to answer. Eli would rather have taken a nap, but he willed himself to respond.

"Forgive me, sir, but we know so little about you. Before we share our story, please, can you explain who you are and why we can trust you?"

Rayorden did not appear put off by Eli's question. "I think that is a wise request. Let me see here, where to begin... Well, I am now little more than a retired old man, but my former profession was something I quite enjoyed. I had the honor of being the royal chronicler."

"What is that?" asked Eli.

"My job was to record the acts and decrees of the High King, basically writing down history on a daily basis. It was always interesting," said Rayorden as he stroked his long beard.

Eli and Kadmiel looked at each other in disbelief.

"You knew King Zaan? Personally?" questioned Kadmiel. "I mean—I assume, as a royal officer, you worked for him..."

Rayorden gave a hearty laugh. "Oh my, yes. I have spent a great deal of my life with the High King. He's a marvelous man."

"That's amazing!" Eli exclaimed. "How did you earn that responsibility, of being the chronicler?"

Rayorden pondered for a moment, then answered simply, "I suppose I was proficient with a quill."

Eli smiled. *I think that I like this man. He seems like a trustworthy kind... Evidently the High King thought so as well.*

"Where is he?" asked Kadmiel.

Rayorden stopped the rocking of his chair in mid-motion, and then his bearded chin sank into his chest in a look of defeat. "I know not. When he addressed his subjects before taking his leave from the throne, he promised that he would return. He was going on a journey that I was not allowed to accompany him on, for my own safety, he said."

"He was going to do battle with Lilith," said Eli.

Rayorden regarded him with a curious expression. "How do you know that?"

Eli hesitated, but didn't imagine that the Search Party was a secret from the king's own chronicler. "We crossed paths with the band of warriors that are searching for any signs of Zaan or Lilith. We were able to learn some things about the history of sorcery in order to better understand the enemies that have come against us," said Eli.

"Did you, now?" asked Rayorden with a small smile. "You were fortunate to meet them—wonderful people, from what I've heard."

"Eli agrees," said Kadmiel as he winked lazily.

Eager to advance the discussion, Eli asked, "What happened here, with Edric? What did he do to you? Is everyone going to be all right?"

Chapter 11: FORTIFY

Rayorden breathed deeply as he recalled what was sure to be a very troubling handful of memories. "He is—or, was, rather—a vile man. I trust that you've met the general populous of the Northern Marshes—you were the ones to rally them together for this battle, yes?"

Kadmiel nodded.

Rayorden beamed at them, shaking his head in wonder. "You must be some very special young men... In any case, you are aware of Edric's atrocities on that front. Fortunately, we did not see much of him in the royal chambers. He gathered us all here, destroyed our escape route, and confined us. He placed enchantments around the library to keep us in and others out. He also posted a couple suits of armor to punish us if needed."

Rayorden seemed to notice the wide-eyed look on Eli's face, and reassured him, "Worry not. Upon killing the man, you destroyed the spirit that he was a host to and you broke his spells. The world is now free from that man's evil influence."

Eli sat back in his seat, able to rest a bit easier.

"The whole ordeal was so awful and happened so quickly," Rayorden continued. "I've had the unfortunate privilege of seeing a great deal of sorcery over the years, in rebellion to the High King's wishes. I must admit that the Brotherhood of Warlocks has made some advancements in their craft recently—never before have the spirits of the dead been invited back into our world to dwell in inanimate objects like Edric arranged for them to do with the suits of armor."

"Never has that happened?" asked Eli.

"Not until now," answered Rayorden. "Spirits have shared their hosts' own bodies before, and drawn upon their life force to sustain themselves. Disembodied spirits can make small influences on reality under direction of a sorcerer. But this..." Rayorden seemed at a loss for words as he rocked in his chair. "What Edric performed was some form of twisted rebirth. He created new bodies coaxed the spirits of the dead to inhabit them and do his bidding. I have not witnessed anything so grotesque. The bodies, these suits of armor, were fragile and hollow. Edric drew these spirits back into the world only to serve him, then shortly to die once more."

Eli felt a twinge of guilt upon hearing Rayorden's words. He had slain many of those spirits without a second thought.

Rayorden must have noticed, because he stopped rocking and looked directly into Eli's eyes. "You've done the right thing today, my boy. You and Kadmiel here, you rescued the Northern Marshes. You put an end to the most evil threat this city has seen in decades. There was nothing better you could have done."

Eli nodded, attempting to take the man's words to heart. However, he still felt numb after killing so many enemies in battle. In the thick of the action, the hollow-looking suits of armor didn't feel like human enemies. To be reminded that all of the faceless suits of armor that he destroyed had their own *souls* was troubling.

Kadmiel spoke up. "What about the ones that weren't killed—the spirit soldiers that collapsed when Edric died?"

Rayorden looked thoughtful for a moment. "I suppose that they were released from this world upon their master's death. They followed him down to the pit of the deceased, from where he led them."

"Hmm," muttered Kadmiel. Eli gave him a quizzical look and he continued. "Well, I just had a strange thought. Now that Edric is dead, I suppose someone could summon his spirit back, right?"

Eli frowned and looked to Rayorden. The old man shook his head, saying, "That's not such an odd question anymore, I'm afraid." He leaned forward, meeting Eli's and Kadmiel's eyes in turn as he said, "You have done well thus far, and you cannot slow down now. The Brotherhood of Warlocks must be stopped, before life and death are imbalanced forever. These sorcerers are meddling with the fabric of our world... They cannot be allowed to succeed."

Chapter 11: FORTIFY

Rayorden's words imbued Eli with determination. For a moment, he forgot his aches, pains, cuts, hunger, and weariness. He wanted to spring up and continue their journey immediately, but there were still a few matters to attend to.

"We have good news on that front," said Eli, deciding to disclose what they knew to Rayorden. So Eli and Kadmiel quickly recounted their journey thus far, and how they had split up with the Royal Search Party to dispatch the sorcerers more quickly. Then the swordsmen briefly discussed their plan to travel next to the Inner Kingdom.

"I just want to see my mother again," stated Kadmiel.

Eli agreed. "And my family as well."

Rayorden gave a sad smile. "I wish there was time to learn all about the two of you. I would love to hear in detail the story of where you came from and the adventures you had when confronting the sorcerer Barid in the Western Plains—I would record it all... It's been a while since I've had something so interesting to chronicle," he said with a twinkle in his eye.

"Well, I think we've covered everything we can in the time we have," said Eli. He held up the scroll, glancing at Kadmiel for affirmation. He didn't seem to mind. "We've gathered that you are a trustworthy man—indeed, even a friend of the High King. Let us have a look at your prophecy, Rayorden."

Eli offered the scroll to Rayorden, who accepted it with a chuckle.

"What is it?" asked Kadmiel.

"It's not quite what you think it is," said Rayorden, examining the document from end to end. "What I hold is not a 'prophecy,' as you have come to know it. Rather, it is the will—the will of the High King."

Eli's mouth parted in disbelief.

Rayorden laughed, rocking in his wooden chair, which creaked beneath the man's weight. "Yes, that is what the scroll is. And it always bears the truth."

Eli immediately thought of its last message coming true: the Search Party being put into great danger for joining their cause.

I hope that they fared well in the Eastern Peaks, and that they are safely on their way to meet us in the Inner Kingdom.

Rayorden slowly began to open the parchment, holding it close enough to his face to suggest that his eyesight had declined over his many years of life.

"What does it say?" asked Kadmiel impatiently.

Rayorden finished reading and closed his eyes. "It says," he began flatly, "that I should disclose to you some information that I have gathered. Information about the wicked sorceress known as Lilith."

Kadmiel suddenly looked as if the color had drained out of his face.

"Don't be alarmed," said Rayorden. "I am going to share with you something that I have not told another soul: Lilith is dead."

Silence fell over the three men for a few moments.

"You mean, King Zaan did it?" asked Eli.

Rayorden inclined his head. "That's correct—the High King was successful when he set out to stop her."

"Where did he go, once he killed Lilith?" asked Kadmiel.

"Again, I do not know about the location of the king. The fact that Lilith was slain was the last information that I ever received from him."

Eli did not know what to think of this new revelation. "I suppose this is good news?"

"Yes and no," answered Rayorden. "The reason that this has been kept a secret is because it is *dangerous* news. I have always feared that if the knowledge of Lilith's death spread, she would become a martyr—a symbol that the other sorcerers in the land would idolize. I feared that they would attempt to bring Lilith back."

Chapter 11: FORTIFY

"There are others, then?" asked Eli. "Sorcerers?"

"Oh, yes. None quite like the Brotherhood of Warlocks, however. You've managed to entangle yourselves in the most crazed bunch of them all."

That actually prompted a smile from Kadmiel.

"Why do you suppose that the proph—well, the will— wanted you to share this secret with us?" Eli asked the old man.

Rayorden breathed deeply, sighing as he considered Eli's question. "Lilith is a restless and evil spirit. The grave will not confine her. She is certainly at work in this entire ordeal— pulling strings, influencing the current events." Rayorden's words sent chills down Eli's spine. He continued. "You must be very cautious, more so than you have been. You must be aware of the spirits of the dead that press in from every side. You must stay vigilant and devoted to your cause—to rescue your families, yes?"

"Yes," said Eli, but his voice felt small. "I suppose this quest has grown much larger than that, hasn't it?"

"It has," agreed Kadmiel.

"You're not just doing this for yourselves anymore," stated Rayorden. "That is quite honorable." Rayorden suddenly stood up and placed his hands on his hips. "But! Before you can think about proceeding any further in this journey, you're going to need a meal or two and a long night's sleep. How does that sound?"

"Marvelous," said Kadmiel.

"I thought so."

Rayorden requested that he could take the will to his study in order to inspect it further, and Eli agreed to allow him the opportunity. The swordsmen were taken to relax in Rayorden's living quarters, where they dozed until a steaming hot soup was brought to them.

The sun was almost ready to rise by the time their bowls

were empty, but Eli and Kadmiel immediately laid down to rest. Sleep overtook them as soon as their eyelids closed.

The companions were allowed to sleep past morning. They awoke to find Rayorden in his study, sipping tea and scribbling something down on a piece of parchment.

Eli yawned and stretched his stiff back. "Did you discover anything with the will?"

"I believe so," said Rayorden mysteriously. "But first, you two wash yourselves off and then I have somewhere to take you."

Eli and Kadmiel cleansed their wounds in Rayorden's bathing room, then redressed and met the old man on his porch.

"Ready, then?" he asked.

The former chronicler led them through the convoluted system of bridges over the Marshes. As they got closer to the heart of the city, Eli noticed that the wooden planks and platforms were stained with blood from the fallen warriors.

The loss had been great.

Eli upturned his gaze, swallowing to get rid of the lump in his throat. The city was a blur of activity, but there was a silence hanging over the people as they bustled about, mopping blood and water or transporting fragments of armor. Men and women who noticed them stopped, straightened up, and acknowledged Eli and Kadmiel with nods, salutes, or other wordless displays of gratitude.

Rayorden walked a few paces in front of them, leading them toward a structure that Eli took a few moments to recognize as the city's forge.

"What are we doing?" Kadmiel asked.

"This," said Rayorden, "is the Northern Marshes' armory."

Rayorden swept aside an entrance flap hanging where a door would go. Stepping inside, they could see that the space had been entirely dedicated to housing the armor and weapons of the battle. Both the stained armor of the warriors as well as the broken spirit soldiers' armor were present.

Chapter 11: FORTIFY

Multiple work stations were set up around the armory; there were women and a few men assigned to various tasks like cleaning, sharpening, organizing, and mounting the weaponry, or melting down anything that was damaged past the point of usability.

After observing the large room from end to end, Eli finally asked, "Where are all of the men?"

Rayorden smiled sadly. "Most are injured and being tended to in our infirmary. Many others are still resting. Before the battle yesterday, they had received little sleep for weeks and worked tirelessly at crafting suits of armor for Edric. They may have died from pure exhaustion if not for the two of you—unifying them and inspiring them to take this city back." Rayorden clapped the swordsmen upon their shoulders and turned back to the workers. "These people are extraordinary. The first thing that they wanted to do was go back to the building where they were held captive and put it to use for something good." The man shook his head in wonder at what he was witnessing. "I've never seen such a bond in this city before."

Eli watched incredulously at the speed of the women performing the different jobs around the armory and suddenly felt very guilty for not helping. However, everyone that met eyes with him smiled appreciatively.

"What will be done with all of this equipment?" Kadmiel asked Rayorden.

"We are going to rebuild ourselves as a stronger society, I think," said the old man, distant in thought. "But the reason I brought you here is because someone would like to see you."

Rayorden gestured to a man at the opposite corner of the building, and Eli tried to crane his neck above the swarm of people to see who was approaching.

"Ah," said Kadmiel simply.

"What?" Eli asked, but then he saw who it was. "Oh. Him."

Eli glanced at Rayorden, who gave him a reassuring smile.

Elmund walked up to the trio with his head slightly bowed. The rude demeanor that Eli and Kadmiel had witnessed before the battle seemed to have vanished. The man now carried himself with an air of humility.

"Sir," Elmund said to both Eli and Kadmiel in turn. "Um, sir!" he added hastily, remembering to address Rayorden as well, who looked amused.

"Elmund, isn't it?" asked Kadmiel.

The man nodded and spoke. "I was wrong to oppose you. Kadmiel, Eli, you have done an amazing service to the entire Tetrad Union by leading our people against Edric. You rescued us..." He trailed off and hung his head.

Eli reached out and touched Elmund on the arm, bending down to meet his downcast gaze.

"You were concerned that we would be leading your people to their death," said Eli. "And we did."

Elmund looked surprised, his eyes darting between them.

"We did," Eli continued. "They chose to follow us into battle, and many of them fell. You weren't wrong. But we did what we thought was best."

"And it worked," Kadmiel added.

"I called you fools," said Elmund with a small voice.

Kadmiel laughed. "Maybe we are."

Elmund seemed to be at a loss for words, so Eli spoke up. "What we're saying is... we forgive you."

The man shook his head in disbelief. "Thank you," he finally muttered.

Kadmiel slapped him on the shoulder. "You put that stubborn will of yours to good work here, all right?"

Elmund smirked. "I'll do that."

"Thanks for speaking with us," Eli said. He and Kadmiel turned to Rayorden to indicate that their visit was done, but Elmund didn't depart.

"One more thing. I have something for you!"

Chapter 11: FORTIFY

The man darted back to the opposite end of the building and returned carrying a wrapped package. It was long and slender, and he handed it with both hands to Eli, who untied a knot and began to remove the paper covering the heavy object.

Eli caught a glimmer of reflected light from within the wrappings and smiled as he realized what it was. "My sword!" he exclaimed.

Elmund wore a proud expression as Eli held his reclaimed blade, gripping the gem-encrusted hilt that fit so perfectly, feeling the weapon's unmatched balance.

"There's no mistaking it—that's Eli's sword," said Kadmiel.

"I retrieved it from the marshes. Knew it was yours because the craftsmanship is unlike anything made here."

The blade had been cleaned, sharpened, and polished. It was in better shape than it had been in a long time.

Eli didn't know what to say. "I can't thank you enough, Elmund. Truly."

"I could say the same."

"What do you have for me?" asked Kadmiel.

Elmund looked stunned at the question.

"I'm only joking," Kadmiel added.

Elmund quickly recovered from his shock and laughed with Eli and Rayorden. "Well, by all means, refill your quiver!"

"That I will," said Kadmiel with a smirk.

Elmund cleared his throat and looked to be gathering his thoughts. "There's one more thing I'd like to say..." He stared Eli in the eyes and took a deep breath. "I know there are more men like Edric out there. I want you to kill them. I want you to destroy the evil spirits with this sword that I've just returned to you... I hope that can be remembered as my service to the Tetrad Union when all is said and done."

With Eli's sword recovered and Kadmiel's quiver full of arrows, plus an entire night's sleep and a few proper meals, the companions were beginning to feel like themselves again.

"That was very noble of you, to forgive that man," Rayorden stated.

Kadmiel nodded. "He's right, Eli. Although, you weren't the one that Elmund tried to kill."

Eli smiled. "My father always said, 'He who offers forgiveness sets both parties free.' I don't want to live with that bitterness for the rest of my life."

"Ah, a proverb that originated from the High King. Wise of your father to pass that lesson down," said Rayorden. Now, are you ready for departure?"

Eli hesitated. "I think there's one more place I would like to stop."

"Where's that?"

"You said there was an infirmary?"

"Ah," said Rayorden. "Of course. This way."

It was a large tent, which was not doing its job of keeping flies away from the wounded. Eli could hear the buzzing from the insects before stepping inside.

Entering the tent, it was a hard sight to behold. Cots after cots lined the walls and the center of the tent, with narrow spaces for the caretakers to traverse between patients. The wounded began to murmur excitedly when Eli and Kadmiel entered, with Rayorden behind them.

There are so many...

Eli had to consciously make an effort not to avert his eyes from anyone, with many of the injured soldiers sporting vicious and bloody gashes. These were men that followed him and Kadmiel against all odds. They deserved his attention and his gratitude. Eli wanted to personally thank each and every patient here, but he knew that he and Kadmiel should have already left for the Inner Kingdom by now.

What if Mikaiya, Idella, and the others have already finished and are waiting for us?

Eli pushed the thought out of his mind. He would deal with that next—for now, the warriors.

Almost of their own accord, Eli's feet began to move and he circled the room, making eye contact with each individual that he passed. Kadmiel followed beside him. The warriors seemed to draw strength from the sight of them, and even those grimacing from their inflictions appeared to regain the resolve that Eli had seen before the battle. Once Eli and Kadmiel had made their way around the entire room, they repeated the circle while facing inward, seeing all the patients that lined the inside of the tent.

It was all worth it, Eli thought. *Seeing these people free again—these strong, resilient people being freed from oppression—has made this whole journey worth it so far.*

Eli smiled at Kadmiel, who couldn't have known exactly what he was thinking right then, but his face showed a similar momentary peace.

"Eli..."

Who said that? It was a small voice. There, at the end of the inner row of cots, was Jacob. It was the boy who Eli had charged with fortifying the entrance to the forge.

His stomach twisted in a tight knot. *What is he doing here in the infirmary?*

The swordsmen hurried to Jacob's bedside and knelt down to the wide-eyed, blond-haired boy. His chin was quivering.

"Are you all right?" asked Eli.

Jacob frowned and glanced downward at the blanket covering his body. Finally, he shrugged. "How are you two?"

"We're just fine," said Kadmiel reassuringly. "I heard that you helped defend the women and children in the forge. You were brave."

Jacob nodded excitedly. "I was! No one could have come through that door. After the good guys won, it took us forever to get back out! We were stuck in there for a while..."

Eli patted the boy on the head and ruffled his hair. "You did perfectly. I knew I could trust you."

Jacob's cheeks turned red, and he murmured something unintelligible.

"Kadmiel and I are leaving now. We have to go finish this war before more people get hurt. Can you look after the Northern Marshes for us?"

"Sure," said Jacob nonchalantly. "I can do that. When will I see you again?"

Kadmiel stood up and helped Eli to his feet.

"After it's all over, maybe the whole Union can celebrate with a big feast," Eli suggested.

"Yeah," agreed Jacob. "See you then."

Eli and Kadmiel turned away, but the boy called out, "The doctor says I'll recover really soon! I don't know, though, it's pretty bad." He held the blankets back and lifted his right arm, showing the swordsmen a scab that had formed around his elbow.

He looks rather proud of his "injury," Eli mused.

"Wow," said Kadmiel. "I sure hope the doctor's right."

The warriors within earshot were grinning, as if Jacob had been the source of their entertainment in the infirmary.

Eli smiled. "Stay strong, my friend."

"Okay!"

Backing up to the tent's entrance flap, Eli did his best to address every one of the wounded. "Thank you, all—it was our honor to fight alongside you. Congratulations on the victory that we claimed!"

There were cheers from all corners of the infirmary tent, then they ducked outside into the bright sunlight of the mid-morning.

Rayorden smiled approvingly. "I'm glad you took the time to do that—your visit should greatly encourage them in their recovery."

"We're glad as well," said Kadmiel. "Now we must be on our way."

"Indeed," said Rayorden uneasily. "But lastly, before you depart the Northern Marshes, there is a final matter that we must discuss…" The man trailed off, as if uncomfortable with continuing.

"What is it, Rayorden? We need to leave for the Inner Kingdom," said Eli.

The former chronicler hesitated. "Yes, you must—but not yet. Come."

Kadmiel hung his head in exasperation. Rayorden ignored the gesture and led them away from town until they were at the southern gate of the city. There, waiting for them, was a simple wooden raft with two paddles. A chest was secured on top, and Rayorden opened the box to reveal a few days' worth of food provisions and a separate compartment to store their armor and supplies.

"We thank you for your continued generosity," said Eli, "but please tell us: what is all of this about?"

Rayorden began to rummage through his pockets, appearing troubled. Then the old man retrieved something that Eli had forgotten about: the will. He rotated the scroll nervously in his hands. Then he sighed and finally met eyes with the two of them. "Something terrible has happened… The new name on the scroll—the next addressee of the will—is Lilith."

Silence fell over the three men as the name seemed to hang in the air.

No, thought Eli despondently.

Kadmiel snatched the will from Rayorden's grasp and inspected it himself. Eli leaned over Kadmiel's shoulder and saw that what Rayorden spoke was the truth. There, inscribed on the rolled parchment, was the name *Lilith.*

"How long have you known?" Eli questioned him.

Rayorden frowned and fiddled with his long beard. "I saw this last night, but I—"

"You *what?*" demanded Kadmiel.

Rayorden spoke urgently. "I kept the scroll with me and held the information from you until this morning in order that you could get one undisturbed night's rest. I knew that this would trouble you, and there was no benefit in telling you sooner."

"Well, what does this mean?" Eli asked weakly.

"It means that somehow, the sorceress is at work in these events, and her plans are most assuredly deadly."

Kadmiel interjected. "But you are certain that King Zaan killed her?"

"Oh yes," said Rayorden confidently. "But why would Lilith let a little thing like death interfere with her gambit for power?"

When neither of the swordsmen answered Rayorden's rhetorical question, the man gestured to the raft that they were gathered around and explained further. "You will need to travel to the Eastern Peaks. Your friends are not safe. They went to confront Fathi, the last of the *known* Warlocks, and he is a mad, deranged man. His mind has been twisted. The Search Party needs the two of you."

Eli could feel his temper rising. "You would send us to the Eastern Peaks when the Search Party members may have already succeeded in killing the sorcerer? We cannot waste time—our people are still in danger! Kadmiel and I have to get to the Inner Kingdom, discover who this fourth Warlock is, and free the captives—our families—if they're even still alive!"

Eli had started to shout without realizing it. He turned away from Rayorden, embarrassed, and began to pace.

Rayorden responded warmly. "The Search Party needs you, and, frankly, you need them. I wish that there was more I could do to help you. I would gather a full army of warriors to send with you, but your greatest advantage right now is stealth.

Besides, the men here need to stay and rebuild this city, fortify it, and defend the women and children within. No, the most I can do is see to it that you are armed, well fed, rested, and have a means of transportation."

Eli took a deep breath and sighed. "Thank you," he mustered.

Rayorden waved away his thanks. "It is my honor."

Kadmiel bumped the raft with his boot. "There's a river to the Eastern Peaks?"

"Yes," replied Rayorden. "It will take you to the foot of the Peaks, where you can scale the mountain unnoticed by the sorcerer. Taking the paved road would be unwise, as it is closely watched by guards charged with dropping stones on intruders. Once you reach the city by an alternate route, you can investigate the fate of your friends and, with fortune, save them."

Eli and Kadmiel thought for a moment, then decided that they were in agreement with the course of action that had been laid out for them.

Eli stepped forward and grasped the man's hand. "I apologize, I should not have become angry with you. You've been truly helpful to us, and there is so much I want to ask you. Perhaps when this is all over, Kadmiel and I can visit. For pleasure."

He wasn't sure, but he thought that a tear may have entered Rayorden's eye.

"I would like that very much."

Kadmiel said his farewells next. "Do you think we can do it?"

"Oh, I have no doubt. I have never met anyone quite like the two of you. Remain close to one another, and you will be just fine."

"Thank you, Rayorden."

"Got the scroll, Kad?" asked Eli.

Kadmiel patted the spot in his tunic in where it was tucked away.

"Good. Let's get moving."

The swordsmen each grabbed one end of the raft and lifted, which was made much more difficult by the weight of the attached chest. Rayorden followed them, but stopped at the gate as Eli and Kadmiel exited the Northern Marshes. The man watched them with a sad smile as they shuffled the raft to the edge of the river, set it down in the water, and tried to board it without it moving from underneath them.

Eli and Kadmiel lifted their paddles to the faint outline of Rayorden, then let go of the riverbank, allowing the rushing water to transport them toward their next destination: the Eastern Peaks.

Chapter 12: **BREAKNECK**

The sun beat down upon Eli all the more on the river. With the combined heat from the sun and from physical exertion, the swordsmen soon found themselves exhausted.

"Ever done this before?" he asked over his shoulder to Kadmiel, who was seated behind him, paddling on the opposite side.

"Not exactly. Yourself?"

"I haven't."

Despite the difficulty, it was both enjoyable and beautiful. In some places the river was steep and quick; in others, the waters were calm. The landscape rolled by in a gorgeous blur of green, looking quite flat just outside the Marshes but taking on more shape as they went.

Steering the vessel turned out to be a lot of work. The river was rarely straight, causing the companions to constantly have to navigate around corners and avoid trees sticking out over the water, disrupting their momentum.

"I can't believe I'm hungry already. Didn't we just have breakfast?"

Kadmiel shrugged. "I could use something."

The swordsmen set down their paddles and opened up the chest that Rayorden had packed them. The box held their armor, and their sheathed swords were secured to it. Eli started by unwrapping some bread and breaking it for the two of them.

The undirected raft soon approached the riverbank, but Kadmiel sat toward the front and draped one leg into the water, with which he pushed off from the wall that they were stuck against.

Eli used the same technique on the opposite corner of their raft, allowing them to maintain a moderate pace as they ate. Afterward, they resumed rowing.

"Another one down," Kadmiel mumbled. "Another Warlock. Another city."

Eli nodded. "Who knew we were useful for more than just fighting one another!"

Kadmiel grunted. "I would go back to just fighting each other if we could."

He quickly agreed. "But that time has gone. Things were much simpler then." Eli ducked under a branch from a low-hanging tree next to the stream. "Are you sure we shouldn't have just walked?"

"No," answered Kadmiel. "But the river *is* speeding up. This should pay off in the end."

"It had better," muttered Eli, pausing his rowing to stretch the sore muscles on his back. His brief break caused them to veer in the direction that Kadmiel was paddling, so Eli hastily tried to adjust their trajectory.

"We'll figure this out... eventually," said Kadmiel with a sigh.

After some time, the sun dipped below the peaks in the east which were just visible above the thinning treetops of the marshes. The water was clearing up, losing the green and brown hues of the marsh and now reflecting the soft orange glow of the sunset.

"This ordeal hasn't been all bad," offered Eli. Kadmiel was silent. "What do you think, Kad?"

"I agree. My favorite part was getting kidnapped for no good reason. No, wait—nearly being killed by two of the most powerful sorcerers alive. What could top that?"

"Can't you look on the bright side?"

Kadmiel smirked. "Yes."

"So you *have* enjoyed some of these moments between the chaos?" Eli pried.

"Yes."

Eli exhaled. "It's so hard to tell with you."

Kadmiel chuckled. "Just keep trying."

"The great Eli Abnerson," Eli mocked himself. "The Champion of Warriors and the Slayer of Spirits... yet he cannot understand women or even his best friend."

His self-deprecation got a real laugh out of Kadmiel, and as the companions continued to row in the silence that followed, Eli wondered if he had surprised Kadmiel with the designation as his closest friend. They had never really addressed the nature of their relationship since agreeing to venture forth from the Southern Shores together, where previously they had only known one another as rivals.

Finally, Kadmiel broke the silence. "How often do you think of them?"

"Every moment," Eli answered without hesitation. "I can't even remember how long it's been since I've seen them."

"Nor can I... I just hope they're still alive." Kadmiel sighed.

As usual, a lump swelled in Eli's throat when he thought of his family in the hands of a Warlock. "But," Eli choked out, "even if they're not..."

"You're not doing all of this just for them anymore," Kadmiel said.

Eli's mind went to all of the citizens of the Tetrad Union that he had met: the brave souls of the Western Plains Uprising, the Royal Search Party, the warriors of the Marshes. "No," Eli stated. "No, I am not." He realized that their journey had caused his mission to evolve from one of vengeance to justice. His mind felt clearer; his thoughts felt sharper. Eli's body seemed to hum with a sense of purpose. Excited, he asked, "Who are *you* doing this for?"

Kadmiel must have contemplated the question for a couple of minutes while the swordsmen snaked along the winding river. Just when Eli wondered if he should repeat himself, Kadmiel spoke.

"I don't know, Eli," he admitted.

He felt a twinge of disappointment that Kadmiel had not shared in his own paradigm shift, but he understood. *The emotions wrapped up in this quest we share are complicated,* Eli thought. "Well, let me ask you something."

"Go on."

"Do you feel... better, now that we have had revenge on two of the men responsible for the attack on our hometown?"

It became evident that Kadmiel had no answer for that question. "What are you saying?"

"I think—" Eli paused. "I think that revenge is not as sweet as it is said to be."

"Hmm," responded Kadmiel. "In any case, they chose the wrong swordsmen to make enemies with."

Eli smiled, always impressed by Kadmiel's confidence. He did not feel quite as certain himself, however. "What do you suppose we will find at the Eastern Peaks?"

"Seeing as we just waged war against an army of possessed suits of armor, I don't see how it could get much weirder."

Eli couldn't take solace in Kadmiel's reassurance, not with Rayorden's warning about Fathi echoing in his mind. Then another question presented itself to him. "I wonder how we will break into the city of the Peaks?"

"Hopefully it will be as exciting as jumping across a moving drawbridge," Kadmiel quipped.

Eli tried to remain hopeful. "Perhaps the Search Party will be at the gates to welcome us, having already disposed of the Warlock."

An uncomfortable silence fell between them as the startling revelation of Lilith's involvement was brought back to mind. Eli shuddered as he recalled the message written in the will for Idella: *Great danger awaits you...*

"I hope they're okay," Eli whispered.

Kadmiel laughed quietly to himself.

Chapter 12: BREAKNECK

"What?"

"Oh, they're just fine," Kadmiel said. "Those girls are tough. If you're not careful, they may claim your title as Champion of Warriors once this is all over."

Eli laughed, took his paddle, and gave a strong backward stroke, hitting Kadmiel across the face with a cold splash.

Kadmiel stared at Eli with his mouth open, aghast as water dripped from his dark hair. "Was it something I said?" he spluttered.

Eli and Kadmiel attempted to sleep in shifts that night, while one stayed awake and kept the raft moving in the right direction. But the water was becoming too fast and too unsteady, so they decided to find a place to stop for the night.

After a painful exit that involved slippery, sharp rocks along the bank of the river, the swordsmen lay flat on the grass next to the water, too exhausted to think about setting up any kind of camp.

And then the sun rose too quickly.

"Good morning, sunshine," said Eli.

Kadmiel yawned. "What's for breakfast?"

Eli rummaged in the chest. "Bread and fruit, I think."

"What do you mean, 'I think'?" Kadmiel inquired.

Eli held up a bright green oval-shaped fruit. "What are these?"

Kadmiel inspected the food. "I don't think these ever made it down to the Southern Shores." He grabbed another, and they both bit down at the same time.

Eli's eyes started to water as he watched Kadmiel's reaction, whose face had puckered up. Eli coughed. "Sour," he choked out.

Kadmiel looked like he was winding up to toss the fruit away, but he stopped. "We don't have much choice out here, do we?"

He frowned and shook his head.

"Sour, mysterious green fruit it is." Kadmiel sighed.

Eli took in their surroundings. The landscape was spotted with tall trees, but not the kind that bore fruit. There were no animals visible around the river, but fish could occasionally be seen jumping above the surface of the water.

"We could try hunting," said Eli, "but we don't have time for that."

Kadmiel nodded. "Rayorden made it clear—every moment matters for the lives of the Royal Search Party. How are you holding up, Eli?"

Eli finished the fruit and rose to stand, but his back protested the whole way up. "Oh, I'm stiff!"

Kadmiel planted his feet and then tried to twist his spine from side to side in order to pop it. "Me too. Who knew that steering a raft used so many different muscles than swinging a sword does?"

Eli stared ahead glumly. "I think I'd rather get back into battle with spirit soldiers than get back on this thing."

"We've got a way to go," stated Kadmiel.

Eli held a hand above his eyes in order to squint at the mountaintops in the distance.

"They don't seem to get any closer, do they?"

"Hand me some bread, please," said Kadmiel.

Judging by the amount of food in the chest compared to the apparent distance between them and their destination, Eli didn't know if their supplies would last them the journey. *We'll just have to do our best.*

After breakfast, the swordsmen carefully lowered the raft over the rocky bank of the river and into the water, careful not to let it get swept away in the current before boarding once again.

The companions opted to trade rowing positions in order to rest the sides of their bodies that were sore from the previous day. That helped invigorate the two, and they covered a good distance at a steady pace.

However, the waters seemed prepared to test their skills.

Chapter 12: BREAKNECK

Eli and Kadmiel had to navigate a number of eddies, tricky portions of the water that were either at a standstill or even going the reverse direction of the current.

"What's that sound?" Eli asked, listening intently.

"Not sure," said Kadmiel. "We'll see around this bend."

And they did.

"Rocks," Kadmiel muttered.

Jagged black teeth of stone stuck out of the river, with white water crashing against them. Eli sat up, looking over Kadmiel's head to try and see the best way to navigate the coming challenges.

No easy route presented itself.

"This is it, Kad."

"What?" he shouted back. The rushing water ahead made it difficult to hear one another as the current picked up speed and pulled them inward.

"We have to work together!"

"You don't say," Kadmiel scoffed, his eyes fixed on the quickly approaching obstacles.

Before either of them could truly prepare for what was about to happen, they were upon the rapids.

Their raft teetered atop a rolling wave, then tipped forward and crashed down the other side. Maintaining their balance and a grip on their paddles was the hardest task at hand. The rapids spit them out into the path of a rock, so the swordsmen rowed furiously to one side.

Just in time, they narrowly escaped the point of collision and hurtled past the enormous rock. They had overcorrected, and now spun toward the stony bank of the river.

"Stop!" Eli called, plunging his oar into the surface of the water and holding it firmly, slowing their momentum. Kadmiel glanced over his shoulder, saw Eli's motion, and did the same on his side. Together, they were able to halt their trajectory and move back toward the center, where the water was deepest and less likely to contain jagged obstacles.

"Not too far!" shouted Kadmiel, watching a group of approaching waves. They were going to be hit broadside if they did not right the raft immediately.

"You paddle backward!" Eli said, as he rowed forward, attempting to turn and face the oncoming threat.

The wall of water hit Eli and Kadmiel before they were able to finish maneuvering. The vessel tipped dangerously over the wave and Kadmiel pitched forward, about to fall into the rushing water. Eli grabbed ahold of Kadmiel's shoulder and then heaved backward, slamming him back onto the wooden planks.

As soon as the wave had passed, another one assaulted them. It happened at the wrong angle, not carrying them over the water but instead submerging the raft beneath its towering height.

Eli's lungs were practically empty when he went under. His vision became dark. The paddle in his hand was tugged ruthlessly away from him by the current, and he tried desperately to cling to the side of the raft.

Then Eli realized that he was upside down; the wave had toppled them and spilled him and Kadmiel beneath the transport.

Heart racing, Eli attempted to resurface time after time, but the boat remained above his head. He slapped and reached wildly, trying to feel his way out from underneath.

At last, he found the edge of the raft and started to pull himself toward it, but something hard slammed into his side and knocked the last breath out of his lungs. He tried to push away from the object, but realized it was Kadmiel. Wrapping his arms around his friend, Eli kicked with all of his might toward the blurry, light blue surface of the water.

Oxygen.

Eli and Kadmiel wordlessly treaded water next to each other as they gasped for air, wildly searching for the raft that they had been separated from. Kadmiel still clung to his own oar, which made Eli feel a twinge of guilt for having lost his.

"There," Kadmiel choked out, coughing water. He was pointing to the side of the river on the opposite end of a large curve that was approaching. Their raft hadn't made the turn but ran into the rocks along the edge, stuck for the time being.

"Watch out!"

They could not do much to alter their course in the current without the transport, and a log stuck out of the water between them and the curve in the river. The fallen tree looked terrifying, with branches that had been snapped to stubby, sharp points.

"Go!" Kadmiel said, swimming with urgent strokes in the direction left of the log.

Eli tore his gaze from the obstacle and immediately began moving to the other side. It was best for him and Kadmiel to split up and go around the threat, to prevent them from getting in each other's way. Eli fought against the stream with what little strength he still had, trying to propel himself away from the jagged tree and toward their target.

If they did not reach their raft before being swept away by the current, they may never be able to retrieve it.

Eager to evade the sharp branches in the water, Eli barely cleared the danger of the tree when he heard Kadmiel cry out in pain on the other side. Turning, Eli saw him being dragged across the tree by the current, unable to avoid it in time. The branches tore at Kadmiel's skin, opening deep wounds across his body.

"KADMIEL!"

Eli swam against the current back toward him. Kadmiel got free of the branches' deadly embrace, but he was badly hurt and moving slowly. There was still a sizeable distance between them and their raft, while the river's current now turned to round the corner.

"Are you okay?" Eli gasped.

Kadmiel could not respond through his clenched teeth, but Eli saw that he was doing all of his swimming with one arm; the other was torn up and bleeding in the water. Miraculously, still in the hand of his injured arm was the paddle. Eli came beside Kadmiel and propped himself up underneath his bad arm. They oriented themselves in the direction of their stranded raft, which teetered precariously on a patch of stone along the riverbank, rocking with each and every wave.

Eli supported some of Kadmiel's weight as they swam in unison. It was slow going.

Too slow.

"We're not going to make it in time," Kadmiel grunted.

"No," Eli answered immediately. "We can do it, just keep—"

Kadmiel wasn't listening. "We need that raft, and I'm slowing you down." He twisted away, letting his injured right arm return limply to his side. "Go, Eli—get it back and then worry about me. Now!"

Before Eli could argue any further, Kadmiel handed him his paddle and let the current sweep him away.

No choice, Eli accepted.

He treaded water and tossed the oar toward the riverbank, which landed with a thud next to the raft about six yards away. Even without Kadmiel's added weight or the paddle to slow him down, it was still difficult to move in the water. The farther away from the center of the river he got, the more the current tried to drag him back toward the curve. Eli focused singularly on the raft, and counted each gained inch as a victory.

I have to catch up to Kadmiel before he gets himself killed.

Finally, he was within an arm's length of the boat. That also meant that he was within reach of all the jagged rocks that were currently holding the raft in place.

Eli was cautious in his approach, and was able to find a place in the rocks where he could wedge himself in order to stay put as he worked on freeing the transport. He grasped the boat

Chapter 12: BREAKNECK

by its side and tried to pull it out from the rocks and back into the current. He realized his hands were shaking; every moment was precious when it could mean the difference between life and death. Eli grimaced at the thought of his friend trying to navigate the rapids with an injured arm.

Redoubling his efforts, he wrenched the vessel loose and pushed it away from the rocks of the riverbank. Within seconds it would be swept away. Eli stood up on the slippery surface of a rock, wobbling with the current pulling at his ankles, grabbed the nearby oar, and leapt on top of the raft. His knees and palms hit the wooden deck hard, but he ignored the pain.

Eli quickly righted himself into a seated position with his paddle at the ready. Quickly taking in his surroundings, he decided on a course through the danger-filled waters.

It was both easier and more difficult to navigate alone. Easier, because it did not involve coordinating direction and speed with someone else. More difficult, because it took twice the work to move.

Eli barely missed rocks on either side as he frantically surveyed the river for any sign of Kadmiel.

Nothing yet.

Eli rounded the bend in the river with too much speed, and had to stroke backward hastily before colliding into the rocky bank. A long stretch followed the bend with no further curves, which would make it easier to spot Kadmiel.

"Where are you?" Eli whispered, already out of breath.

There.

Kadmiel's head popped out of the water briefly, about fifteen yards down the stream.

"KADMIEL!" Eli screamed. "Hang on!"

He wasn't sure if he could be heard, but it made no difference. All that mattered was getting to his friend. Eli rowed as fast as he was physically able, but was constantly having to alternate sides to remain on target. Kadmiel floated down the center of the river, his head bobbing below the water between short breaths, clearly losing energy.

Eli tried not to let panic set in, but relied on the focus that had made him a champion warrior. He kept his eyes fixed on Kadmiel's location and did his best to navigate the jagged stones and logs sticking out of the water.

Four more yards. Three more yards. Almost there.

"Kadmiel!"

"Eli," he gasped, turning to face the raft. He looked exhausted, pale in the face and sluggish. Eli stretched out a hand, which Kadmiel took, and Eli pulled him to the side, where he clung on with his good arm.

"Let's get you up here!"

"Wait," Kadmiel said weakly, with a nod of the head indicating another turn in the river. They had come to the end of the straight stretch.

With Kadmiel still holding on to the right side of the raft, Eli reluctantly left him to paddle. The river took a hard right turn, but Kadmiel was able to hold on while he maneuvered.

What Eli saw rounding the corner made him gasp. A treacherous stretch of river lay before them, riddled with stones like knives jutting out in all directions. Numerous downed trees lined the riverbanks, leaving no option for escape.

"We're getting you on the raft, NOW!"

Eli dropped the oar next to the chest, then crouched near Kadmiel, who was shaking his head.

"No time—you need to be steering—"

Eli wasn't listening. "You'll get torn to pieces. I'm not leaving you in the water," he said as he grabbed Kadmiel by the collar and turned him so his face was pointing away from the raft. Eli planned to drag him onto the transport, and did not want to break Kadmiel's nose on the way up. Despite himself, Eli stole another glance at the daunting obstructions before them. His heart quickened.

Chapter 12: BREAKNECK

Focus.

Eli grasped Kadmiel firmly under the arms. "Ready?"

Kadmiel nodded and Eli heaved, pulling him upward. But the swordsman did not move very far.

Why do you have to be the taller one? "All right, I'm going to have to dunk you. One... two... three!" Eli plunged Kadmiel under the water, submerging him once more, then stood up from his crouching position with as much momentum as possible. It worked, and Eli locked his knees while holding Kadmiel close to his chest. The boat would have toppled but he immediately fell backward, bringing Kadmiel on board with him.

Kadmiel was not quick to rally himself and find his own spot on the raft. Eli could feel warm blood from the man's injuries seeping onto him. The transport wasn't wide enough for a grown man to lay across, and the rescue had left Eli with his head hanging over the side.

He didn't see the rock until it was too late. Impact.

"Eli!" Kadmiel screamed.

The cry echoed in his mind as the world spun and his vision blackened. The sounds of the rushing waves faded away, and his consciousness was snuffed out.

Eli awoke with a splitting pain piercing his skull.

"Whoa, lay down!"

Eli blinked repeatedly, propped up on one elbow. The voice was Kadmiel's.

"What's going on?" he asked groggily.

"You're okay," Kadmiel said with evident relief. "You've been asleep for a while."

Laying back down, Eli realized amidst his spinning thoughts and sensations that they were still on the raft Rayorden had given them. Eli clenched his eyes shut again. The light hurt and made the headache even worse. He lifted a hand to his temple.

Oh my. His head was swollen. His jaw was sore. Eli shuddered.

"You all right?" Kadmiel inquired.

"No," he said honestly.

"You're alive."

"Mm... You've been navigating us this whole time? How long have I been asleep?"

Kadmiel shifted from sitting to kneeling, then rolled his shoulders. The wounds on his arm and chest from the downed tree trunk had started to dry. "Yep, I have. And I lost track of how long you've been out—since yesterday."

Eli's eyes snapped open, wide. "Are you joking?"

Kadmiel was silent.

"You mean the sun set after I was knocked out, it rose again, and now it's *tomorrow?*" Eli couldn't believe it.

"Technically, it's today," said Kadmiel, smirking. "But yes."

"Did you stop for the night?"

"Did I stop for the night?" Kadmiel repeated, incredulous. "Of course I did. The worst part of the rapids was finished as soon as you hit your head. If only you could have held on for another few minutes," he teased.

Eli looked at Kadmiel with newfound awe. "Where did you stop?"

"I just wedged the raft in a calm corner of the riverbank. No way was I going to try and haul you onto dry land."

"Hey, I hauled you *onto* the raft. That's actually where this whole thing started, remember?"

"Oh yeah," said Kadmiel.

After a few moments of silence, Eli asked, "Were you worried about me?"

Kadmiel shrugged then winced at the pain in his shoulder muscles. "Knew you were alive. You do know that you snore, right?"

"I'm sorry."

Chapter 12: BREAKNECK

"It's okay. I couldn't sleep, so I stayed up all night and ate the rest of our food."

Eli hadn't realized that he was so hungry until Kadmiel mentioned eating. His stomach felt hollow; he was ravenous. "You're going to make me cry."

"Please don't." Kadmiel unlatched their container and tossed Eli the strange fruit from the Northern Marshes. In that moment, it was as appetizing as any food he had ever seen. "I miss Rayorden," Eli stated through a mouthful.

"Him, or his comfortable seats and regularly scheduled meals?"

"Regularly scheduled meals..." said Eli slowly, taking another bite. "I think that my life is going to contain a lot of those, once the last sorcerer is killed and we move on."

Kadmiel chuckled quietly.

"You'll join me sometimes, won't you? We'll see each other?"

"We'll see each other often," Kadmiel confirmed.

No sarcasm that time, thought Eli. *I think I'm really getting through to him.*

Once Eli could sit up without a skull-splitting ringing in his ears, the companions traded rowing duties in shifts with their single remaining paddle. While one would handle the raft, the other would eat, tend to their injuries, and sleep.

They drew nearer to the Eastern Peaks, which loomed above them threateningly. The air was turning cold to where the swordsmen could see their breath.

For the most part, the river remained tame, and Eli was thankful that they had left the most dangerous part far behind them. *Never again*, he told himself. Every time he recalled the brief memory of hurtling toward the rock, Eli would flinch unwittingly. Kadmiel may have noticed, but did not comment.

As night fell once more, Kadmiel asked something that struck Eli as humorous. "When are we getting off?"

"Uh... I have no idea," Eli said. "Never been here."

"We didn't travel the Union much, did we?"

Eli shook his head. "Never imagined my first trip would look like this."

"It's beautiful," Kadmiel stated simply.

Eli stopped rowing mid-stroke and looked around. He had been too preoccupied to notice, but Kadmiel was right: the moon reflected off the surface of the water, a gentle breeze swayed the trees back and forth, and a few sparse fireflies flitted about, making pinpricks of light in the dark canvas of the surrounding scenery. *Yes, it is beautiful.*

Then, slowly, Eli felt the heat of anger boiling up inside of him. *How could someone dare to try and usurp this land, claiming it all for themselves? The High King gave this land to the people freely. Now, in his absence, these sorcerers—these monsters—insert themselves as our rulers. They cannot succeed.* Eli noticed himself rowing at double speed.

"What's going on?" Kadmiel asked, looking over his shoulder as if to see if they were being followed.

Eli sighed. "I'm just eager," he said flatly.

His slowly burning rage propelled him through the night, past the time when he was supposed to wake Kadmiel up for his shift. The pain in his heart distracted him from the pain in his skull, although the swelling had finally stopped. He fixed his mind's eye on his loved ones, and put more strength into each stroke of the paddle. After rounding another curve in the river, it seemed they had arrived.

A sandy incline extended from the left side of the water onto a beach at the base of the Eastern Peaks. Eli shook Kadmiel by the shoulder to wake him, then directed their raft toward the sand. Stepping off, his legs jerked beneath him like he had forgotten how to walk. Kadmiel moved slowly with eyes half-lidded. Without the constant exertion of steering the boat, the chilly night air was starting to steal Eli's body heat. He pulled the vessel completely out of the water and onto the beach, then collapsed onto the soft sand. Kadmiel stretched out next to him, shivering. The swordsmen sidled closer until they were lying with their backs touching, sharing each other's warmth, and then were immediately taken by sleep.

Chapter 13: **ASCEND**

E li dreamed of normal life and how it had been before this year's Championship of Warriors. He was doing the usual things, like fishing on his family's beach and playing with his sister Gabbi. Life in the Southern Shores was so simple, yet so fulfilling.

He awoke with a jump, and a tear formed in his eye. The dreams just made the constant ache in his heart more prominent. Meanwhile, the sounds of a crackling fire could be heard nearby. Slowly, Eli uncurled his tense body on the sandy floor of the beach and stretched every tight muscle in his body.

"Good morning."

"You're cooking breakfast, Kad?"

"I am."

"You're a wonderful man," said Eli.

"I am."

Eli yawned and got up. His head still hurt, but the pain had reduced from its initial debilitating state to one comparable with the throbbing sensation his whole body felt.

He saw that Kadmiel's bow was out and that the warrior had retrieved two rabbits, which were now being slowly rotated over the flames of a campfire.

"You've been busy! Sorry I slept so long," said Eli.

"Don't mention it—you took much too long of a shift last night anyway. You must have been exhausted."

"Maybe, but we can't afford to feel exhausted on a journey like this," said Eli, lifting his eyes to examine the peaks towering above them. The sun had started to rise but was still concealed by the Eastern Peaks, leaving the land cold and misty.

Once the rabbits had been fully cooked, Eli accepted his portion gratefully and tried to eat it slower than he could have, enjoying the meal.

"Almost ready for the climb?" he asked.

Kadmiel shrugged. "Ready as ever."

"What should we do with Rayorden's raft?"

"What raft?" he asked, grinning.

Eli turned his head to look across the beach, back toward the river. The transport was gone. Turning back to Kadmiel, Eli suddenly understood. *The fire.*

"You used it for firewood?"

"Some of it," Kadmiel said. "As you can imagine, much of the wood was pretty wet."

Eli didn't know whether to be impressed or to feel guilty that they had destroyed Rayorden's gift to them.

Kadmiel seemed to know what he was thinking, because he said, "It's okay, Eli. I can't really see Rayorden taking the raft on a trip down the river at his age, can you?"

Eli chuckled. "Not at all," he answered honestly. "We barely made it out of there alive. Speaking of which, is your arm doing all right?"

"I'll be fine," said Kadmiel. "It'll take a lot more than that to stop us."

Eli reached for more to eat, but Kadmiel shot him a look and said, "Not so fast. That's for later—we're taking it with us."

"Ah," said Eli, beginning to package it up. "Don't know what you'll be able to find once we're up in the mountains, right?"

"Exactly."

The swordsmen collected their meager belongings from around the camp. After untying their swords and removing their packs from the supply chest, they found themselves both staring out at the river that they had come from.

"I don't know if I'll ever make that trip again," Eli muttered.

Chapter 13: ASCEND

"Ready to ruin hiking for yourself as well?" Kadmiel asked, half turning toward the Eastern Peaks.

Eli sighed. "I suppose."

The climb started out smoothly, with gentle inclines and few obstructions. But as the morning wore on, their endurance waned. Eli and Kadmiel packed their armor, food, and supplies on their backs, which made them have to fight that much harder for every step. It was difficult to hold any kind of conversation while trying to maintain a steady climb. Instead, Eli focused on admiring the beauty of the mountainside, with its tall and narrow trees, boulders covered in moss, and chirping insects.

As the swordsmen continued on their trek, Kadmiel had to remind Eli to stay hydrated. They had filled up their waterskins at the river but did not know when their next opportunity to refill would be, so Eli drank sparingly despite the dryness of his mouth.

After a few hours, there was still no Eastern Peaks city in sight.

"Are you sure we're going the right way?" Eli asked.

"Up," Kadmiel said, shrugging.

The way was getting harder. Eli tried to keep them oriented in the direction of soft dirt paths, but patches of loose rocks were appearing more frequently, which threatened their balance and made them more cautious with their steps.

Eli visualized the act of rescuing his loved ones from their captivity, and let that image propel him forward. Not the thought of them in danger, but the thought of seeing his family set free and the smiles on their faces as he rejoined them.

"Enough," Kadmiel eventually rasped.

He did not stop. "Come on, we're doing so well! Just a bit further—"

"No," Kadmiel interrupted. "We've gone without food and water for too long. We've climbed all day. Rest before you run yourself into the ground."

Eli knew that Kadmiel was right, but was reluctant to give up their momentum. The duo had reached a plateau in the cliffside after hiking into the afternoon. Stopping and seating himself, Eli began to feel the aches in his body and the empty groaning of his stomach. "What can I do to help?"

"Nothing. No cooking," said Kadmiel, shrugging his pack off and retrieving their food.

Eli took off his pack, forgetting it had been there. His body felt twice as light without the heavy load.

"Last of the fruit," Kadmiel said with a frown, handing Eli a portion. "Bread. Some meat. There you go."

"Thanks, Kadmiel. How are you doing now?" Eli asked, beginning to eat.

Kadmiel took a bite of his own before answering. "I'm all right. Trying to enjoy the view and take one step after another."

"It *is* amazing."

The swordsmen were seated on a large rock on the plateau, where the rapids could only be seen as a small sliver of their vision below. From this height the clouds appeared to be moving quickly, casting dark shadows on the land beneath them as the wind carried them across the sky. They finished their meal in silence, appreciating the scenery and the rest. Afterward, Eli remained seated, not wanting to offer the idea of leaving again.

Finally, Kadmiel gave a great sigh and he rose to his feet. Eli followed suit, stretching his legs. He tightened his boots, trying to prevent his feet from becoming more sore than need be in the journey to follow.

Donning their packs, they set out for the top of the Eastern Peaks once more.

The evening stretched onward, hours passing unremarkably in a series of trees, rocks, and dirt paths. Eli found himself pressing his palms to his knees, using arm strength to compensate for his tired legs. He was determined to reach the top.

Chapter 13: ASCEND

"Hold up," Kadmiel said, short of breath.

Eli turned to see him inspecting a tree closely. Low to the ground, there was something caught on the bark of the tree trunk.

Kadmiel grabbed it and held it out in his palm. It was a tangled clump of scruffy, white hair. "What is this?" he asked.

Eli took the ball and rolled it between his fingers. The hair was rough and shaggy feeling. "Huh. You tell me—you're the hunter!"

"Didn't have those back home," said Kadmiel.

"Hopefully nothing too big or vicious."

So far, their climb had been devoid of any threatening creatures. Eli and Kadmiel took drinks from their waterskins while they were stopped, then pressed onward. At last, the companions neared the top of a peak. Although not the highest of the range, it would afford them a great view of the surrounding area.

The trail had grown so steep that the swordsmen had to use their hands to scale the last portion before the high plateau. Hoisting himself up, Eli sat on the cliffside and extended a hand to Kadmiel. Grasping him tightly, Eli pulled him onto the ledge beside him.

"Look!" he said excitedly. "We can see everything."

Kadmiel was in awe, taking in the landscape.

The view from the mountains was unlike anything they had seen near the Southern Shores. Three other peaks could be seen around them, extending outward at an angle, like giant stone waves frozen in time.

"Aha," said Kadmiel, gazing downward.

"What do you see?"

He pointed. There, far below them, were two mountain goats resting in the dying light of the sun.

"I think that was the hair you found!" said Eli.

"That's my guess. They don't look too vicious," said Kadmiel.

"No."

They were quiet again as they watched the sun begin to set over the horizon in the west.

Eli squinted at something in the distance, at the extent of his vision. Looking downward into the center of the Tetrad Union, there appeared to be a small city. It was difficult to see with the backdrop of the sun, but the light cast what appeared to be castle structures into silhouettes.

"No... could that be? Kadmiel, is that the Inner Kingdom?"

"I think you're right, Eli," Kadmiel said softly.

One particularly tall tower protruded from within the city, stretching toward the sky like a spire. Eli found it intriguing. Then something began to trouble him.

"I still wonder if we're making a mistake in coming to the Eastern Peaks, Kadmiel. We told the Search Party that we would meet them in the Inner Kingdom. What if they've already slain Fathi and are waiting for us there?" asked Eli.

Kadmiel rebutted immediately, not one to consider changing plans. "I trust Rayorden. If he thinks that our allies are in danger, then we need to go to them. They are the only other warriors left in the Union—we'll need their help."

Eli sighed and tried to relax, leaning back on a stone behind him. "You're right."

Atop the peak, the companions rested again while the sun disappeared, casting the land into shadow. Their breath was soon visible as a chill settled over the mountains.

"You got any more climb in you tonight?" Kadmiel asked.

Eli's calves were burning and his thighs were protesting the idea of any further exercise. "I'm out," he answered.

"Good." Kadmiel chuckled. "Me too."

"Let's set up camp," said Eli. "It's getting freezing up here."

"We could build a fire, but I don't want to draw attention."

Everything was fairly flat and open atop the peak they had climbed, so they decided to leave and look for an area secluded enough to conceal them while they slept. The companions

Chapter 13: ASCEND

backtracked down the cliffside, which proved to be difficult in their exhaustion and in the absence of daylight. Without the shadows the sun had created, the rock face had deceptive handholds and surfaces of uncertain depth. With caution, they made it down to a clearing which had a generous amount of trees surrounding the perimeter.

Eli had difficulty getting the fire started with his cold hands, which were stiff and numb in the night air. He had to pause and warm them in the folds of his clothes. Kadmiel set out their bedrolls and laid their packs next to the firewood. At last, a flame caught, which Eli nurtured into a modest blaze. Then he collapsed onto his bed, appreciating the heat from the fire.

After a few moments of enjoyment, a question occurred to Eli. "How will we keep this going the whole night?"

Kadmiel groaned. "Whoever wakes up first has to tend to it, I suppose."

Eli chuckled. "I think my parents had a similar arrangement for Gabbi, when she was a few years old. Whoever woke up from her crying first had to take care of her."

Kadmiel smiled, then hoisted himself upright. "Come on, Eli, let's grab some more firewood. Neither of us are going to want to get up and go rummaging around in the middle of the night. We would be so sleep-deprived that we'd walk right off the cliff, anyway."

Eli slept fitfully that night, losing track of the amount of times he was awoken by the chill of the air, only to restart the flame beside him. He inched his bedding closer and closer to the fire until he was touching the surrounding rocks, but the Eastern Peaks seemed eager to snatch away his body heat. Curled up in a ball, Eli held on to his knees, and his teeth chattered.

By the time he woke, he was almost excited to resume their climb up the mountain in order to warm up. The morning air was still cold, but the sun was beginning to burn away the mist that hung over the peaks. Eli was drawn to the edge of the clearing, where he hung on to a nearby tree as he surveyed the landscape once more.

"Come look at this!" he said excitedly.

Kadmiel stretched and came over to stand beside him. "What?"

Eli pointed toward the center of the Tetrad Union, to what they suspected was the Inner Kingdom. "See that, right there... Is that building *bigger* than it was before?"

Kadmiel squared his jaw, looking like he was mulling the question over. "Could be... I don't exactly remember from yesterday."

"I do," said Eli, "and it has definitely gotten taller! I wonder what's going on."

"Does it have to do with breakfast? Otherwise, I'm not really interested," said Kadmiel, turning his back on the view.

"Oh, lighten up. We'll figure something out once we get to the city. We must be close."

Eli and Kadmiel packed their supplies and prepared for another day of climbing. Leaving the clearing of their campsite, the companions immediately set out for the last leg of their journey to the Eastern Peaks.

Returning to the high plateau they had discovered the previous night, they followed a winding route along the clifftop for a few hours. It was not steep, but was made difficult by patches of snow and strong gales of wind that threatened to topple them.

A fog hung around Eli and Kadmiel that grew thicker as they got higher, making it hard to see, and with the air thinning, even harder to breathe. When they couldn't see but a short distance ahead, the pair marched on in the general direction that they hoped would lead them to the city of the Eastern Peaks.

At one point, Kadmiel asked, "Are we in a cloud?"

"I don't know," said Eli, teeth chattering. He was rubbing his arms, trying to maintain body heat. He had gotten snow in his boots. "I don't think we're *that* high up. Hanging in there?"

"I say we go back to the Northern Marshes, visit our friends Rayorden and Elmund, call it a day, and let someone else finish up the Brotherhood of Warlocks for us."

Eli appreciated the touch of humor, which helped make the day a little brighter. "Do you think—"

"What?" Kadmiel shouted. The wind had picked up again and was whipping around Eli and Kadmiel, filling their ears with the noise of rushing air.

Eli shouted back over his shoulder, "Do you—"

He was stopped mid-sentence, and mid-step, by something large and solid that was obscured by the fog. The impact dropped Eli to the ground. Holding his jaw in one hand and sitting himself up with another, he saw that it was a massive boulder the height of a grown man.

Kadmiel rushed to his side to help him up, but Eli waved him off hurriedly as he realized that the boulder was shifting.

"Quick, grab it! These are the stones that Rayorden told us about!"

Kadmiel sprang toward the moving boulder, which was tipping slowly over what was sure to be a steep overhang.

Eli pushed himself to his feet as Kadmiel wrapped his arms around the wide rock and dug his heels into the ground, attempting to stop it from falling over the cliff. Indeed, Eli now noticed that rocks like this one were lined up on either side, extending past the point of visibility among the fog. The presence of these boulders meant that the Eastern Peaks city was nearby, and if any fell to the ground below it would be heard for a mile around, potentially alerting the sorcerer to their presence.

Eli stepped up behind Kadmiel and grabbed him by the belt, leaning back and tugging as hard as he could to pull the stone back to its resting place. It was a massive weight, but they managed to heave it over a bump and back into the divot that the stone had been sitting in.

Eli and Kadmiel collapsed to the ground, chests heaving from the exertion. After catching their breath, they retrieved their waterskins and drank deeply.

"I'm out," said Eli.

Kadmiel gave him the last few drops he had, and then they stowed the empty skins until they could be refilled.

Kadmiel looked at him with disbelief, shaking his head as if he did not have the words to say.

"What?"

"Of all the things that you could have walked headfirst into, it had to be the Eastern Peaks' line of defense, huh?"

Eli laughed then got up and went to the cliffside where the rocks were lined up. Careful to give them a wide berth, he chose a gap between the stones and peeked over the edge. Far below was a winding footpath, paved for the use of merchants and travelers.

Kadmiel joined him and commented, "That looks quite inviting. We had to invent our own way to the city, and this was here the whole time."

"So were these," said Eli, gesturing to the human-sized stones stationed above the path like guardians.

"But... no one is manning them," Kadmiel pointed out.

"That's true," Eli said. "You're right. It's mid-morning, and there's no one out here—"

"Let's go," said Kadmiel, suddenly in a hurry. "Maybe the watch is on a break or switching out with another guard. This may be our best chance to get into the city."

Eli agreed, then the swordsmen pointed themselves in the direction that the Eastern Peaks must be in and set off at a quick pace. Though it was difficult to see through the fog, Eli had a suspicion that the city would be nestled against the highest mountain to provide a high-ground advantage against any intruders or attackers.

His hunch turned out to be correct. Nearing the tallest peak, the city walls began to become visible through the morning fog. The walls were extremely tall and built out of the mountain, surrounding the entire city.

Eli's mouth parted at the sight of the enormous structure looming before them. It was breathtaking.

Still jogging toward the city, Eli began to wonder how he and Kadmiel could possibly sneak inside, when he noticed something peculiar. The city's main gate was wide open.

Chapter 14: **ILLUSORY**

In the center of the city's large walls was a gate that could be lowered and raised above a cobblestone street that extended into the Eastern Peaks' market. Eli could see the inhabitants of the city milling about, doing business and recreating.

"Kadmiel!" Eli shouted, slowing to a halt with his eyes still fixed upon the activity within the city. "Kadmiel, they've done it!"

He looked at Eli skeptically.

"The Search Party, they've killed the Warlock! These people are free!" Eli was amazed; he had started to doubt that their comrades were successful. "Come on," he said, laughing. "The city gates are open!" Just as fast as before, Eli resumed running toward the city with Kadmiel beside him.

The size of the Eastern Peaks struck Eli again as he passed underneath the gate, where the cobblestone road stretched in front of him at an incline as far as he could see, and with the city extending in every other direction. Then he saw something that made him choke with emotion: children playing games in the street, carefree and joyous. It was an encouraging sight, and it again reminded Eli of what was driving him. He took a moment to observe all the many people within the city, young and old, men and women, wandering the market or relaxing and enjoying the sun.

Kadmiel flagged down a young man carrying a basket, who was passing them on his way out through the city gate. "Excuse me," said Kadmiel. "How did it happen?"

"Visitors, eh? Welcome to the Eastern Peaks! Now, how did *what* happen?" the man asked.

The response took Eli off guard. "You and your people are free! We are asking about the sorcerer, of course."

No response from the young man.

"The Warlock?" asked Kadmiel. "The man that took over your city?"

The stranger smiled, finally understanding. "Oh, you mean Fathi?"

"Yes!" Eli exclaimed. "Is everything all right here? The situation appears to be under control," he said, indicating the activity around them.

"Oh, oh, oh. Yes, you're talking about Fathi, our new leader. Things are great—never been better, actually."

Kadmiel scowled, confused. "'New leader'?"

"Yes, Fathi."

"He's not dead?" asked Eli, stunned.

The man looked taken aback. "Of course not. He just got here! I think you two will really like him. He's great. Goodbye now!"

The stranger resumed his departure from the city and began whistling to himself.

"I'm so confused," said Eli.

Kadmiel shook his head. The swordsmen approached two other passersby, and had similar interactions. The inhabitants of the Eastern Peaks appeared to be quite enamored with Fathi, their new leader, who they insisted was very much alive.

Eli's heart sank. Just when he thought that things were actually looking up. "I'm getting that feeling again," he said.

"What feeling?"

"That feeling you get when you're invading the city that a Warlock has overtaken."

"Right," said Kadmiel. "We're getting used to that feeling, aren't we?"

Although quite confused by the state of the city and its populace, Eli and Kadmiel decided to take advantage of one of its best offerings: food. The main street was lined with carts of fresh fruit, cooked meat, and goods from the bakeries.

Chapter 14: ILLUSORY

The companions used their coins from the Southern Shores, and purchased enough to feed themselves and refill their stocks for a while.

Eli tried to enjoy the meal, but despite the carefree attitude of the citydwellers, knowing that Fathi was nearby did nothing to put him at ease.

They finished eating and approached one of the shop owners whom they had purchased from. Eli leaned over the counter and spoke to the man in hushed tones.

"Are you aware that your new leader, Fathi, is a sorcerer?" Eli asked.

"It makes no difference to me," the older shop owner whispered back.

"Are you being forced to say that?" Eli asked, concerned. "Has he threatened you and your people?"

"No!" the man exclaimed, genuinely appalled at the idea. "No, no. Fathi has done us no harm. Go visit him yourself at the castle if you must. See for yourself."

"Thank you, sir," said Eli as he turned to leave the shop. Then another thought struck him and made him stop. "Sir," he continued, "has there been any news from the other regions in the Union as of late?"

"No," he said. "Of course not—everyone is busy with the Championship of Warriors in the Southern Shores. We don't expect to get any visitors for some time."

Eli frowned. "That doesn't strike you as suspicious?"

The shopkeeper raised an eyebrow at Eli, appearing irritated by the questioning. Eli dipped his head and exited the shop with Kadmiel.

"They've been bewitched," Kadmiel whispered.

Eli shook his head. "That's brilliant, if you think about it. Fathi doesn't need to contain or threaten the inhabitants when he can just convince them that everything's fine." He looked around the city, finding it hard to believe that the Warlock had so effortlessly inserted himself into the lives of all of these individuals. "And no one is challenging him," said Eli.

"Until now," said Kadmiel, firmly. "My thought is this: we need to infiltrate the castle and confront Fathi before word reaches him that there are strangers in the city, asking a lot of questions."

"Probably wise," Eli grumbled, still frustrated by the genius of Fathi's plan.

"But first, one more stop," said Kadmiel.

"Weapons?"

Kadmiel nodded. His quiver of arrows was running low.

It wouldn't hurt to purchase a couple of knives as well, thought Eli, remembering that theirs were becoming dull.

The companions set off on the city's main road, searching for a weapons dealer. Eli and Kadmiel watched separate sides of the street as they traveled at a quick pace. After a few minutes they had traveled the length of the shops, but no weapons were to be found, not even hunting equipment.

Eli stopped at a fruit cart that was being managed by a kind-looking older woman and approached her.

"Excuse me, ma'am, I have a question."

"How can I help you?" the woman rasped, gesturing down at her produce for sale.

Eli grinned good-naturedly, made a small purchase, and then continued. "Do you know where my friend and I can find a place to refill our quivers and maybe sharpen our knives?"

She chuckled. "Not from around here? Well, let me tell you the good news. The people of the Peaks no longer need to arm ourselves. Fathi protects us all."

The hair on Eli's neck stood up.

"No arrows for hunting game, no knives for skinning?" Kadmiel inquired.

The woman shook her gray-haired head. "None of it. Fathi brings what we need. You don't have to worry about hunting anymore!" she said with apparent glee.

Chapter 14: ILLUSORY

*
**

Having donned their armor, Eli and Kadmiel approached the castle of the Eastern Peaks. It was easily the tallest building around, built into the back wall of the city's defenses which were pressed against the highest mountain.

The swordsmen had traveled a series of switchback roads with hairpin turns, climbing higher and higher to reach the castle which overlooked the rest of the city below. There was an impressive view of the Tetrad Union from where they stood, for the fog had cleared up and Eli had to tear his eyes away from the beautiful lakes and forests that sprawled before him.

It was still difficult to breathe as Eli and Kadmiel were not accustomed to being this high up in the atmosphere. They stopped to catch their breath once more before going to the castle entrance itself.

Eli could see no guards stationed outside, and he could tell that Kadmiel was searching the area as well. They looked at each other, confused.

So far, this has been all too easy, he thought.

After their breathing had regulated, Eli hesitated to resume their advance on the castle, not knowing what they could possibly encounter.

"Are you ready?" he asked.

Kadmiel looked down at his hands, then at his supplies. "Three arrows... old hunting knives..." He smirked. "I've got my sword and I've got you. I'm ready."

Eli grasped Kadmiel by the forearm, and Kadmiel returned the gesture. The swordsmen locked their gaze, and Eli spoke, "Hold closely to who you are. We've seen that this sorcerer is capable of tampering with the mind. I don't want to lose you."

"Same," he responded.

Eli saw a burning confidence in Kadmiel, and trusted that they would be okay.

"Then now is the time," said Eli, releasing his arm and gripping the ornate handle on the gate surrounding the castle.

"I'm going to assume this is unlocked because everything else in this city has been unusually inviting," said Eli.

The door opened without resistance.

The companions crossed the courtyard in front of the castle and walked up the steps that lay before the grand front entrance. The doors were twice the height and twice the thickness of a grown man, so Eli and Kadmiel had to pull one together to make it move. Again, unlocked.

"So we agree this is a trap, right?" asked Kadmiel.

"Undoubtedly," said Eli.

There was a ringing sound as Kadmiel drew his sword and stepped into the castle's foyer. "Good," he said. "As long as we're both clear on that detail."

The swordsmen entered.

The king did not reside in the Northern Peaks, but the structure was home to the royal subjects that served him and oversaw the region. Decorative support columns and high ceilings with candelabras gave an aura of power and beauty to the building. Eli was in awe, as it was much more regal than anything he had ever encountered.

As Eli and Kadmiel proceeded through the entrance and the main hall and deeper into the building, there was a feeling that pervaded the old stone walls: emptiness. The castle felt lonely and neglected. Fireplaces were left unburning, dust and webs collected in the corners, and the castle had become dark and cold.

"I don't think that Fathi has kept the caretakers on staff here," said Kadmiel darkly.

"I would agree," replied Eli.

The companions were not familiar with the castle layout, nor did they have an idea of how to locate the sorcerer in the sprawling edifice. Eli just hoped that they would find Fathi, and not the other way around. He and Kadmiel wore their helmets with the visors up, ready to shut them at a moment's notice at any sign of the enemy's presence.

"Do you think we're going the right way?" asked Eli as the swordsmen continued passing under archways and through rooms and hallways.

Kadmiel shrugged, looking confused. "This appears to be the only way to go."

Indeed, it struck Eli that they had yet to be presented with any real choices or branching paths.

The companions proceeded along for several more minutes. Their progression through the castle appeared like a blur to Eli; he could not remember many of the rooms and halls that they passed through, only that the way forward seemed clear, that is, until they came upon a closed door. Eli stopped and looked at it, blinking.

"You okay, Kad?"

Kadmiel grunted. "Mind feels fuzzy. There's something wrong with this castle."

Eli agreed. "Fathi doesn't want us to be here," he stated, gripping the handle of the closed door. "He's scared. We can't afford to be."

Kadmiel gave a half-smile of agreement, then took a deep breath and squared his shoulders.

Opening the door before them felt like an important occasion, as the castle thus far had been laid out plainly before them. Not knowing what to expect, Eli pried open the entrance and followed after Kadmiel. What lay beyond was a hallway that stretched almost as far as their eyes could see, lit sparsely by chandeliers far above on a distant ceiling.

"Just a hall." Eli breathed with relief.

"A long, long hallway," Kadmiel agreed, taking the first step.

They walked rather slowly toward the door on the other end of the corridor, staying alert for any signs of an ambush.

"You know," Eli whispered, catching up to Kadmiel, "this really would be the best time for Fathi to spring an attack on us."

"If he knows we're here," said Kadmiel uncertainly.

The swordsmen walked side by side until their shoulders kept bumping.

Kadmiel was clearly getting irritated. "Walk behind me!" he finally snapped.

Eli fell back a number of paces so Kadmiel could proceed before him.

I thought this passage was large enough for two men to walk next to each other...

Eli looked over his shoulder to where they had come from and saw that his suspicion was confirmed. The hallway seemed to be getting smaller.

Odd.

"Are we almost there?" Eli asked nervously, trying to peek around Kadmiel at the remaining distance.

Kadmiel didn't respond immediately, but answered in a growl, "It doesn't look to be getting any closer, honestly."

Eli noticed that the ceiling, which had appeared to be many stories tall when they entered the long room, was now encroaching downward on them. Eli could almost reach up and grab the hanging chandeliers.

Kadmiel halted and turned to examine the hallway behind them and the ceiling above, observing the same things that Eli had noticed. He looked confused, saying, "This isn't just me, right?"

Eli shook his head. He tried to blink and rub his eyes, but whatever he did, the hall appeared to be shrinking.

Kadmiel slammed a fist against the wall close by. "Fathi," he muttered.

Eli held up a palm to silence him. "Yes, but don't alert him to our presence. We can go back and find another path if you would like."

Chapter 14: ILLUSORY

Kadmiel gritted his teeth. "You know as well as I do that there was no other way. He wanted us in this trap."

Attempting to remain optimistic, Eli said, "Let's go then. This isn't all bad. We've fought an army of armored dead, navigated a vicious river, and slept outside in the cold. At least we've got a roof over our heads at the moment—"

"A roof that is closing in on us, you mean?"

Eli smirked, then passed Kadmiel to take the lead and proceed deeper down the hallway. Being in front made the whole ordeal even more unnerving. He could see the end of the hall had a door that matched the one they had entered through, but it never seemed to get any closer. The walls and ceiling, on the other hand, closed in with every step the warriors took.

Twice Eli stopped to speak with Kadmiel and reconsider their plan, but he would not meet Eli's eyes or allow him the opportunity to falter, and instead pushed him to keep leading.

The experience was unsettling, but it became even more so when the narrowness of the hallway caused Eli to turn his shoulders parallel to the walls in order to fit. The ceiling was just inches above his head now, and no more chandeliers hung from it. The corridor became darker and darker as the companions left the wider, lit area behind them.

The continuous plodding of Kadmiel's steps behind Eli helped him keep up the pace despite the hammering of his heart. He was scared, and had never enjoyed tight spaces. But this was unlike anything he had ever experienced before.

Soon, Eli could not move without his back touching one wall and his chest touching the other. He could no longer see in front of him for the darkness in the hallway.

How was I able to make out the door back then? he wondered. *I can't see anything now.*

Facing forward into pure blackness, Eli squeezed further down the passageway. Kadmiel gave him more of a lead to avoid running into him in the darkness, and Eli did not say so, but he would have preferred Kadmiel closer.

A loud thump sounded as the top of Eli's head smacked against the ceiling. He was stunned for a moment and rubbed the sore spot, which throbbed along with his bruise from rafting. Taking a deep breath, Eli tried to continue onward without thinking too much about what was going on.

He had to crouch, but the width of the hallway was now too small for his knees to bend very far.

"We're stuck," he whispered to Kadmiel.

"Not yet," the swordsman answered. Eli felt Kadmiel push him down by the shoulder, which made him fall into a crawling position, only he was still on his side with his body parallel to the walls.

"Are you serious?" Eli asked, bewildered.

"I think so," said Kadmiel, as he slumped onto the ground behind him.

Eli kept attempting to calm his racing heart, but claustrophobia was setting in. It was difficult to crawl forward on his side with a shoulder, hip, and leg touching the floor, especially with armor restricting his movement. Eli reached his arms forward and tried to pull himself along the tight walls. He wasn't sure how much longer they could keep this up before getting stuck between the sides of the corridor.

Suddenly, Eli could touch the ceiling again. It was barely an inch above his head. He felt tears forming in his eyes, and wanted to say something to Kadmiel but decided not to risk his voice wavering.

I have to stay strong.

Reaching his hands to feel ahead, Eli found that the constricting path was rotating from a vertical orientation to a horizontal one, where the ceiling was threateningly close to the ground and the sides were just wide enough for his shoulders.

This portion would have to be crawled through on their bellies.

Chapter 14: ILLUSORY

Eli clenched his eyes shut and tried to expel the cold blanket of fear that wrapped around his mind.

"How are you doing, Kad?"

When no answer came, Eli began to panic at the thought of being alone. His body convulsed as he tried to whip his head around to see behind him. Looking into the blackness proved useless, but Kadmiel's voice emanated from a point close behind him.

"Don't worry, I'm here," said Kadmiel. "I'm doing okay. It gets even worse up ahead, doesn't it?"

"How did you know?"

"Because, Eli... you've stopped."

Eli growled. "What kind of hallway is this?"

"Something from Fathi's imagination," Kadmiel suggested.

"I get the feeling that he's a very twisted man," said Eli.

Kadmiel chuckled, despite their situation. "I think I'd have to agree with you."

"We can't say for sure, but we do know that he has another person's soul living inside of him," said Eli, attempting to use a light tone.

"Mm," said Kadmiel. "Now, stop stalling."

Eli sighed. *He's got me there.*

Inching forward, he twisted his body until he was flat on his stomach. He could not prop his head up to face whatever darkness lay before him as seemed natural, but had to lay his face flat against the cold, stone ground in order to fit his head through the passageway. He could not crawl on his hands and knees but pulled and pushed himself forward, inch by terrifying inch.

The tears welled up again. He had heard of people wedging themselves in small caves around the outskirts of the Southern Shores for sport before, but that kind of adventuring had never appealed to him.

And it never will. This is enough claustrophobia for a lifetime.

For a moment, Eli's mind drifted to the outdoors and the sunlight, and he heard the sounds of birds chirping in his mind. He could almost feel the sensation of wind whipping past him like it had atop the peaks they had climbed hours earlier. Then he had to shake the thoughts free of his mind and focus on the task at hand.

"Kadmiel, once this is over and we've killed the Warlock, can we go outside?"

"I'd like that."

Eli was not sure how long they spent in the crawlspace. It could have been a matter of minutes, or it could have been hours. The time stretched on painfully, and there were no visual cues to measure their progress. The only sounds heard were from their heavy breathing and armor scraping against the walls, and everything else remained the exact same, except when feeling the passageway closing in even tighter.

But suddenly, Eli lifted his head and felt no ceiling. He crawled a little further and the pressure on his sides lessened.

Slowly, the swordsman rose to his hands and knees, then spread out his arms. There were no walls on either side for him to touch. Eli almost felt lost in the unforeseen openness. He spun around to try and find Kadmiel, and he could clearly see him rising to his feet. No longer shrouded in darkness, Eli was able to make out Kadmiel and the hallway behind him in the abrupt light.

Eli blinked and stared, then blinked again. The hallway looked as it had when they first entered, like any common corridor—no narrowing walls or sinking ceiling. A chandelier hung high above their heads.

Kadmiel's jaw dropped. He kept looking from the hallway to Eli, bewildered.

"I can't believe what I'm seeing," Eli finally muttered.

Kadmiel shook his head. "I can. It's what I *was* seeing that I can't believe."

Chapter 14: ILLUSORY

The swordsmen stood there, stunned, for a few more moments. Then Kadmiel suggested, "Onward?"

"Onward," Eli agreed weakly.

Eli swung open the door that they had found at the end of the shrinking hallway. What could be seen past the threshold was a solid wall of darkness. The room had no light emanating from within, and none penetrated from outside.

He stretched his arm out and stuck his hand through the door frame. Instantly, his hand became shrouded in shadows, and he was unable to see it. The room felt cold and damp. Snatching his hand back, Eli shivered at the thought of passing his entire body over the threshold and into the mysterious room.

"After what we just made it through, I think we can do anything," said Kadmiel. "So what are we waiting for?"

Eli swallowed then moved aside for Kadmiel to take the lead, who obliged and stepped up to the door frame. After steadying himself with a deep breath, he plunged into the darkness.

Instantly feeling alone, Eli hurled himself into the darkened room before he could change his mind. All of the warmth was sapped from his body in an instant. The clothes that he was wearing felt cold, and hung off of him as if wet. Eli turned to look back at the hallway behind him, but through the darkness nothing could be seen.

Kadmiel? Eli said. Or, rather, attempted to say. No sound came from his mouth. *Kadmiel!* he tried to shout. His mouth was free to move, but the shadows seemed to snatch the air from his lungs like it did the warmth from his body.

Where do I go?

Eli quickly lost his sense of direction, and he had no idea which way was forward. He did the only thing that he could do: stretch out his arms and feel around. *I can't die in this room,* Eli thought, panicking. He longed to touch something familiar:

a wall, a door handle, Kadmiel—anything. But he could find nothing with his extended hands. Eli began to run, thinking he must surely meet a wall any moment.

But no. The room must have been vast, for Eli ran at full speed for what felt like a minute without any contact. He felt helpless. He tried to call his companion's name again, but it was no use.

This is it, thought Eli. *There's nothing I can do.*

Suddenly, the black room began to come alive with noise, first starting slowly, then increasing in volume until it was a constant hum. Eli was surrounded by the sounds of a hundred rattlesnakes.

He was unable to see the creatures, but their tails were unmistakable. A multitude of angry hisses caused Eli to step back, trembling with fear. Then he felt something around his ankles, slithering past him.

Eli jumped into the air and kicked his legs out, swatting at his boots as he landed back on the ground. A soundless scream racked his lungs, and he had never felt more afraid in his life.

The rattles surrounding him were unrelenting. There was another brushing sensation against his boot and Eli kicked instinctively, although he knew he should try not to upset the unseen creatures. Everywhere Eli spun, he was met with the intimidating threats from the rattlesnakes, making their presence known.

He felt his knees wobble, and for a moment he thought he might faint. Just then, he felt something touch his hand.

Eli almost jumped out of his skin, reeling back before realizing that it could not have been a snake. He took a deep breath and extended his hand back in the direction of the touch. It was a human hand, still open where Eli had left it. The hand was warm and inviting, and it gripped his tightly.

Kadmiel? Eli thought. He was pulled by the unknown guide

in a direction that he did not know. Eli followed, not resisting the person's help.

He noticed the noise from the angry brood of snakes dying down; their hissing became less frequent, and the rattling tails faded into the distance as the one guiding him marched onward.

The longer Eli held the hand, the more he started to doubt that it was Kadmiel's. It felt too soft, maybe even belonging to a woman.

Eli hesitated, unsure if he could trust whomever he was with. How could he or she see in this blackness? If this indeed was not Kadmiel, then he could not just leave his friend in this room. Slowing to a stop, Eli felt three very insistent tugs on his arm as he dug his heels into the ground, refusing to go any further.

The hand, if it could have communicated emotions in that dark and silent room, seemed furious and anxious to keep moving forward.

I don't know who you are or where you're taking me, Eli tried to say, but the enchantments of the room stole the words from his mouth. The grip was growing stronger, and with a heave Eli wrenched his hand free. As he did so, the snakes seemed to close in all around him once more. He was alone again.

I don't know if I made the right choice, but I'm starting to think that this room and that hallway before are some kind of tests. And that hand seemed to want me to turn back.

Eli spun on his heel in his best approximation of 180 degrees, orienting himself in the opposite direction that the mysterious person was taking him.

If this is a test, I'm about to pass it, Eli thought, steeling himself. Putting his head down, he began to sprint forward as fast as he could. The snakes responded in anger, hissing louder and louder. The sound filled Eli's ears until it was all he could hear, but still he ran forward.

Eli concluded that the room was made to keep him from finding the Royal Search Party members and the Warlock Fathi. He then began to doubt the existence of the serpents, which lent him more strength as he barrelled recklessly through the pitch-black room. Eli started to feel them brushing against his feet and his ankles, trying to trip him. He took even longer strides, touching the ground as little as he could.

All of a sudden, Eli seemed to be past them. The rattling and hissing of the beasts began to fade away. He breathed deeply, not realizing how long he had been holding the air in his lungs. Eli slowed and then stopped, resting his hands on his knees as he gasped for air, his sides burning.

Then he heard something coming from above. A cold chill ran from the top of his skull to the base of his spine as an echoing hiss emanated from above, belonging to what must have been a snake double his height. Eli felt the forked tongue of the snake tickle his face, and he trembled as the ground vibrated when the beast moved.

Eli was frozen with terror. His legs were not moving as he was telling them to. He focused on leveling his breathing instead.

Trying to rationalize the situation, Eli thought to himself, *If this snake was real, I would probably be dead by now.* Somehow, the thought did little to calm him.

He could hear the serpent's tongue darting in and out of its mouth. Then the snake spoke, but its words sounded inside of Eli's mind and not aloud. It said: *"Turn back, foolish warrior. This castle belongs to one far more powerful than you and your friend."*

Eli raised his chin defiantly, unsure if the creature could see him or not.

"You will lose. You stand no chance," the snake continued, hissing its words into Eli's mind. *"You will die, just like those who came before you."*

Chapter 14: ILLUSORY

He reeled at the serpent's words. *The Search Party?* Eli wondered. Then he berated himself for letting information on his allies come to the top of his mind while the enemy seemed to be occupying his thoughts. *Although my slip won't matter if they've already been killed,* he reasoned.

A deep-seated rage started to boil up inside of Eli at the mention of Mikaiya, Idella, and their companions. Then Eli decided that if the snake wanted to speak with him, he had some thoughts to share with the creature.

"If Fathi laid a finger on my friends, I hope he has his affairs in order, because it's the last thing he'll do. I wish that the coward would show his face and we could put these childish tricks to rest. I've grown tired of his illusions."

The massive snake stirred at Eli's thoughts, rattling with ferocity. Two red orbs lit up above Eli, and he realized that they were the snake's glowing eyes with dark slits for pupils, fixed in a glare. The fiery light shone on the surrounding area, revealing the serpent's maw parted into a vicious snarl, with gleaming fangs the size of daggers. The great snake gave one last hiss before its head rapidly descended toward Eli, its movement a blur.

He could have turned his back on the snake and ran for his life, but he knew that was exactly what Fathi would have wanted. So Eli planted his feet and closed his eyes, ignoring his every urge to escape and run for safety.

But it never struck. The room suddenly became silent, making Eli realize just how deafeningly loud the snakes' den had been. He willed himself to look, yet saw nothing before him. Not the nothingness of a room covered in darkness, but the emptiness of a dank, vacant cellar.

Eli's heart threatened to pound out of his chest. He turned to look for Kadmiel, but the room was completely empty, with an identical entrance and exit door.

Assuming it was the way forward, Eli approached the door that the giant snake had been guarding. He quickly swung the door open and was relieved to see Kadmiel on the other side, who greeted him with a blank expression. Eli couldn't help himself; after slamming the door firmly behind him, he threw himself at Kadmiel and embraced him.

"Whoa," said Kadmiel. "Good to see you, too."

"That was insane!" Eli shouted. "Did you see the big one at the end?"

Kadmiel shrugged. "Sort of. I was too busy walking right past it."

Eli raised an eyebrow. "You are kidding, right? That thing was terrifying!"

Kadmiel chuckled. "I've seen a lot of snakes. This, on the other hand—this is a whole other story." He was pointing to the centerpiece of the room that they had just joined each other in. It was a staircase that extended as far as Eli could see as he craned his neck up to follow the massive series of steps. Higher up, the structure got narrower and the steps became steeper.

"The worst part?" Kadmiel said. "Not even any railings."

Kadmiel was not mistaken: the sides of the towering staircase were unprotected.

"Maybe you weren't too shaken by the serpents back there," said Eli, "but I say they make this pile of steps look easy."

Kadmiel was already off. "Let's get moving then."

Eli darted past Kadmiel and bounded up the first few flights of stairs, eager to put distance between himself and the serpents. "Keep up," he wheezed to Kadmiel, who was making his way up the flight below him.

"Pace yourself," said Kadmiel. "We've got a long way to go."

He paused and gazed upward, getting dizzy as he peered over the edge of the staircase and up toward the ceiling, only the ceiling could not be seen above the seemingly endless steps extending upward, like the Eastern Peaks themselves, reaching for the skies.

Eli placed his hands on his hips and sighed.

Kadmiel joined him. "What?" he asked.

"I don't understand," said Eli. "The hallway. The snakes. This staircase..." He trailed off and shook his head. "I don't know what to make of all this. I have a hard time believing it's real, but look!" Eli bent down and touched the stairs in front of him with his hands.

"Do you know how crazy you look right now?" Kadmiel asked. "Maybe Fathi is rubbing off on you."

Eli smiled. "No, see. These steps are here. I can feel them. They seem real, but how could a staircase like this be possible?"

Kadmiel began to walk again, taking the next step and brushing past Eli. "There's no time to discuss all of this while the Search Party is in danger. Just add it to the list of things that we need to speak with Fathi about when we find him."

The companions' waterskins were empty, and Eli's muscles screamed at him with each step that he climbed—if the obstacles he and Kadmiel were facing could still be classified as "steps."

Gradually, the staircase had grown steeper. The steps themselves had become narrower, and the space in between them had grown substantially, every step becoming taller. The swordsmen must have scaled a hundred flights, each set of steps doubling back on itself as they were carried higher and higher toward the indistinct roof of the mysterious castle.

Eli and Kadmiel could no longer scale the stairs side by side, as one would push the other off of the confined space. There was no more room for error; though their hands were sweaty and their limbs were beginning to shake, they had to move precisely, or one slip would be their last mistake.

Pausing for yet another break, Eli and Kadmiel sat with

their backs to the tall steps behind them and let their arms hang at their sides.

Eli took in a deep breath and exhaled shakily. "What a relief. My legs are so tired."

"You would think all of that sword practice would prepare us for a day like this," Kadmiel agreed. He peered over the steep edge of the staircase, then whistled. "If we fell... do you think we could grab onto one of the wider flights below us?"

Eli scoffed. "Let me know how that works out."

"Okay..." Kadmiel mocked hesitation and pretended to lower himself toward the side of the staircase.

"No, don't!" Eli reacted abruptly, extending an arm to hold him back.

Kadmiel chuckled. Eli quickly retracted his hand, feeling embarrassed. There was a moment of silence before Kadmiel asked if he was okay.

He tried to relax again and leaned his head back on the steps. He stuttered a response, not knowing how to express what was on his mind, then he said simply, "I just couldn't do this without you." Kadmiel looked at him dubiously, about to object, but Eli cut him off. "I mean it. Imagine me on this staircase, alone. Imagine me dying in that river without you to protect me. There are so many times that I might have turned back and given up without you." Eli shook his head and tried to fight back a lump that was forming in his throat.

Kadmiel appeared to be taken aback.

Calming himself, Eli muttered, "What I mean to tell you is... thank you, friend."

Kadmiel slowly pushed himself up from his seat and stretched his arms and legs. He then took a perilously long step downward to reach Eli, grabbed him by the forearm and pulled him to his feet.

Looking Eli straight in the face, Kadmiel said something

that gave him the strength to climb another hundred flights of stairs. "You are a great man, Eli. It is my honor to be making history alongside you. Now let's show Fathi that he can't stop us."

Another couple of grueling hours passed with little evidence of progress, but the companions kept each other going.

Eventually, the end of the staircase came into view. A final flight made of the steepest steps they had encountered yet towered before them. The stairs ended at the base of an eight foot wall that rested underneath a trapdoor in the ceiling.

This last flight was now thinner than their own bodies, causing their feet to hang over on either side, even with their boots pressed together.

Kadmiel fought to reach the top, then stood in front of the wall. Eli cautiously followed up the remaining steps, his muscles screaming in protest at the continued exertion.

He stopped and considered how to make it to the trapdoor high above as he shook and wobbled slightly on the stairs beneath.

"Well, that's that," said Kadmiel. "I think we should turn back."

Eli chuckled, shaking his head and racking his brain for the best and safest course of action.

Kadmiel turned to face him and pressed his back against the wall, holding his hands out to create a place for Eli to step. "Climb up me," he said.

Eli hesitated. "Are you sure?"

"Better idea?" Kadmiel asked.

"No," said Eli.

"Go."

Eli joined him precariously on the last narrow step, then raised his right foot and placed it on Kadmiel's open palm and paused for a moment.

"What are you waiting for?" Kadmiel snapped.

"This is a good stretch!" Eli said excitedly. "Oh my legs—they're killing me."

"Mine are too, so let's get going."

Eli prepared to shift his weight and placed his hands on Kadmiel's shoulders, who inhaled and steadied himself.

He pushed up, stepping into Kadmiel's hand and extending his leg. Kadmiel was strong but tired, and could not support his full weight for long. Immediately, Eli started to wobble. He quickly grabbed onto the trapdoor above and pulled it open, then lifted his other foot up and placed it on Kadmiel's shoulder for more balance. He yelled at the contact and Eli remembered that his arm was injured from the river.

"I need to be higher!" Eli shouted, reaching for the hole in the ceiling.

Kadmiel grunted, his arms shaking as he bore the weight.

"Just a little more," Eli urged.

"I can't!" he cried.

Eli lunged for the ceiling and grabbed on to the opening, holding himself up.

Kadmiel exhaled in relief. "Can you make it?" he asked.

Unable to answer, Eli gritted his teeth and hoisted himself upward, trying to get a leg through the hole. Once he did, he quickly crawled through the trapdoor and rolled onto his back. He took a moment to catch his breath.

"What's up there?" Kadmiel asked.

"Nothing—just a normal hallway," Eli answered. "Here, grab my hand."

Kadmiel stood on his toes and reached as Eli leaned out the opening and pulled him up.

Once they were both safely in the hallway, Kadmiel kicked the trapdoor closed and sighed, saying, "I never want to see another staircase as long as I live."

At the end of the short hallway, lit by a single torch on the wall, was a door. It was plain and unremarkable, but Eli was drawn to it as if by a magnet.

"This feels like the one," he said warily, freezing with his hand on the door handle.

Kadmiel appeared to agree, for he armed himself with his bow and held an arrow at the ready. Eli took a steadying breath, lifted the latch without making any noise, and pushed inward. The room was dark inside, lit only by moonlight spilling in at the other end of the room. Eli stepped in quietly, followed by Kadmiel.

From what he could see, it appeared to be some kind of study. The walls were lined with bookcases, and tables and desks were densely packed in the room, covered in stacks of books and unlit lamps. A giant window decorated the far wall, through which a nearly full moon could be seen above the Eastern Peaks.

The companions tiptoed deeper into the study, attempting to move noiselessly. Kadmiel swiveled from side to side, aiming his bow at each spot that an assailant could be hiding. Eli felt like their entire journey within this castle had led to this very room. What it could possibly contain, he had no idea.

His eye was drawn to one peculiar feature near the center of the study: a vast chandelier that hung from the high ceiling down within reach. Its shape was unusual, wider at the top and long and narrow at the bottom. For whatever reason, the chandelier stole Eli's attention, and his gaze was locked on it as they approached the center of the room.

"Eli..." whispered Kadmiel uncertainly.

"Yes?" he asked in a hushed tone, not removing his eyes from the odd feature.

Kadmiel held Eli back by the shoulder and spun him around. "Something's not right."

Eli could barely make out the look on his face in the moonlit room, but he could tell that Kadmiel was concerned.

"I won't let my guard down," Eli asserted, trying to sound more confident than he actually was.

Kadmiel nodded and released him, raising his bow again in a ready position. As Eli turned back to face the center of the room, a realization hit him. The long shape was not part of the chandelier; something was hanging off of it. Or someone.

Chapter 15: **RECLAMATION**

Eli trembled as he ran the last few paces toward the chandelier, and then his boots splashed in something on the ground around the person. It was blood. A woman was hanging upside down, her feet fastened to each end of the light fixture. Her hair and arms hung limply past her head, and she was utterly still. Eli's heart was hammering, and he immediately began trying to think of some way to help, searching around without knowing what to look for.

"Kad..."

The swordsman knelt next to the inverted body, examining its face. Kadmiel swallowed and looked up at Eli with wide eyes.

"This is Mikaiya," he said.

All of the warmth drained out of Eli's body in an instant. *No. It can't be her. It can't be her.*

He frantically searched the face of the woman hanging from the chandelier, but no matter how strongly he willed it not to be her, there was no denying her identity. Kadmiel was right.

Wave after wave of conflicting emotions washed over Eli: fear, rage, despair, determination, helplessness.

Eli screamed into the quiet study, letting lose a ragged cry born from a mixture of the feelings coursing through his mind and heart, caring not who heard him. He *wanted* Fathi to hear him.

Kadmiel took a step back, as if giving him space for whatever his fury might cause him to do.

But Eli did not know what to do. With tears welling up, he turned to face Kadmiel. "Who could ever do this?" he asked, gesturing to Mikaiya behind him. "What did the Search Party do to deserve this? All they ever did was dedicate their lives to something greater than themselves! They never harmed anyone!" Eli choked and bowed his head, embarrassed of the emotions that were channeling through him unchecked.

Kadmiel bowed his head as well, matching Eli's posture. "This is one of the strongest women I have ever met. Fathi will surely pay for his deeds this night."

"Kadmiel," Eli spoke hurriedly. "The rest of them. We need to find them. Maybe we can save them. We need to find Idella."

Kadmiel's gaze flickered from Eli's face back to the hanging body behind him, and Eli knew what thought had just flashed through his mind.

Eli walked up and placed both hands on Kadmiel's shoulders, looking directly into his eyes. "Don't think like that. There's still a chance we can save them. We have to..."

"Yes," agreed Kadmiel, with an attempt at a smile. "We have to try."

Eli could not help but break eye contact with Kadmiel to glance over his shoulder one more time at Mikaiya.

"We will return for her," Kadmiel assured him.

Just as the companions were preparing to move, a hair-raising scream echoed from the other end of the study. It went on and on, making Eli feel sick to his stomach.

It was the cry of a young woman, afraid and in pain.

Eli froze and hoped beyond hope that Idella was somewhere else in this castle, somewhere safe. He heard slow, faltering footsteps approaching from across the room. Looking for the source of the noise, he saw a door swinging loosely on its hinges, creaking as it settled into place. A shadowy figure limped through the doorway and came nearer, stepping in front of the large window that overlooked the city below, and a swath of moonlight bathed her face.

Eli's heart skipped a beat. It was Idella. A brief wave of relief washed over him as he saw that she was alive, but the sentiment disappeared as he noticed the sheer horror that was etched into her face. She looked as if she was ready to unleash another scream, and each step appeared painful for the girl.

Eli went to her, sprinting as fast as he could and crossing the distance between them. He could barely breathe.

What has Fathi done? Is he following her? Is she all right? Where are the other Search Party members?

Idella released another cry that was cut short as her voice gave into a hoarse rasp. A lump lodged firmly in Eli's throat as he desperately made his way to her, leaping over desks and low tables, unable to form any coherent words.

I'm almost there, Idella. I'm almost there!

Eli's eyes kept darting to the open door Idella had entered through, wondering if Fathi was in pursuit. A quick backward glance at Kadmiel confirmed that he had readied his bow and was watching the doorway. Turning his sole focus to Idella, Eli shoved the last chair between them aside and threw himself forward, wrapping her in an embrace.

"It's me! It's Eli," he said weakly, removing his helmet after realizing it was hiding his face.

Idella looked up at him with vague recognition, not with the relief that he expected.

Eli's heart sank, and he searched her eyes. "Idella, do you remember me? Idella, are you okay?"

She would not speak. Just as Eli started to wonder what atrocities Fathi may have committed to place her in such an imbalanced and confused state, he heard the *twang* of a bow from Kadmiel's end of the study. There was a whistling sound as an arrow flew through the air, and Eli glanced up to see Kadmiel's target. But no one had entered the room, and Eli heard the arrow strike with a *thump* next to him.

He felt Idella tense up in his arms. Looking down at her, Eli realized with horror that the missile had found its mark in her neck.

Idella's eyes were wide with shock. "Eli?" she sputtered.

His mouth fell open, and he looked at Kadmiel with a glare of confusion and anger. Kadmiel approached with his bow lowered; his face looked concerned, as if an accident had just occurred.

"Eli?" Idella spoke again, growing paler and paler in the moonlight as the life faded from her limbs. "You were... supposed to be..."

Eli carefully reached for the arrow protruding from her skin, unsure what to do. Blood pooled around her now, just like her older sister.

"Yes, Idella?" he asked, trying to speak in a reassuring tone.

"You were sup—supposed to be... dead." With that, the girl took one last raspy breath, and her head fell limply over his arm.

Kadmiel had reached them and removed his helmet, running a hand through his hair as he surveyed the scene. "Eli..."

He gently lowered Idella's body, resting her head upon the hardwood floor, then wasted no time in pushing himself to his feet and launching himself at Kadmiel. Eli tackled him, slamming him to the floor and landing on top of him. Before consciously deciding to, he had wrapped his hands around Kadmiel's throat.

"WHAT WERE YOU THINKING?" he demanded.

Kadmiel grappled with Eli's hands around his neck, unable to give him an answer. Tears filled Eli's eyes, and he wiped them away furiously. Kadmiel caught his wrist before he could regain his grip.

Kadmiel looked fierce but understanding at the same time. "I know you're confused, Eli! Look! She was holding a knife!"

No explanation could appease Eli. Idella had just died in his arms, and someone needed to pay for that. The someone who had fired the arrow.

He wrenched his arm free and threw a punch at Kadmiel's ribs, who buckled under the blow. Kadmiel twisted beneath Eli, throwing him off and slamming his side onto the hard planks

Chapter 15: RECLAMATION

of the floor. Kadmiel then kicked him away, putting distance between them.

"Eli, I'm sorry! LOOK!"

No longer trusting of Kadmiel, Eli was wary not to take his eyes off him. Seeing his hesitation, Kadmiel raised his hands up to show they were empty, and he circled around to Idella's body. Slowly kneeling down, Kadmiel gestured to a knife that was wrapped in Idella's cold grip.

Silence settled over the study.

"She pulled this out when you took your helmet off," Kadmiel stated simply.

Eli was reeling, trying to understand what it all meant. "And that's when you...?"

Kadmiel nodded. "What was it that she said to you?"

He had to pause and try to remember amongst his scattered thoughts. "She said I was supposed to be dead."

Kadmiel looked like he shared Eli's confusion. "I don't think Idella was herself, Eli... She may have been under control—"

"Kad!" Eli cried, pointing at the body on the ground.

It was beginning to transform.

Within moments, the still figure lying between Eli and Kadmiel had changed from the likeness of Idella to that of a man. As her appearance faded away, the anguish Eli had felt began to dissipate, but he wasn't sure what to believe.

Where the girl had lain, they now looked upon Fathi of the Brotherhood of Warlocks. The old man appeared frail, his skin withered with age. His face held the wrinkles of many decades, and his eyes had a wild look to them, even in death.

"It wasn't her!" Eli exclaimed.

A final whisper of breath escaped the Warlock's lips, followed by a loud tremor that shook forth from the dead body as wisps of dark energy dissipated before them. Fathi's body had been destroyed, and both his spirit and the one he hosted were sent to the unseen land of souls.

Eli's knees shook from the blast, but Kadmiel was closer and was thrown onto his back. Eli roused himself from his shocked state and hurried to help Kadmiel, pulling him up by the forearm.

Kadmiel groaned and stretched his back. "I always forget about that part."

"It's no joke," Eli agreed, pointing to the arrow that had taken Fathi's life. It now lay in splinters, discharged from the sorcerer's body and broken to pieces.

"That was one of my last arrows," Kadmiel quipped.

"I'm so sorry," Eli said earnestly. "For attacking you."

Kadmiel sighed. "You handled that pretty well, all things considered."

"But how did you know?"

Kadmiel shrugged. "The knife, I suppose. Didn't think Idella would pull a weapon on you—that, and Fathi has been messing with our minds this whole time."

Eli's eyes widened as understanding gripped him. "And the townspeople," he suggested. "Fathi's been tricking them."

"No doubt. It's probably all he could manage to do without any physical strength to speak of."

Somewhere a wolf howled in the distance, reining Eli's thoughts in and bringing him back to the present. Realizing where they were standing, he asked, "Is this the longest conversation you've ever held over a dead body?"

Kadmiel barked a laugh, still recovering from the rush of adrenaline.

Then his gaze fixed on something over Eli's shoulder, and he grew solemn once more. With a sudden onset of dread, Eli knew what he was thinking. Turning to face the same direction, he said, "Mikaiya."

"You never know. If Idella was an illusion, then maybe..." Kadmiel trailed off as he caught up to Eli, who was slowly approaching the chandelier and the back of the body hanging beneath it.

Chapter 15: RECLAMATION

"Don't let me hope," said Eli firmly. "The rest of the Search Party could still be hung up somewhere in this castle." It pained him to say it, but he was trying ardently to manage his expectations.

Circling the chandelier, they turned to face the body. The carcass was even more grotesque than before. To be certain, this body did not belong to Mikaiya or any other woman. The hanging figure was distinctly male but disfigured and difficult to recognize. Its skin was deteriorating. A curled mustache revealed its true identity: Edric the sorcerer.

Eli shuddered, not sure how many more surprises of Fathi's he could take. A stench came from the waterlogged body that had not been present when it was shrouded in Mikaiya's likeness. Eli and Kadmiel recoiled from the smell.

"So he pulled Edric's body out of the river and strung him up in here," Eli said in awe.

"And he laid all of those traps for us—or deterrents, I should say. I think when he found out that Edric was killed, Fathi became afraid. He kept trying to get us to turn back."

Eli nodded. "This bodes well for Mikaiya and the others," he said. "Were they killed, he could have just used their bodies."

"I would agree, but..." Kadmiel trailed off, and Eli shot him a questioning look. "I'm not supposed to let you hope," he finished with a grin.

"Right," Eli said, placing his hands on his hips and assessing the study. He couldn't help but shake his head in amazement.

"What is it?" Kadmiel inquired.

It took him a moment to form a response. "I just never thought we could actually do it." He gave a short laugh. "Now look at us. We're standing in a room with two of the sorcerers that we killed, and we've won back the Eastern Peaks for the people of the Union, just like we have at the previous locations. Kadmiel, we are really doing it!"

Kadmiel's smile grew broader as he listened, then he chuckled. "You know what the Search Party says about our off-the-charts energy power or whatever."

"Yes," said Eli, clasping his hands together. "Let's go find them."

The castle had regained its original state of normalcy that had been robbed by the Warlock Fathi. The sorcerer's tricks and enchantments faded away along with his life, leaving the Eastern Peaks palace feeling decidedly ordinary.

However, Eli's sense of unease did not disappear along with Fathi's supernatural effects. He wouldn't rest until he found that the Search Party members were safe and whole. Fortunately, he and Kadmiel did not have to wander the castle's corridors for long. After a couple winding hallways and dead ends, they saw a door that was held shut by a chain. Undoing the lock and throwing the door open, they found five men and women who flinched in unison.

The warriors of the Search Party were seated on the floor against the walls of a small, bare room; they stared up at the swordsmen with wide, bloodshot eyes, appearing tired and terrified. Eli's relief was overwhelming, and he sagged against the frame of the doorway, ecstatic that they were all alive.

When the group continued to eye them dubiously, he became concerned. Although the swordsmen wore no helmets, Idella, Mikaiya, and the rest looked at them with unknowing gazes. Eli glanced at Kadmiel, who appeared equally unsure of how to proceed.

In the back corner of the room, Idella burst into tears and placed her head in her hands. Mikaiya put a hand on her sister's knee without taking her eyes off them.

"What's wrong?" Eli choked out. "It's us."

Chapter 15: RECLAMATION

Mikaiya glared at them deeply. "Did you kill them, sorcerer?" she snarled, starting to rise slowly to her feet.

Eli raised his hands and took a step backward, feeling nervous. Kadmiel grabbed the hilt of his sheathed sword, but Eli waved him off.

"Did you steal their appearance, Warlock?" Mikaiya continued, shouting as she pushed herself up. Suddenly, her knee buckled and she crashed back to the floor, with her leg splayed beneath her. Idella continued to sob, and the men surrounding them looked protective, but afraid.

The horrors they must have endured, Eli thought with a heavy sadness. "It's us," he repeated as a tear fell from his eye.

"We killed Fathi," Kadmiel stated firmly. "He's gone."

A flicker of hope crossed Elhart's face, but he shook his head violently and slammed a fist against the ground beside him. "You're not supposed to be here! You were to go to the Inner Kingdom. How would you have known—"

Suvien kicked the man speaking, glaring at him incredulously as if he had just divulged private information to the enemy. The whole exchange was too much for Eli to bear, breaking his heart. He turned away from the room to collect himself.

"You can trust us," Kadmiel urged. "You're safe."

"You have told us that before," Mikaiya spat. "Begone, Fathi. You will wrest no information from our party. The least of us is stronger than you."

Eli was moved by her show of devotion, and he turned to face the group again. "Yes! Yes you are. So very strong. And I am so glad that we decided to travel here. We've missed you all." He emphasized every word with sympathy and sincerity so they would know he spoke the truth.

The contempt on Mikaiya's face was replaced with questioning as she searched Eli's eyes. He smiled back at her, wordlessly trying to convince her to believe.

There was an abrupt silence in the room as Idella halted her weeping. She grew very still, and her shoulders stopped shaking.

The hair in front of her eyes slowly fell away as she raised her head. Meeting Eli's gaze, she whispered, "Wait."

It was a word full of hope, spoken with trembling. Idella closed her eyes and extended an open palm in Eli and Kadmiel's direction. Eli noticed that her hands and arm appeared bruised, causing a spike of pain in his chest.

"Wait," she whispered again, fingers shaking.

"Be careful!" Mikaiya snapped. "Don't open yourself to—"

"It's them!" Idella exclaimed. Her eyes snapped open, and she gave a smile that illuminated the room. "It's Eli and Kadmiel!" she shouted, springing to her feet. Kadmiel stepped aside with a grin as Idella propelled herself through the doorway and into Eli's arms.

He was overtaken by joy, reunited with Idella and confident that the Search Party was going to be all right. Each time Eli tried to pull back and look at her, she held him tighter.

"You came," Idella said.

Eli locked eyes with Kadmiel, who had helped the other members to their feet. He smiled approvingly.

Idella released him temporarily and grabbed Kadmiel by the arm, pulling him in to join them in a three-way hug. The Search Party laughed, looking like an enormous weight had been lifted from their shoulders. Mikaiya was standing while leaning on Marrick for support, her leg looking weak beneath her. She smiled through the pain, enjoying the celebratory moment.

Both the Search Party and the swordsmen were ready to leave the castle and put its haunting memories behind them. Eli and Kadmiel led them back the way they had come, but deviated to avoid the castle's study. Progress was slow going, with Mikaiya and her team members having suffered a wide range of afflictions at Fathi's hands. The individuals were not ready to discuss any specifics of their torture, but opted instead to repeat some variation of the statement: "I kept your identities a secret," for which Eli and Kadmiel were endlessly grateful.

The group descended an average-sized staircase, passed through a lit and vacant room and finally, crossed a corridor without shrinking walls or ceiling. Eli and Kadmiel marveled silently at the simple rooms that had contained the objects of nightmares only a few hours prior.

The cool, thin air of the Eastern Peaks washed over them as they threw open the castle doors. Eli held one of the tall doors while Kadmiel propped open the other, allowing the Search Party passage out of the building in which they had been confined. They murmured their thanks to the swordsmen as they breathed deeply of the night air and admired the stars. The castle doors swung inward when Eli and Kadmiel released them, closing with a *boom*.

The city that sprawled beyond the courtyard lay utterly still and quiet—a city full of people who did not know the significance of what had taken place that night.

Eli smiled to himself as he imagined the townspeople waking to unclouded minds and untethered wills. He surveyed the gathered companions with gladness, but his eyelids were heavy, and everyone else looked just as tired.

"Sleep?" he suggested simply.

They all quickly agreed with that.

While the castle courtyard would have been as good a place as any to rest for the night, the group still wanted to be out from underneath its foreboding shadow. Marrick, who had grown up in the Eastern Peaks before joining the Royal Search Party, guided the company to a park where they could lie down. It was then that Mikaiya realized that they were without their belongings; weapons, rations, bed mats, and various supplies had all been taken from them at the time of their captivity.

"Yeah, being kidnapped isn't great," Kadmiel said. "I wouldn't recommend it."

Eli winced upon hearing his attempt at humor, but a few of the Search Party members found it within themselves to laugh.

"If you would like, I can go back to get—" Eli began.

"No!" Mikaiya interjected. "You are not stepping foot back in that castle. You're staying here with us."

Eli grinned sheepishly, privately grateful that Mikaiya had refused his offer.

It was late, and the group was eager to settle down for the night. They plodded around momentarily, searching for soft patches of land, but in the end decided it did not matter very much. It would be their first peaceful night of sleep in days, and the hardest of ground would hardly disturb their slumber.

Eli gladly removed his pack, letting it slump to the ground as he stretched his shoulder muscles. Unbuckling his bedroll from his belongings, he was about to unfurl it onto the grass in front of him when an idea struck him.

Immediately making up his mind, Eli walked a few paces to the spot where Idella had laid down.

Her eyes are already shut, Eli noticed. She was lying on her side, looking comfortable and content with her hands folded beneath her cheek.

Careful not to wake her, Eli laid out his bedding and gently moved her to rest on top of it, then removed his cloak and draped it over the girl, covering her bare arms. He did all of this quietly, but Idella stirred and her eyes fluttered open. Looking up at Eli, she smiled and parted her lips as if to say something, but sleep took her again before she could speak.

Returning to lie next to Kadmiel, he noticed a sly look coming from him. Eli raised an eyebrow, wondering if Kadmiel was going to tease him for his show of kindness. Instead, he sighed and sprung upright, then gathered his bedding in a bundle under his arm.

"Where are you going?" Eli asked.

"You think I can lie down comfortably on this bedroll after watching you sacrifice so nobly?" Kadmiel stomped away with a huff, bringing his bedding to Mikaiya.

Eli collapsed onto the damp grass and looked up at the stars, more vivid than he had seen them from elsewhere in the Tetrad Union. There was a cool breeze blowing through the park, but despite the chill of the night, Eli felt warm.

He awoke slowly, with the sunlight seeping in through his eyelids. Yawning and stretching, he got up from his bed of grass. The memories of the previous day rushed through his mind, and he remembered all that happened.

"Good morning, Eli," said Idella.

He smiled and greeted her back, noticing that she had rolled up his bedding and returned it to him. She appeared well-rested and wore a thankful expression, and Eli was glad he had been able to return the favor that she had first extended to him.

"Where's Kadmiel?" Eli asked.

"He's with Marrick, hunting," Mikaiya answered.

Eli had been the last to wake up, and the sun had already traveled some distance west. Looking out into the city, he could see people beginning to stir and come out of their homes, some with confused looks on their faces.

"Do they know the good news yet?" he asked.

Idella shook her head. "We saved that honor for you."

Eli stood up and gathered his belongings. "Come with me, all of you. The people must know what happened last night!"

He was eager to be off and to inform the city inhabitants of Fathi's demise, but Mikaiya hesitated to accompany him. Then Eli remembered her injury, and he felt guilty for being so excited to leave.

"I'm sorry, Mikaiya—you should remain here with our things, shouldn't you?"

She smiled sadly. "I can do that."

Eli, Idella, Suvien, and Elhart entered the Eastern Peaks city and split up in different directions, spreading out from

233

the main junction. As it would have been difficult and time consuming to gather all of the inhabitants in one place and address them, Eli had decided on a word-of-mouth approach.

Eli spotted an older woman nearby on her front porch, looking like everyone else in the city: dazed. Her eyes were glazed over, and she kept looking from side to side. He greeted her, but the woman barely seemed to notice.

"Mm," she mumbled, nodding slightly in his direction, but her vision was still fixed far in the distance.

"Excuse me, ma'am. How are you feeling?"

"What? Oh... oh, I don't know. I can't seem to remember what I was doing yesterday—or the day before... Just part of growing old, I reckon."

He felt pity for the confused old woman. "I understand that you must be very disoriented today. I can help you with that—my name is Eli."

"Hi, Eli," she said absently.

"Do you remember Fathi?"

The woman flinched. "I remember something about a man named Fathi arriving here—everything in my recollection from that point is a little fuzzy."

Eli stepped up onto the porch and placed a hand on her arm. "He was an evil man—a sorcerer—and he has been tampering with your mind."

The old woman looked aghast and turned to look Eli in the face.

"Not only *your* mind, but everyone's in this city. He tricked you into believing that he was a fit ruler for your land."

"I don't believe it..." She trailed off.

Eli sighed sympathetically. "I'm sorry. I know that this is a lot to take in. Fathi played with my mind as well."

"Really? So you feel it?"

He frowned. "Feel what?"

The woman raised her hands to her temples and clenched

her eyes shut. "There was this pressure around my mind, suffocating my thoughts... When I woke up this morning, it started growing smaller. I think it's going away."

Eli considered it for a moment. "I'm sorry, ma'am, I'm not feeling the effects that you're talking about, but I think your neighbors are." He gestured to the other citydwellers beginning to wander out of their homes with bewildered expressions. "You have all been under the influence of the sorcerer for some time," said Eli sadly. "But he was killed last night, and his magic is breaking."

"Will I ever feel normal again?" the woman asked with glimmering eyes.

"You will," Eli said, feigning full confidence. Realizing that he had yet to ask her name, Eli inquired of it.

"My friends call me Mag."

Eli shook her hand. "It's nice to meet you, Mag. I'm going to need your help today. The rest of this city needs to know that they have been freed, and that they will recover in time. Can you assist me in spreading the word?"

Mag nodded. "How did Fathi die?"

Eli paused, unsure how to answer the question without giving the long and detailed story. "You can tell them—" he started. Then, making up his mind, he said, "Tell them that the servants of the High King are protecting his kingdom, and making way for his return."

Mag's lips parted, and her eyes grew wide. "You are a servant of King Zaan?"

"I am."

Mag pulled Eli into a warm hug. "Bless you, child. Bless you. I thought that the king had abandoned us."

Many of Eli's interactions with the townspeople unfolded similarly. Soon the dull confusion of the morning gave way to an excited buzz that spread throughout the city, as neighbors rushed to tell others of Fathi's fate and began to celebrate their freedom.

The more individuals that Eli met, the more he grew to despise the memory of Fathi. The Warlock had invaded these people's minds, taking one of the most sacred things a person can have: their own will.

Some men and women were in better condition than others. There were a few townspeople that would not respond to Eli, as if they had become both blind and deaf. *I just hope they come to, eventually,* he thought sadly. The children generally fared the best, adapting to the change quickly.

Eli regrouped with the others back at the park, where Kadmiel and Marrick brought their catch from the morning. Mikaiya was helping prepare the meal, and Idella, Elhart, and Suvien were just returning.

"How are the townspeople reacting to the news so far?" Kadmiel inquired.

"Fairly well," Eli answered. "For being told that their minds have been manipulated, everyone seems to be remaining calm."

Suvien raised his eyebrows. "Not my experience. There were some men who couldn't believe that we killed Fathi..."

Mikaiya looked astonished. "You mean they *supported* him?"

"No, no. They think he should have been publicly tortured for his crimes. They became upset when they learned that his life was ended quickly and 'painlessly.'"

"Kadmiel, you killed the sorcerer wrong," Eli teased. "Way to go."

Kadmiel chuckled and the group laughed along with him.

Turning to face the city, Eli observed the townspeople. "I think that in general, they're doing well. They will bounce back."

"Some of the people seem rather hollow," said Idella.

"One does not recover immediately from a Warlock's oppression," Mikaiya said with her eyes downcast.

There was a pause in the conversation.

Chapter 15: RECLAMATION

"How are you all?" Eli asked, afraid of what they might say.

In the full daylight, the abuse that the ex-captives had gone through was even more evident. Bruises, cuts, and burns were visible on their skin, which had sunken inward from malnutrition during their captivity. No one seemed eager to speak first.

Finally, Elhart said, "Well, I think that Mikaiya is in the worst shape."

She was seated with her bad leg stretched out, to keep the knee from bending. She looked embarrassed, like she did not enjoy the attention that her injury afforded her.

"Marrick helped me hunt today—showed me the best places to look," said Kadmiel. "But his arm needs attention. He can't pull the bowstring himself."

"You all need a doctor," Eli said firmly.

The collective members of the Search Party responded immediately with looks of defiance.

"No!" Idella exclaimed. "We have to go with you to the Inner Kingdom!"

Eli turned his back to the group and began to pace with his head down. He felt conflicted. "I want you to come with us."

"But?" Idella prodded.

"But there's no way I can take you in your current state. You're not fit for travel or combat," said Eli.

"But—" Marrick began to protest.

"Kadmiel?" Eli interjected. "What are your thoughts?"

The swordsman contemplated long and hard before answering. "I agree with Eli. You have all done enough, and we need to get you medical attention. The Eastern Peaks has doctors you can see, yes?"

Marrick nodded shortly.

"Good. You can stay here and get looked at," Kadmiel continued, "and you can oversee the townspeople's recovery."

"You can also help the original government become reinstated," added Eli. He was glad that Kadmiel agreed with him.

As much as he desired Idella and the others to accompany them, he knew that it would be unwise for their health and well-being. The group had endured trauma for his and Kadmiel's sake, and had already done all they could.

"We can't thank you enough, for what you did for us," said Eli solemnly.

"Yes, thank you," Kadmiel added. "Fathi would have stopped at nothing to learn the identities of the men who are killing their Brotherhood, but you managed to protect us and, thereby, our families."

The team seemed to swell with pride.

"Can't you wait for us... to recover?" Idella asked hopefully.

Averting his eyes, Eli answered, "No."

There was no further argument and indeed little discussion at all amongst the group from that point. They ate mostly in silence, and some of the Search Party members laid back down to rest after they had finished eating. Eli and Kadmiel continued their preparations to depart the city, replenishing their food supplies and performing basic maintenance on their weapons. Kadmiel was even able to restock his arrows in town now that the city had been released from Fathi's dark spell. Eli tried to enjoy the last moment of peace that their journey might afford.

Chapter 16: **ELEMENTS**

B y late afternoon, they were ready to leave. Eli's stomach
had tied itself in knots throughout the day, as he dreaded
saying farewell to Idella.

They returned to the Search Party's makeshift campsite, Eli
walking a few paces behind Kadmiel and dreading the interaction that would follow. The whole of the Search Party's eyes were
on them, filled with a mixture of gratitude, sadness, longing,
and perhaps even jealousy. These were men and women who
always wanted to be in the thick of the action, not hanging
back to recover.

"Are you sure you don't need our help getting to the doctor?"
Kadmiel asked.

"You must go," Suvien asserted. "We will be just fine."

"Marrick will show us the way," Mikaiya said with a nod.

Eli started to speak, but his voice cracked. Clearing his
throat, he said, "Well done, all of you. Few people in the
Tetrad Union could have ever stood up to a sorcerer like you
did. Kadmiel and I are fortunate to have met you and to have
called you our allies."

"We are *still* your allies, Eli," Idella corrected him. "And
should you and Kadmiel run into too much trouble in the Inner
Kingdom—should you become captured like we were—then
know that we will be close behind."

Eli couldn't help but smile at that. "Thank you. It's good
to know that you have our backs."

"As long as you serve the king and his kingdom, we are with
you," said Mikaiya.

It seemed that all that could have been said was already
said, so Eli and Kadmiel approached each Search Party member
individually to exchange their goodbyes.

Eli gripped the forearms of the men, exchanging words that he would immediately forget, as his mind was elsewhere. He skipped over Idella to speak with Mikaiya, who pulled him into a quick embrace and kissed his forehead.

"We believe in you," she said.

Then there was no further avoidance. Eli went up to Idella and fell into her arms, and she held him as tightly as her frail frame could. He could not keep the tears from pooling up in his eyes.

"It's okay, Eli... I will see you again..."

"You're so brave," he said. "I can't believe what you have been through."

"Yes you can," Idella countered. "You are going through the same things. We are fighting the same war."

"I hope I won't be too long." Eli sniffed.

Idella squeezed him. "Only one more. Just one more sorcerer."

Staring over Idella's shoulder, Eli knew that it would be best not to mention the scroll and its revelation that Lilith was somehow involved. Instead, he nodded and pulled out of the embrace, looked Idella in the eyes, and said, "I will see you soon."

"I will miss you."

"I too."

Eli must have glanced backward a dozen times as he and Kadmiel left the Eastern Peaks through the city's main gate. He barely took notice of the dazed townspeople that he was passing on each side, some of them mumbling their thanks or reaching out to greet them. Kadmiel did a better job of accepting the gestures that were extended.

The Royal Search Party members had hobbled alongside them from the park to the main city street, where they stopped and bid one last farewell. There the team stayed, waving goodbye to Eli and Kadmiel as they departed. Looking back,

Eli thought he could just make out a smile on Idella's distant face, and then the two companions passed under the arched gateway of the city, and the Search Party members atop the steep road were out of sight.

Eli let out a long, quavering sigh, and Kadmiel patted his shoulder.

"We did it."

"Hmm?" he asked, absentmindedly.

"They are free, and they will recover. Fathi is dead."

Eli kicked a pebble in his way and continued beside Kadmiel down the main road leading from the city and winding down the mountainside. They could now travel this path without fear of the line of defensive boulders surrounding the cliffside.

"You should be celebrating, Eli," Kadmiel continued.

Eli knew that his friend was right, but his heart did not seem to acknowledge the truth.

Kadmiel mostly left him to his own tumultuous thoughts that day, and thanks to the paved walkway, the swordsmen had already reached the base of the mountain by nightfall. At the path's end was a bridge that passed over the river, and tied to it were two beautiful horses.

They were arranged for Eli and Kadmiel courtesy of a breeder in the Eastern Peaks. The man had been gracious enough to bestow the steeds upon them as a token of his gratitude for setting him and his family free of Fathi's influence. One was gray, named Silverbell, and the other was tan, called Dixen.

Eli and Kadmiel shared the same excitement: the horses would make the trip far quicker and much less exhausting. They were even outfitted in saddles with supply containers and buckles made for holding swords.

The animals were tied in such a way that they were able to drink from the river and graze, so the swordsmen left them as they were for the night while setting up camp. Eli was grateful for the gift from the breeder, for he knew that any energy saved for the final confrontation at the Inner Kingdom would be priceless.

Eli woke feeling not entirely different than he had the night before. His dreams had been restless, full of images of his family, Idella, and Lilith. Though for the sorceress, his mind's eye had no frame of reference with which to conjure what she looked like, so his dreams portrayed the woman as a tall shadow or a mysterious silhouette, screaming vile curses upon him and Kadmiel.

Shaking his head in an attempt to clear his mind, Eli got up from his bedroll and began to pack it away. That was when he noticed it once more: Idella's scent, left from the night in the park.

The cool morning air and the dawn of a new day provided a sharp clarity to Eli's mind. He was ready to ride hard to the Inner Kingdom and do whatever it would take to dismantle the Brotherhood of Warlocks' last member and remove their blight from the Tetrad Union.

Eli bent over Kadmiel, who was still resting, but beginning to stir in the dawn's first light. Eli clapped him on the shoulder and reached for his hand.

"Come, Kadmiel. Today is the day." Eli pulled him to his feet and was greeted with a look of approval.

"Someone is eager to be off," Kadmiel stated with a grin.

"I am eager to be back home."

Kadmiel mocked confusion. "Home is that way," he said, pointing southwest.

Eli chuckled. "There are a few people that I need to pick up first. Do you mind?"

"Not at all."

The swordsmen had packed up the campsite and were now preparing their food for the morning. The horses' packs were already filled with food for the beasts: apples and cubes of sugar, gifts from their former owner.

The companions ate lightly, not wanting to stuff their stomachs, in anticipation of the bumpy ride that was to come. They did not intend to travel leisurely.

"How is your experience with horses?" Eli asked.

"Moderate," said Kadmiel. "And yourself?"

"Same," Eli answered. "So if you can handle a horse, a sword, and a bow and arrow, you really could take the entire Championship of Warriors someday, couldn't you?"

"Who, me?" Kadmiel asked. "I'm flattered."

Eli paused, reflecting on the competition. "To think... I used to wield this sword just for sport. Now I have saved my life with it, and taken the life of others."

Kadmiel appeared deep in thought as well while they finished their breakfast. "We've been forced to grow up rather quickly, eh?"

"I have," said Eli. "You did that years ago, when you started looking after your family."

Kadmiel shrugged, conceding the point. "Let's be off, then!"

They tied all of their belongings down to their horses' saddles, Eli choosing to take Silverbell.

"Got everything?" Kadmiel asked.

Eli took a moment and examined the bare patch of ground where they slept. "I don't think we forgot anything," he said with a smirk.

The companions oriented their horses west, pointing directly at the Inner Kingdom, which was a small dot on the horizon. Then they rode without break, abstaining from their waterskins in order to prevent stops. Dixen always tried to ride in front, much to Eli's annoyance. The landscape rolled beside them beautifully, with green hills on either side.

It was not until halfway through the day when they stopped to rest, more for the horses than for themselves. Eli offered

Silverbell an apple and patted the horse's long neck before sitting down with some food of his own.

Neither of them had anticipated the strain on their bodies that riding would cause.

"It hurts to stand," groaned Kadmiel with his mouth full of bread.

"It hurts to sit," Eli added in agreement.

Kadmiel heaved a great sigh and collapsed onto his back, disappearing beneath the tall grass. Eli could hear a multitude of insects all around them, and birds chirping in the sky above.

"Does it hurt to lie—"

"Yes," said Kadmiel.

Eli chuckled. His eyes wandered toward their destination—the heart of the Tetrad Union. "It's definitely becoming taller, Kad."

Kadmiel propped himself up on his elbows and followed Eli's gaze, observing the tower that extended from within the Inner Kingdom up toward the sky.

"See it?"

Kadmiel frowned. "We were looking down on it from the Eastern Peaks last—maybe it just appears to be getting taller as we draw near."

"I don't know."

Once the two had finished their meals, Eli asked, "Shall we continue?"

As if in response, Dixen decided to lie down in the grass. Eli's horse followed suit, resting its head on the ground.

"Evidently not," Kadmiel stated.

Eli woke with a start. His eyes darted to the position of the sun in the sky, almost touching the horizon in the west, casting the Inner Kingdom into a silhouette.

"Kadmiel!" Eli shouted. Panicked, he called his friend's name again.

Chapter 16: ELEMENTS

"What is it?" Kadmiel asked groggily, sitting up.

"We slept," he said, dismayed.

Kadmiel groaned and pushed himself to his feet, and Eli did the same. They stretched and popped their backs, sore from lying on the ground.

"We were more tired than we knew," said Kadmiel distantly.

Eli was disappointed in himself for making such a simple mistake when people's lives were in danger. He was mentally berating himself, and Kadmiel must have noticed.

"Hey, we would have had to stop and sleep at some point. We just got our resting out of the way. Now we can ride through the night."

Eli supposed he was right. "I'm sure the horses didn't mind." He walked over to his gray steed. "Did you?" he asked, patting the beast on the nose.

The horses appeared well rested and ready to cover more land, so they rode even harder that night, eager to make up for lost time. It was frightening for Eli to be riding at such high speeds through unfamiliar landscape under the cover of darkness, but he tried to trust Silverbell's instincts and not worry. No accidents had befallen them, and everything seemed to be going smoothly.

Until the companions noticed the storm chasing them.

Flashes of lightning and rolling thunder alerted the swordsmen to its presence, drawing ever nearer to them from behind. Dark clouds covered the night sky in pitch blackness, snuffing out the valuable light from the moon and the stars. Eli and Kadmiel could faintly see sheets of rain drenching the land and following them westward toward the Inner Kingdom.

For some time, they did their best to press onward and outrun the storm. But the clouds were traveling impossibly fast, and would soon overtake them. A crash of thunder rattled Eli's teeth and stood his hair on end. The sounds of the storm roared louder as it pressed in on the companions.

"What do we do?" Eli shouted, barely audible above the din.

Kadmiel kept glancing over his shoulder at the looming clouds, weighing their options. "Shelter!" he finally shouted, sounding defeated.

Eli and Kadmiel slowed their horses to a trot and then jumped down.

"Let's start there!" said Kadmiel, pointing to a large tree near them.

Eli grabbed Silverbell's reins and began pulling toward the tree, but the animal was difficult to direct and kept tossing his head to the side, trying to sidle away from the storm. "Come on!" Eli shouted. Kadmiel looked like he was having the same difficulty with his steed.

The swordsmen were struggling, and the thunderclouds were gaining on them quickly. After much delay, they arrived at the tree with their frightened and stubborn horses. Kadmiel gave Dixen's reins to Eli, who gripped one set in each hand. He dug his heels into the ground, trying to hold the horses in place and prevent them from running away. Kadmiel quickly unloaded the saddles and darted toward the tree with their supplies.

Right then, a bolt of lightning streaked down from the sky and exploded on the ground in a burst of white-hot light. The place of contact was within a hundred yards from them.

The horses were spooked, neighing furiously at the blinding light. Silverbell reared back on its hindlegs, and the sudden pull caught Eli by surprise. He fell onto his hands and knees, losing his grip on both sets of reins.

"Kadmiel, I can't hold them! What are you doing?" Eli roared.

"Gathering what we need for our shelter, what—"

But it was too late. The beasts were fleeing as fast as their four legs would carry them over the grassy plains. Another bolt of lightning struck in the far distance, and the horses split up, losing each other in the chaos.

Kadmiel growled.

"Should I—" Eli began to ask.

"Just help me," Kadmiel interjected.

They were going to try and weather the storm beneath the tree, which was tall and covered in dense leaves. Kadmiel collected downed branches and laid them across the canopy of the tree, hoping to create more of a sealed shelter that they could sit underneath. Eli joined him at once, feeling guilty about the horses. He hadn't noticed it starting, but rain was already falling on them, and it was growing heavier every minute. Soon they had collected all the loose branches within the vicinity.

"What can I do to help?" Eli asked urgently, seeing the storm clouds closing in.

"Bedrolls. Blankets," Kadmiel said curtly.

Eli gave him a questioning look, unsure why he wanted to put those items out in the storm.

"Look," said Kadmiel, pointing at the tree's covering that they had reinforced. "This isn't enough. We need more," he said, digging through his own supplies. "Do you want just your bedding to get wet while it covers you, or do you want to get soaked along with everything you're carrying?"

Eli didn't argue. He tossed his bedroll to Kadmiel, who scrambled up the tree and stretched the bedding out above them. He used the loose branches they had collected to hold the coverings in place. With the few spare minutes they had, they created a small shelter. The swordsmen huddled closely together beneath the makeshift roof, hugging their knees tightly to their chests for warmth. No sooner had they gotten in place than the downpour reached them.

The rain was thick, with heavy drops that splashed upon the ground. Its sound was deafening, and Eli and Kadmiel had to yell in order to be heard.

The tree and bedding kept them mostly protected from above, but gusts of wind blew rain into their shelter from the side. Eli's clothes were drenched and water constantly dripped down his face and neck, but he tried to tell himself that things could be much worse.

Chapter 17: **BOUND**

By the time Eli and Kadmiel arrived at the Inner Kingdom, their clothes had finally dried. The storm had been in no hurry to pass them by, and they stayed huddled beneath the tree for what felt like hours while lightning tore at the landscape all around them, and an onslaught of rain blocked their vision.

Once the tempest had moved on, it was already well into the night. The swordsmen were not eager to chase the storm's tail, and wanted to give it a wide berth. They opted to sleep up among the leaves so as to avoid the puddles and muddy terrain below, strapping themselves to the branches in order to prevent themselves from falling.

Without their horses, the remaining distance to the Inner Kingdom took the entire day to traverse on foot. The warriors were weary and wet but determined to make it to their destination without resting again. That day, the forces of nature were favorable, and they came upon their destination without incident.

This was the royal palace from which the High King ruled the Tetrad Union a quarter century ago. It was at the very center of the Union, equal distances from all four of its parts.

Eli took a deep breath as he and Kadmiel crested a hill over-looking the city. He had expected more. The castle within the Inner Kingdom was relatively small—smaller perhaps than the one at the Eastern Peaks. It looked ancient, simple, and humble.

There was not much to say in regard to defensive measures. There was no moat around the kingdom like the Northern Marshes had surrounding its city, only a simple wall from which archers could be posted and a gate that was currently open.

There were other establishments that dotted the courtyard, like barracks for the king's personal guards, a bakery, and the like. But not much more than what someone would need for survival, and certainly not much for a king to pride himself on.

There was one striking feature, however, that held Eli's and Kadmiel's attention with an iron grip. There, amongst the abandoned castle and surrounding buildings, was the city's new development: a great tower that stretched toward the stars, looming over the Inner Kingdom and, indeed, over the Tetrad Union. It was made of wood that creaked and swayed dangerously in the wind, and the tower looked as if its construction had not yet been completed. There were empty gaps in its walls where windows would go, and a winding staircase could be seen inside. The steps wrapped around and around the tower, which was wider at the base and slowly became more narrow toward the top. Eli could barely make out the pinnacle of the tower from where he stood, but it looked unfinished, like it had been abandoned by its workers in the middle of the project.

"Kadmiel, maybe I wasn't imagining things," Eli said without removing his eyes from the spire.

The swordsman had his arms crossed, examining the tower from top to bottom as if he were critiquing its construction. "Hmm?" he asked absentmindedly.

Eli shook his head, amazed at the sight of this new structure that hadn't existed before, but could likely now be seen from all reaches of the Tetrad Union. With his hand on the pommel of his sword, Eli went to Kadmiel's side and rested his other arm upon the man's shoulder. Together, they took in the unbelievable view.

"This tower has been growing taller," Eli said. "I knew it when we were going to the Eastern Peaks."

"Someone has been here," Kadmiel agreed, nodding slightly. "Someone has been constructing this tower relentlessly."

"I think we know who's been here, and who has been forced

to erect this structure," Eli said, excitement creeping into his voice. "Kadmiel, let's go!"

Ever since the day of the disaster at the Championship of Warriors, Eli had tried to suppress the hope of ever seeing his family again. Now that three members of the Brotherhood of Warlocks were dead, and now that they had traversed the many miles in pursuit of their enemies and their people, he could not keep himself from feeling excited. Ecstatic. Invincible.

"Be careful, Eli. Be cautious. We don't—"

"No, Kadmiel!" Eli interrupted. "Let the last sorcerer show himself! Let Lilith do her worst! We've made it this far, and there is nothing that will keep me from my loved ones tonight!" Eli's voice had risen, but the look on his face was one of wonder and awe. "There's nothing that can stop us, Kadmiel. We have nothing to fear. We will be victorious again."

Kadmiel's mouth was a thin line as he listened. Nothing Eli said seemed to have an effect on him.

Eli grabbed him by the shoulders. "Are you not ready? Don't you miss them?"

Kadmiel's eyes fell, and he hung his head. Next, his shoulders shook, and Eli forced him into an embrace. Kadmiel choked out a sob.

"I do," he whispered. "More than anything."

"Are you afraid?" Eli asked, bewildered by the sudden show of emotion from his quiet companion.

Kadmiel did not answer, which was an answer in itself.

Eli clapped him on the back and moved to see his face. "We have each other, Kad. Don't leave my side. I need you tonight. But it is time that we found where our people are being kept. They may have lost all hope, and they could be hanging onto life by a thread. They may have been tortured like the Search Party was. They need us."

Kadmiel nodded and blinked the last bit of moisture from his eyes as something close to a smile formed on his lips.

*
**

The swordsmen set out to find the people of the Southern Shores. The size of the Inner Kingdom was actually smaller than their hometown, which Eli never would have guessed. That being considered, the question remained in his mind: *Where would a sorcerer be hiding a city's worth of people?*

Eli and Kadmiel finished searching the perimeter of the castle for any signs of life, and had moved on to examining the various structures throughout the area before it occurred to Eli.

"The tower," he said suddenly.

Kadmiel glanced at him inquisitively before peeking through a shop window.

"There's more to it than we can see—beneath," he explained. "It's so tall, the foundation must reach below the surface of the ground. Otherwise it would have already been blown over by the wind."

Kadmiel shrugged and followed Eli on his hunch. Together they crossed the distance to the tall tower, this time with their eyes scanning the ground around it.

The pair split up and circled the structure, searching for any hint of a passage.

"Here!" Kadmiel called from the opposite end.

Eli dashed around the other side, not noticing that he hit his shoulder against the tower as he did so. "What is it?"

Kadmiel was crouching in the grass, inspecting a wooden plank wedged into the ground. "Trapdoor," he stated.

Eli's heart began pounding restlessly like a hammer in a forge. Suddenly, his knees felt weak and he was becoming dizzy. "We're so close," he mumbled.

"Don't let your guard down," Kadmiel warned, eyeing Eli from head to toe. "Are you all right?"

Chapter 17: BOUND

He shook his head vigorously, trying to clear it. "Stop worrying about me, Kad. This is it." He knelt down next to the trapdoor and gripped a metal handle fastened to the plank.

"Wait," Kadmiel snapped.

Eli had to enlist a great deal of restraint to keep from opening the door behind which he hoped to see his parents and sister once more. "Yes?" he asked flatly.

"How do you know this is a good idea?"

He rolled his eyes and began to pull on the door, but Kadmiel slammed a hand down on top of it and halted the trapdoor's movement.

"This could be exactly what the Warlock wants you to do. This could be a trap."

"I'm done running. I'm done hiding."

Kadmiel let go and folded his arms. Through gritted teeth, he said, "Go. I'll wait outside."

Eli's mouth fell open. "Kadmiel, come with me! What are you thinking?"

"I'm thinking that it's too dangerous to lower ourselves into a confined space underground, presumably surrounded by our unarmed friends and family, when the last member of the Brotherhood is surely somewhere nearby, wanting to kill us!" Kadmiel's voice had steadily risen until he was shouting.

Eli pursed his lips and considered Kadmiel's warning for a moment before nodding. "Understood. I won't take long. I just need to know that they're all right."

Kadmiel turned his back to Eli and the trapdoor and drew his sword, releasing a shrill ringing sound into the night.

Eli lowered himself down the rungs of a ladder that was placed beneath the trapdoor. There was only pitch blackness past the reach of the moon's light through the hole in the ceiling.

His boots touched the stone floor at the bottom, and the word escaped his lips before he decided to speak it: "Hello?"

A round of gasps echoed from an unseen chamber beyond Eli's vision. He heard the rustling of clothes and the sounds of numerous people clapping hands over their mouths, then all was silent once more.

"Hello?" Eli asked again, with his voice quavering and his hands shaking.

Then, on the far end of the room a fire was uncovered that danced upon a torch, and the flame illuminated a row of faces. Eli immediately recognized the one holding the light. It was the bearded, wrinkled, and kind face of his father, Abner.

Eli's heart skipped a beat, and his voice caught in his throat.

Abner squinted in the firelight, unable to see past the few yards of visibility that the torch afforded him. "Eli? Is that you?" he whispered.

Tears streaked down Eli's cheeks at the sound of his name spoken by that old voice. He could not answer, but finally he willed his legs to move and he ran forward. Abner's mouth was agape and he handed the torch to someone beside him before Eli threw himself into his father's arms. There Eli stayed, weeping with joy as he held on. He felt warm splashes on his cheek as Abner's tears joined his own.

"It is him!" Abner gasped. "It's my boy. It's Eli."

The room resounded with a collective gasp once more, and Eli pulled back from his father to see as torch after torch were lit around the dingy underground cellar.

There, beneath the tower in the Inner Kingdom, was gathered the entirety of the Southern Shores villagers, whom Eli had not dared hope to ever see again. The captives were chained by the ankles to the grimy walls behind them, and they were all gaunt, dangerously slim, and filthy, yet their joy in that moment was undeterred. The villagers beamed at Eli with a hope in their eyes that struck him as beautiful.

Eli blinked in the sudden firelight and turned slowly back to Abner, holding his breath. Then relief flooded through him

Chapter 17: BOUND

as his eyes met those of his mother, Lana, standing next to them with tears on her face as well, wearing the biggest smile he had ever seen.

"Mom," he croaked, reaching his hand out to take hers. Her fingers were cold and feeble, and Eli squeezed them with all the love he could muster as she pulled him in for an embrace.

"You're alive," Lana whimpered with glee.

"*You* are alive!" Eli exclaimed. "And Gabbi?" he asked frantically, searching but not seeing her.

Abner gestured with a tip of his gray head to the line of captives along the wall to their left, where Gabbi lay curled up in the arms of Tabitha, both fast asleep on the cold stone floor, their legs chained to the wall.

As relieved as Eli was to find his loved ones and his neighbors alive, seeing his little sister and oldest friend in chains ignited a fierce desire for justice. There was something wickedly wrong with what he beheld, and resolve filled him as he tore his gaze from the deplorable sight.

"You've been forced to build this tower?" Eli questioned.

"Yes," Abner confirmed. "A watchtower for the Brotherhood of Warlocks. We think that they intend to overthrow the entire kingdom."

"And they are paranoid of invasions," added Lana hurriedly. "The tower is not yet finished. We cannot stop building until one can stand on the pinnacle and see past the Tetrad Union, into the lands beyond."

"This is what you were taken from the Southern Shores to do?"

Abner nodded sadly, looking out over the gathered faces of their people, who were watching the exchange quietly.

Eli placed his hands on his hips and began to pace. "Why can't you leave?"

"We have been blighted by a curse of dark magic," Abner replied. "We must remain in contact with the watchtower at all times, or pain and madness will take us."

"The spell is growing weaker, though," said Lana. "Little by little, we have felt the magic coming undone."

Eli's heart leapt. "The sorcerers! We have been killing the Warlocks! So their power over you has been waning," he said with wonder.

"'We'?" Lana asked.

"Kadmiel and myself, we—"

A woman wailed behind Eli. He spun to see who it was, but she was shrinking to the ground just outside the reach of firelight. He went and knelt beside the woman, who moaned and held a shaking hand in front of her lips.

"What is it? Are you all right?" Eli asked.

"What did you say?" she whispered, gripping him by the shoulders. "What was that name?"

Then Eli understood. This was Kadmiel's mother. "Kadmiel," he said gently.

The woman clenched her eyes shut as tears streamed down her face. She let go of Eli and hugged her knees to her chest, rocking slowly. "He's alive..."

A lump formed in Eli's throat as he watched her take in the revelation.

"He is," he finally managed to say. "And he is a great warrior. Together we have taken the Tetrad Union back."

She was overwhelmed by Eli's words, so after a few long moments, he straightened up and excused himself as Kadmiel's mother continued to cry.

He returned to Abner and Lana, who were watching him and embracing one another.

"You have done so well," Lana said, shaking her head in wonder as Eli drew near.

"But my task is not yet complete," said Eli. "The spell still binds you?"

"It does," said Abner. "Each morning we are brought our rations, and then our bonds are released. Then we are forced to build the tower, taller and taller, until long after the sun has set once more."

Eli bowed his head. "As we feared. There is another sorcerer: a fourth Warlock."

Lana shook her head abruptly. "Eli, it's not safe for you here! You cannot visit us—this sorcerer will know you've come! You must flee this cursed tower!"

"No, Mother," Eli said slowly. "I may not be safe here, but my mind has been made. Should I draw the despicable being out of hiding, so be it. The Brotherhood of Warlocks will be destroyed this night, and their spell will be undone."

Abner raised his chin as he looked upon Eli with a newfound perspective. Lana clung to Abner's arm and looked desperately into his face, silently pleading with her husband to persuade Eli against his plan.

With a deep sigh, Abner shook his head. "Eli has decided in his heart, Lana. We cannot deter him."

Eli squared his shoulders, trying to project confidence and ease his mother's worries. Lana looked upon him with a mixture of deep sadness and pride that he did not quite comprehend.

Abner stepped forward, pulling against the chains that bound him to the stone wall. Then the man gripped Eli by the forearms and he spoke, looking directly into his eyes. "If this is your course of action, my son—if you will confront the sorcerer—do not divert your gaze. Do not give a foothold to doubt and never falter. Never question yourself. Do what must be done, whatever the cost, if you know that your heart is true."

Eli cherished the contact with his father and absorbed the wisdom he spoke. With conviction, he replied, "I promise."

Chapter 18: **DECEPTION**

Atop the ladder, Eli knocked on the trapdoor above. Kadmiel opened the passageway and extended an arm to help him up. "It's them!" Eli exclaimed.

Kadmiel waited expectantly as Eli caught his breath from scampering up the ladder, eager to hear more.

"They're all there. They've been forced to work on this watchtower for the sorcerers—they're alive! Your mother, she—" Eli gasped. "She's so relieved to hear that you're okay."

Kadmiel gave a pained smile and exhaled his pent-up breath.

"It's safe!" Eli exclaimed. "Go to her!"

"No," Kadmiel said quickly. "No. I will go to her the moment the Warlock has been killed, and no sooner."

Eli wasn't sure he understood, but didn't press him. "No sign?" he asked.

"None. This abandoned kingdom is utterly still."

Eli paused, looking over the dark landscape that sprawled around them. Kadmiel was right—not a living being or creature could be seen above the ground. "My parents said that the sorcerer would know we're here—that he would come to kill us."

"Let's be ready for him then," Kadmiel stated.

Eli pounded a fist against the watchtower's wall next to them. "I am ready," he said with resolve.

"No," Kadmiel said, shaking his head. "Let's be ready for him," he repeated, gesturing to the tower.

Eli caught his meaning. "We'll climb it and watch as he comes."

Kadmiel nodded.

The swordsmen began the long journey up the winding

steps of the watchtower. A door at the base allowed them inside, which revealed a staircase that wound around the inner section. The wooden steps were loose in places, held together with crooked nails. Only a gentle breeze stirred outside, but the tower swayed in the night, becoming more noticeable as they climbed higher.

Eli spent the majority of their time recounting his visit with the Southern Shores' captives, to which Kadmiel listened without question or comment. Eli was elated to have discovered that their people were alive and were going to be free once the night was over.

Impatient to encounter the final sorcerer, he took two steps at a time. Kadmiel followed at a reserved pace behind him, despite Eli's urging to speed up. He did not want to be separated from Kadmiel, so he waited at the empty pane in the watchtower wall where a window was meant to go. He looked out over the Inner Kingdom, which appeared even smaller from that height. Still no movement or sign of their unknown adversary. Then a sickly feeling formed in Eli's core as a thought occurred to him.

"Kadmiel..."

"What is it?" he answered, joining him at the window.

"What if the Warlock is atop this tower?" Eli asked, eyes wide.

Kadmiel sighed and squared his jaw. "He could be. You're right. Now stay quiet and stay alert."

Eli's bravado slowly faded at the realization that every step he climbed in this staircase could be leading him to his last confrontation with the Brotherhood of Warlocks. He kept his sword at the ready and rounded each corner of the staircase with caution, now far more comfortable with Kadmiel's speed.

Adding to his anxiety, Eli couldn't help but notice their height. *We must be nearing the top,* he thought, carefully avoiding the glimpses of the city below through the gaping window holes. The swordsmen were now uncomfortably high, able to see much further than they had ever wished to.

Chapter 18: DECEPTION

At last, there were no more bends in the staircase. Instead, a gap separated the inner and outer walls of the tower, revealing the night sky above the unfinished structure.

Eli turned to Kadmiel with wide eyes and a pounding heart as he tried to remember the courage he had felt only a short time ago. Kadmiel met his gaze with resolve, and Eli found himself indescribably thankful once more for his companion. Wordlessly, the swordsmen gripped one another's shoulders and prepared themselves for what they might confront.

"Go," Kadmiel said.

Eli nodded, turning back to the steps' dead end. It would be a bit of a climb to reach the top of the tower, and he wondered if the villagers would have brought a ladder with them the next day as they continued their forced labor.

He shook his head, clearing the thought from his mind and standing on the top of the staircase. He placed his sword softly on the lip of the tower so he could grip the wooden platform with both hands.

Eli heaved himself up and over the edge of the watchtower's inner wall. Scrambling onto his feet, he quickly scooped up his sword and looked from side to side, alert for anything or anyone that may have been expecting his arrival.

The watchtower appeared to be vacant.

"There's no one here," Eli whispered over his shoulder to Kadmiel, who was preparing to climb up.

Kadmiel grunted as he pulled himself onto the side of the wall. Eli extended a hand and helped him up.

The platform was a temporary covering over the walls of the watchtower, not meant to be a permanent ceiling. The tower and its accompanying staircase would continue to be constructed ever upward, until the Warlock's paranoia was satisfied. *Or their lives snuffed out,* Eli thought. *Whichever comes first.*

The top of the watchtower was largely barren, with little besides Eli and Kadmiel resting upon its creaky wooden boards. There were a few beams and wall frames around the edges, waiting to be fortified and built upon by the sorcerer's captives.

A gust of wind made Eli break into a cold sweat as the tower leaned in the breeze, and then tottered back to its rightful balance. The shift was minimal, but standing atop the structure made any movement feel like an earthquake.

"He's not here," Eli muttered. "I expected the Warlock to be lying in wait."

Kadmiel glanced about nervously, as if not convinced of the sorcerer's absence.

"Where are you?" Eli wondered aloud, crossing to the edge of the tower and holding onto a narrow wooden beam for support as he examined the landscape below.

Nothing.

He circled the watchtower twice, ignoring the sickening sensation that the height gave him as he searched the Inner Kingdom grounds and surrounding areas for any sign of their enemy's whereabouts.

"Perhaps he forfeits, Kadmiel. Perhaps our reputation precedes us and this mysterious Warlock wishes to avoid the same fate as his brethren." Eli sheathed his sword abruptly, shaking his head.

Kadmiel had not spoken since the swordsmen had arrived atop the tower.

"Kad, what's wrong?" Eli asked.

Kadmiel eyed him with an uncertain look and let out a long, shaky breath. The tendons in his hand flexed as he gripped and re-gripped the pommel of his sheathed sword. "Eli, the fourth sorcerer is not coming to meet us."

"What do you mean?" Eli demanded. "How do you know?"

Kadmiel smirked, and something flashed in his eyes. "It's me, Eli. I am the fourth member of the Brotherhood."

Chapter 18: DECEPTION

"Very funny," Eli sighed, heart still pounding from adrenaline.

Kadmiel just stared at him flatly.

Eli raised an eyebrow and waited for Kadmiel to indicate that he wasn't being serious, which usually followed after his attempts at humor.

No such admission was given. There was a foreboding feeling in the pit of his gut, but his heart was trying fervently to believe that it was still some sort of joke.

"What are you saying?" Eli asked weakly.

Kadmiel drew himself up and raised his chin, speaking with a louder voice. "I am the fourth sorcerer, Eli. I am he."

Eli's entire body went numb, and he felt like rigor mortis had set in. A thousand possibilities ran through his mind to try and make sense of Kadmiel's words, but the man seemed to believe what he was saying.

"You're kidding, Kadmiel. You're just—"

"NO!" Kadmiel shrieked, pointing an accusing finger at Eli. "Don't be naive. I speak the truth."

Eli found the will to move his feet and took a careful step backward, followed by another. He could see that Kadmiel was harboring a rising rage, and although his mind was racing with questions, he wanted to try and keep the situation as calm as possible.

Kadmiel, it seemed, had a different idea in mind. The man took confident, threatening steps forward until he was inches from Eli's face, pressing him against the insecure wall beams of the watchtower.

Kadmiel spoke in a hushed tone and with a wild look in his eyes: "You are here because I made it so. The other Warlocks are dead because I wanted them out of the way. There is only one man that will leave this watchtower in victory tonight, and that man will be *me!*"

"Kadmiel, stop this," Eli pleaded. "I don't understand—what

madness has taken you?" His vision blurred with tears. "Do you hear yourself?"

"Oh," said Kadmiel with glee. "I hear myself. Yes, and I have waited a long time for this moment."

"What do you mean, you're one of them?" Eli exclaimed, at a loss. "How could you be? You command the spirits of the dead?"

Kadmiel's eyes flashed again, a dreadful darkness swirling within their steely gaze. "The dead are loyal to me. They serve me and fulfill my every wish."

"Kadmiel, how long have you deceived me?" Eli shouted.

Kadmiel turned away from Eli and placed his hands on his hips. "The entire time, Eli. You have been too blind to see. This has *always* been the stratagem." Kadmiel turned to look at Eli with a blank expression. "I am sorry that you thought this quest was about your family and your people, but I have far more in mind."

Kadmiel's words were daggers to Eli's heart. "*Our* families! *Our* people! Do you not care for the captives beneath this tower?"

Kadmiel grimaced. "Care? The people of the Southern Shores afforded me none. Why should I for them? No, after tonight, they will have no choice but to care about me."

Eli gasped. "You want to rule! You want the throne!"

Kadmiel dipped his head and spread his hands. "And is it not quite time that someone stepped up and succeeded the missing king?"

"Not a sorcerer," Eli spat. "Not a deceiver. I trusted you! I loved you!"

At those words, he thought he saw a look of pain upon Kadmiel's face, but it was gone in an instant and was replaced by a deep scowl. The man began to pace, and his breathing grew heavier.

"Kadmiel, listen to me! There is no loyalty that you can win tonight. The life you pursue is one of deception and tyranny. That is not true power."

Chapter 18: DECEPTION

Kadmiel whirled on him, looking as if he were ready to strike. "You know nothing of power! Do not speak of it—you are weak!"

Kadmiel's lips curled in an unnatural snarl. Eli barely recognized the man. *He's battling with something inside of him,* Eli realized. He observed as Kadmiel roamed back and forth upon the watchtower, growling and working himself up into a frenzy.

"Kadmiel," he spoke gently. "You took on a spirit host, didn't you?" Kadmiel stopped pacing dead in his tracks and looked at him through the dark locks of his hair. "You've opened up your soul and shared it with another being," Eli continued. "You've lost control."

Kadmiel's nostrils flared. "She chose me," he said with evident pride.

"Who?" Eli asked faintly, already knowing the answer.

A grin spread slowly across Kadmiel's face as he reached within his tunic. His hand darted into a pocket and came back out bearing the scroll, the will of the High King. Upon the ornate document was written the name that the will had borne since Rayorden had read it: the name *Lilith.*

Eli's heart threatened to beat out of his chest as Kadmiel's fingers traced the scroll until he found the edge of the paper. Then the swordsman closed his eyes and did what Eli could never have expected in a hundred lifetimes.

Kadmiel opened the scroll.

The will fell open effortlessly within his grasp, and his smile only grew wider as he beheld the look of shock etched across Eli's face.

"Now you understand, brother," said Kadmiel. "The great Lilith has chosen me as her vessel, and I have carried her this far."

The watchtower creaked as Eli fell to his knees, burying his face in his hands.

"You are right to bow, very good!" Kadmiel said, sounding less and less like himself every moment.

Eli's shoulders shook with the strength of his weeping, and his breath was short. "Kadmiel," he rasped. "Do not give in to evil! We've come so close!"

Kadmiel slowly approached Eli's kneeling figure, and then crouched beside him. "Don't cry, Eli. Though you are helpless before me, your defeat is not inevitable. Stand up."

Kadmiel extended his hand as if to help him rise, but he pushed himself to his knees and his feet without assistance, staring into Kadmiel's unrecognizable eyes. The man looked stung by Eli's rejection, but placed a hand upon his shoulder.

"Look," he said, gesturing with his other arm, still clutching the open document. "Tonight, I claim this kingdom for my own. The Tetrad Union—everything you see—will be under my command, for no one can destroy me."

Eli's shook his head, grieved by the poison of power that had consumed his companion's heart.

"You have been useful to me, Eli. You've been instrumental in displacing the Warlocks who would split the kingdom among themselves. For that reason, I extend to you my most generous offer: serve me, as the highest in my command." Kadmiel looked at Eli expectantly, as if he thought the proposition was actually worthy of consideration.

Eli let Kadmiel's hand fall from his shoulder and faced him with as much courage as he could muster, remembering the promise that he had made to his father Abner. "I have heard enough, Kadmiel. You are lost to Lilith—she is just using you, a willing puppet. She will rob you fully of your mind, just to accomplish her own goals. You have no part to play in this scheme, Kadmiel; Lilith will destroy the balance between life and death, and you will forfeit your soul in the process."

Kadmiel screamed in response to Eli's admonishment, filling the night air with unnatural energy. Eli could feel a dark presence growing thicker atop the watchtower, as if Lilith was gathering her strength. He summoned the remainder of his willpower to sustain him for the confrontation that was about to come.

"You fool!" Kadmiel shouted. "You fool! You fool!" he repeated over and over again, running his hands through his hair, turning about and striding the length of the watchtower. Kadmiel stopped and pointed the open scroll at Eli, shaking it at him in defiance. "I suspected that you would reject my reign. I knew you would never submit!"

Kadmiel then seemed to remember what he was holding and drew the scroll in toward his face, turning to illuminate its contents beneath the moonlight. "*This is your final chance to heed my law, Lilith sorceress.*' Bah! The missing king makes empty threats as usual." Kadmiel tossed the will aside and it slid across the floor, coming to a stop in front of an unfinished wall. Kadmiel turned to Eli and glared fiercely while taking a steadying breath. "I was afraid it would come to this, my friend, but so be it." Eli's heart sank as he considered the possibility that Kadmiel had yet another dark surprise.

"If you will not join me," the sorcerer continued, "then it appears we will have our Championship of Warriors after all."

Kadmiel closed his eyes, and his lips began to move rapidly as the man whispered to the spirits of the dead surrounding them. Eli heard a faint *thud* as the trapdoor to the captive's cellar was thrust open far below them, followed by screams coming from those within.

Eli watched in horror as one by one, the villagers of the Southern Shores were dragged by unseen forces from their prison onto the Inner Kingdom grounds. Still bound by chains, the captives attempted to flee but were held in place by the spirits under Kadmiel and Lilith's command.

The people of the Southern Shores were being placed in a large circle surrounding the tower, at a distance that allowed them to watch the swordsmen atop the crudely constructed spire. The men, women, and children yelled in terror as they were pulled along the ground.

Eli's eyes filled again with tears of pain and pity for those he had come to rescue, and for his companion who had plotted against him from the beginning.

Once the last captives were summoned from underground and their chains stopped rattling, Kadmiel sized up Eli as if they were facing off in the arena back home.

"There," Kadmiel said. "We have our audience, we have our sparring grounds, and we have our swords." There was a mad gleam in his eye, like all of his fantasies were finally coming true. "Now we will determine who the stronger warrior is! *Draw your weapon!*"

Eli stood in defiance, trembling with fear. "No."

"Draw your weapon!" Kadmiel hissed, unsheathing his blade in a burst of fury.

"I will not fight you."

Kadmiel rushed at Eli and backhanded him across the face with his gauntlet. Eli reeled back, trying not to fall off the tower.

"Are you too afraid, *champion?* Am I too much for you? TELL ME!" Kadmiel roared.

"I will not fight you, Kadmiel. You were like my brother. I love you too much."

Kadmiel swung his sword with a mighty downward blow at a partial wall, cleaving the wood in two. "Love! What is *love?* Where does it belong in this forsaken kingdom?"

"Kadmiel, resist her! Submit no more to Lilith—she doesn't care about you!"

The Warlock grabbed Eli by the collar and lifted him off of his feet. "Fight me, you coward. If you will not join me, then meet me in battle!"

Kadmiel dragged Eli to the center of the watchtower and addressed the terrified villagers below. Somewhere, watching from the grounds of the Inner Kingdom, was Kadmiel's mother, but he seemed to recognize no one. "Behold, your savior! Your champion! Eli Abnerson."

Chapter 18: DECEPTION

Kadmiel released him and held up his sword in a ready stance, but Eli refused to match his posture. Kadmiel growled and drew Eli's sword from its scabbard, holding it out for him to take. But still he remained motionless.

"Take your sword, Eli."

"I shall not repeat myself, Kadmiel."

Kadmiel roared and lifted his boot. Rearing back, Kadmiel kicked Eli square in the chest with more force than a normal man could muster on his own. The blow sent him stumbling back, and would have pushed him over the edge had he not slammed into a wooden beam along the perimeter of the platform. Eli's head whipped backward on impact, sounding like something had been broken. He leaned against the vertical plank, attempting to regain the breath that Kadmiel had knocked out of his lungs.

Thud. There was a sudden sharp pain under Eli's collarbone, and his vision went white. He was struggling to maintain consciousness, breathless and in agony. When his vision returned, Eli recognized the pommel of his own sword protruding from his chest. Kadmiel had thrown the weapon at him, pinning him to the wooden structure.

The beam behind Eli groaned in the wind, weakened from the trauma. He could feel warm blood seeping from where the sword had penetrated between his right shoulder and collarbone.

Kadmiel's eyes were wide, his teeth bared, and his veins pulsing with fury. As quickly as Eli blinked, the sorcerer crossed from the other side of the watchtower to join him at the edge.

"Look! The champion, defeated!" Kadmiel gloated desperately. "Helpless! Humiliated!"

The captives below wailed as they watched Eli's life draining in a stream of red.

"SWEAR TO SERVE ME!" Kadmiel bellowed, with only inches separating the swordsmen.

Eli looked upon his old friend with a deep sadness.

A strong gust of wind caused Kadmiel to lose his footing and fall back a few paces, while the beam that Eli was fixed to swayed dangerously. The breeze also caused the king's scroll to move, rolling into the space between him and Kadmiel. Looking down, Eli could see that the will now bore his own name once again, just as it had at the onset of their journey.

Kadmiel scooped up the will and scoffed, striding over to Eli and gripping the hilt of the sword that held him to the tower wall. Kadmiel jerked on the hilt violently, causing Eli to wince and cry in pain as the steel ripped his flesh.

"Your fate is sealed, Abnerson. You cannot cheat death this time." Kadmiel surprised Eli by holding out the will on the palm of his hand. "Read your prophecy. It will surely speak of my reign over the kingdom. And once the last shred of hope has abandoned you, I will end your life and declare myself king."

Eli gritted his teeth and took a painful breath as he moved his left arm to retrieve the will from Kadmiel's outstretched hand, every muscle, ligament, and bone screaming in protest as the sword tore his body. Grabbing the will, he let it fall open.

'Eli, you are born to the royal line of the High King, he who claimed victory over the dark sorceress Lilith and established his victory over the evil forces of the dead. By your birthright, you carry the very same authority over the wicked one. Command the unclean spirit, and it will obey you. A great and terrible sacrifice is at hand, for the freedom of the many.'

The words of the will resounded in Eli's mind like the sharp notes of a bell, and with them came a peace that washed over his entire being, leaving a clear sense of purpose in its wake. He knew what must be done.

"Lilith, depart from him!" he commanded.

Kadmiel's eyes grew wide and his mouth was agape as he realized what Eli had done. Immediately, Kadmiel's body grew rigid and his limbs hung at odd angles as something lifted his

Chapter 18: DECEPTION

feet from the ground. Lilith's dark presence was torn from him like a patch being ripped from a piece of cloth, then Kadmiel dropped his sword and fell limply to the ground, looking sickly and pale. The wicked spirit's aura hung in the air for a moment, gleaming in the moonlight. It looked both terrible and beautiful at the same time. Kadmiel writhed in horror as Lilith drifted away from him, screaming for her to return.

Eli's pity for Kadmiel grew as he saw how much the man had grown to depend upon the sorceresses' intoxicating power. Then suddenly, the spirit of Lilith surged forward and enveloped Eli, forcing itself through every pore of his body. He felt the weight of all evil bearing down upon him. His eyes rolled back into his head as the spirit fought for dominion, but he did not resist, for he knew what must occur for balance to return to the kingdom.

A great and terrible sacrifice is at hand...

"NO!" Kadmiel screamed.

In a flash of panic and rage, Kadmiel retrieved his sword and swung the weapon with all his might. His aim was true, and the blade entered Eli's neck before lodging itself in the wooden beam behind him.

There was a blast upon Eli's death that pushed Kadmiel off his feet and sent him sprawling onto the floor. A blinding light filled the night sky as Lilith's essence was destroyed by Kadmiel's fell stroke. As her spirit faded from existence, the cries of the dying sorceress could be heard distantly, as if from another plane of reality.

The shockwave crippled the beam to which Eli was fixed, and the unfinished piece of the watchtower fell along with his ruined body, beginning its long descent to the ground below. Kadmiel screamed in terror at the act which he had just committed, and his cries mingled with those of the people watching below.

Epilogue: **MONUMENT**

The moment Lilith's soul had been destroyed, the Warlocks' power was erased and the villagers had been freed, their bonds released.

Abner and Lana went to Eli's body at the base of the watchtower, after it crashed forcefully to the earth. The other villagers joined them, and they filled the night with the sounds of their mourning until the sun rose, their eyes were dry, and their voices were hoarse.

Kadmiel escaped the Inner Kingdom before Eli's parents had risen from their place of despair, but Abner told the men not to pursue him. "Enough blood has been spilt."

Most heartbreaking of all, the children did not seem to fully grasp what had happened, Gabbi included. Abner knew not how or when to answer her questions, but he held her close.

The people remained solemn through the entire journey back from captivity, taking shifts carrying Eli's body, enclosed in a makeshift casket made of pieces of wood from the watchtower.

Now Lana stood behind her son's grave, facing the assembled villagers of the Southern Shores. A day had passed since the town's inhabitants had returned, attending immediately to their fallen comrades in the ruined stadium. The crying and wailing of the people still echoed in Lana's mind as she shifted her weight, trying to maintain a semblance of composure.

"We are all well acquainted with loss," she choked out. The crowd listened in complete silence. "I don't claim to have lost more than any of you, but... it feels like I'm losing my Eli for a second time." She couldn't hold back a sob that racked her frame.

On the other side of the grave, Abner stared at the freshly turned ground, unable to meet his wife's eyes. Tabitha rushed to Lana's side and wrapped an arm around her. Gabbi clung to Abner's leg, watching with her lips parted.

"When my son wasn't captured with the rest of us, I thought he must have died in the arena. Even as the sorcery that bound us weakened, I didn't allow myself to hope that it was actually him. But then—there he was, in our midst, sword in hand, ready to do anything to free us."

Members of the crowd nodded, their tears joining Lana's.

"And he did it. He exchanged his life for ours, and found his destiny... I couldn't possibly be more proud. I miss him dearly—always will... but I'm thankful that he was able to show us what true love looks like."

If Lana had tried to say anything further, it was drowned out by the sudden thunderous cheers that rose from the crowd. Lana looked downward sheepishly and her eyes came to rest on Eli's grave. She started to move back to Abner's side, but Tabitha did not release her embrace.

"Wait," said the young woman. She turned Eli's mother to face her directly and spoke, "We have something for you. It's not much, it's just..." Tabitha trailed off, searching for words. "We can never repay you, for what was taken from you... but this is yours." From her pocket, Tabitha produced a beautiful necklace. It shimmered in the sunlight, a dazzling array of precious stones. Lana held up a hand to decline the gift, but Tabitha was already moving to fasten the jewelry for her. Lana acquiesced and lifted her hair so Tabitha could clasp the jewelry behind her neck. A gem rested on Lana's collar that made the ornate chain pale in comparison.

"This is Eli's third Champion of Warriors jewel. It's rightfully yours."

Tears streamed down Lana's face anew as she beheld the gift.

Tabitha comforted her, rubbing her back. "This would

Epilogue: MONUMENT

have been added to Eli's sword, but I think you should have it, and the Championship conductors agreed," she said, gesturing to a few smiling individuals, "and we got right to work on it yesterday. We thought you'd want to carry something of Eli's with you."

Lana couldn't manage to voice her gratitude, but her face said it all. The onlookers cheered again as the women stepped around Eli's grave and retook their place in the crowd.

The noise died down as Abner took solemn steps forward, leaving Gabbi with her mother. In his hands, he held Eli's sword. He had cleaned the blood from the blade, and shined the hilt. He gripped and re-gripped the pommel as he summoned the will to speak.

"Thank you for coming. I know that everyone here has a lot to attend to." His voice was raspy, and he looked like he hadn't slept at all. "There's only one reason my son is buried here today," he continued, "and only one reason it's him instead of us. That's because he allowed it to happen. We all saw it. He willingly took the blow."

Abner lifted his gaze to the sky and his mouth trembled. "He could have killed his enemy—struck the boy down." Abner slashed Eli's sword through the air as he spoke. "But he didn't. He proved his strength by not showing it."

Here Abner paused to survey the crowd, looking from one individual to the next. "Do you all agree that is what took place atop the tyrant's spire?"

Several people shouted their affirmation, but Abner held up a finger to silence them and proceeded. "This is what I know beyond a shadow of a doubt—Eli would not wish us to live another day as victims. If there was ever a victim, it was he. But Eli shed that lesser identity for one of a hero. Thus, on behalf of my son, I beg you... live as free men and women. Let go of the wrongs done to you and rebuild—a stronger life! A life marked by the kind of sacrifice that Eli showed us."

Chants of "Rebuild!" started up among the assembled villagers, then Abner joined until every voice partook in the mantra. When the din had reached its peak, Abner raised Eli's sword above his head and plunged it deep into the earth. The sword stood above his grave, serving as a headstone. Abner folded his hands upon the pommel and addressed his neighbors earnestly once more.

"Friends, you are Eli's legacy. You were bought with my bloodline. All I ask is that I can see my son in you."

Abner nodded at Lana, who grabbed Gabbi by the hand and went to join him beside the grave. There the family knelt and placed their hands upon Eli's sword, heads bowed together.

The crowd watched silently as Abner, Lana, and Gabbi said goodbye to Eli. When they finally stood up, a line had formed behind them and Eli's family stepped aside. Households approached the burial site one by one and knelt at the sword to pay their respects, grabbing the handle, thanking Eli, and kissing the pommel.

The sun had started to set, but the villagers who had not yet given their regards remained in line to do so. Abner beamed and Lana couldn't help but smile.

"Let's go home," said Abner.

Abner froze on the doorstep, with his hand holding the latch. He took a deep, steadying breath and looked at his wife. "Ready?"

"No," Lana admitted quietly, her nose red and eyes puffy. "But we have each other."

Gabbi frowned. Abner ran a hand over her hair and took another breath. "Let's go."

Abner did not remember in what state they had left the house. Was it messy? Would there be spoiled food on the counter? So much had transpired that these concerns seemed trivial.

Epilogue: MONUMENT

The door swung open, and Abner stepped over the threshold of their house.

Kadmiel was seated at their dining room table.

Lana gasped and clutched Abner's arm, shrinking back behind him. Abner handed his daughter to Lana and said, "Go— go to the neighbors." Lana looked terrified and hesitant to leave Abner's side, but he insisted.

The girls left. Abner closed the door and faced Kadmiel. He looked as if he had not eaten since leaving the Inner Kingdom. His clothes were hanging onto his gaunt body by shreds, his long hair was unkempt, and he looked distressed—as distressed as Abner had seen anyone look.

The man was unarmed, and barely acknowledged Abner's arrival. His head was bowed and his teeth were clenched. He sounded like he was fighting for every breath he drew, and his shoulders shook with the effort.

Abner crossed the distance and took the chair across from Kadmiel, lowering himself into it slowly. Finally, Kadmiel met his eyes. They were bloodshot and teary.

"Kadmiel," Abner said simply.

Kadmiel let out a muffled sob. "I came for you to kill me," he mumbled.

Abner stared at him blankly.

"I've come close to doing it myself so many times since... since..." Kadmiel shook his head. "And I can't. I can't take that from you."

"You think you deserve to die?" Abner asked.

Kadmiel slammed his fist on the table. "I am a murderer! A traitor! Your son trusted me, and I just *used* him. I'm the worst kind of criminal," he rasped. "You would be doing me a favor."

It was as Abner feared. "All that occurred—this was of your own free will?"

Kadmiel buried his face in his hands. "It was."

"Tell me," said Abner calmly. "Tell me everything."

Kadmiel drew an unsteady breath. "Must I?"

Abner did not answer and only stared into Kadmiel's wandering eyes until he conceded. "I suppose I owe you everything—anything you could ask of me...

"The night before the championship finals—when Eli and I would battle—that's when the sorcerers found me and spoke to me. They explained that they had crafted a spell to allow dead spirits passage into this world, and... and I thought of my father."

Here Kadmiel wept and rocked in his chair. Abner gave him the time he needed to collect himself.

At last, he continued shakily. "The Warlocks told me that they were planning an attack to destroy the warriors that would oppose them, but that they had received a scroll of prophecy, warning them. It read: *'A Champion named Eli stands between your efforts and success, and you shall not be permitted to take his life.'* They decided that they needed someone else to kill Eli for them, and they chose me..." Kadmiel gasped for air. "I was so tempted by the idea of finally being stronger than him, I really didn't think that I would beat him... So I said yes, only if they would lend me the power I needed. So they took me in when they performed the spell. I was there when they rent a hole in reality and four spirits of the deceased entered our realm, one inhabiting each of us. It was the most vile feeling." He shuddered.

"And it was Lilith who chose you?" Abner asked.

"Yes, Lilith chose me. The sorcerers never knew which spirit I became host to—they could not summon specific beings that had passed. Before I left, they threatened me that if I should fail in killing Eli, they would find me, torture me, and end my life slowly." Kadmiel leaned back in his chair and hung his head backward, anguish upon his face. "I loved the power that the spirit brought me, but I didn't actually want to kill Eli before the competition—I just wanted to be better than him. I wanted him to—to... Ah, I'm ashamed."

"Continue," Abner spoke.

Kadmiel sighed wearily. "I wanted Eli to submit to me—to declare me as the better swordsman at last. My entire experience with the sorcerers made me uneasy, and I didn't trust them. I knew that they were using me as their weapon against Eli, since it was foretold that they could not defeat him. That was when I decided to use Eli against *them*. I broke my oath to the sorcerers and befriended him, warning him of the Warlocks' impending attack. This was moments before the contest was about to begin, and the sorcerers struck. I think that they tried to kill me right then. They thought I had entered Eli's tent to slay him, and then they brought it down around me in flames. They didn't care about me—they wanted me dead and out of their way." Kadmiel grimaced darkly. "Little did they know, Eli and I would be their undoing."

Abner nodded. "Thank you for telling me all of this, Kadmiel."

The young man snorted. "It makes no difference—you already know well the depths of my depravity."

"I do," Abner agreed. "What I don't understand is this—you traveled with Eli. You fought beside him. You overcame enemies with him—and through all that, did you feel nothing for him?"

Abner could see his words striking like hammer blows. Kadmiel groaned and tightened his fists.

"I did," he whispered. "Eli was the closest friend I've ever had... I was just so blinded by my greed. Lilith fed on that—she thrived on my thirst for power."

A tear fell from Abner's eye and ran down his cheek.

Kadmiel looked horrified. "I'm so sorry for what I've done. I'm so sorry to you and to your family... I'm so sorry..."

Then Kadmiel gave in to the full strength of his grief, and his body shook with the force of his misery. Abner stood and turned away from him, looking out the window with his hands clasped behind his back.

A minute passed without either's posture changing, but then Kadmiel regained his breath and he stood from the table. "If you will not kill me, I cannot bear to be in your presence any longer."

Abner bowed his head but said nothing.

"I'm so sorry," Kadmiel repeated. Then he marched out of the dining room and out of Abner's home, his sobs trailing behind him.

Lana quickly entered the house alone. "I dropped Gabbi off—I was listening... I—"

Abner went to meet her and she threw herself into his arms.

"You're okay! But he's getting away, Abner. Kadmiel just left—"

"I know, dearest," he said. Abner turned away and tightened his belt, then donned his cloak that hung by their doorway, pulling it over his shoulders and fastening it in the front.

"You're going after him?" Lana asked, searching her husband's face.

Abner grabbed a walking staff and pulled Lana into a tight squeeze. "I am."

He stepped out the doorway and looked to the horizon. Kadmiel's outline grew smaller as the boy fled the Southern Shores.

"What will you do when you find him?" Lana asked.

Abner started to run. "I'm going to forgive him!"

The End